DEATH BY GRAVITY

ALSO BY
SHARON LINNÉA

FICTION

Death in Tranquility (Bartender's Guide to Murder 1)

These Violent Delights

WITH B.K. SHERER:

Chasing Eden • Beyond Eden • Treasure of Eden • Plagues of Eden

YOUNG ADULT, WITH AXEL AVIAN:

Agent Colt Shore: Domino 29

NONFICTION

Princess Kaiulani: Hope of a Nation, Heart of a People

Raoul Wallenberg: The Man Who Stopped Death

Chicken Soup from the Soul of Hawai'i

Lost Civilizations

America's Famous and Historic Trees with Jeff Meyer

AS SHERIDAN SCOTT:

Now You Tell Me! 12 Actors Give the Best Advice They Never Got

Now You Tell Me! 12 Army Wives Give the Best Advice They Never Got

Now You Tell Me! 12 College Students Give the Best Advice They Never Got

THE BARTENDER'S GUIDE TO MURDER

DEATH BY GRAVITY

Arundel
PUBLISHING

SHARON LINNÉA

THE BARTENDER'S GUIDE TO MURDER

Book 2: DEATH BY GRAVITY

ISBN: 978 1 933608-18-1 (*paperback*)

ISBN: 978 1 933608 19-8 (*ebook*)

First Edition December 2020

Cover Art and Cover Design by David Colón

Interior Design by Phillip Gessert

For Bob
Cheers, my love

TWENTY YEARS AGO

Seven-year-old Davy Edison awoke alone in the dark. He had a moment of frightened confusion before he was able to orient himself.

He was in a tent that he and his older sister, Misty, had concocted out of sheets and chairs downstairs in the television room.

Davy loved it when their parents went out and Misty babysat. They always thought of fun trouble to get into—like building a fort out of blankets, eating barbecue wings, and watching shows of which their parents didn't approve.

However, the television was now off and the sleeping bag next to him was empty. Misty must have gone up to bed.

Davy briefly considered going back to sleep, but he had to pee, and his real bed was more comfortable, anyway. He used the downstairs bathroom and walked through silent halls to the staircase in the bedroom wing. To his right at the first landing, the door to the staircase that led to his parents' floor was closed, which meant they'd come home.

He padded down the long hall toward his room.

When he passed Misty's room, he was surprised to find the door slightly ajar. He pushed against it silently and opened it a few inches to see if she was still awake.

Her bed hadn't been slept in. One of the French doors to her balcony was open.

"Mist?" he whispered, as he stepped into the room.

The sheer curtain by the outside deck fluttered, and he stopped.

He could see shapes outside. More than one.

This threw him enough that he didn't hear the person who

stepped up behind him until the man grabbed him firmly with one hand and planted his other hand over Davy's mouth.

Davy heard him kick the hall door closed behind them.

"What the hell are you doing here?" asked an angry whisper.

Davy did the first thing he thought of: he chomped down on the top of the hand over his mouth.

"Where's my sister?" he hissed.

"You are in so much trouble, you little freak. You've got two choices. You shut up, now, right now, and you stay silent, *silent*, till morning, or your sister and your parents all die. We have your sister already. I can shoot your parents before they even wake up!"

Davy was thinking fast. He'd heard about kids who were kidnapped and their siblings keeping quiet way too long because they were scared. That wasn't him. He had to pretend to go along.

He nodded his head. When the man took his hand away a few millimeters, he said, "Okay. Okay! I'll be quiet. Just don't hurt her! Put me down. Let me go to my room!"

"Fat chance, idiot kid," said the voice. It sounded rusty, like it had to bounce over lots of nails to get from the voice box to the air.

"Put me down," he said, with a bravado he didn't feel.

The man put him down, but awkwardly, so he landed on the dude's shoe and lost his balance.

The kidnapper was suddenly furious. His other hand grabbed something, and suddenly there was steel against the boy's throat.

"No!" Davy cried.

"First you, then her," came the raspy reply.

And everything went black.

Davy woke up in Misty's bed while it was still dark outside. Her balcony door was closed. She was gone.

He knew he had to sound the alarm as soon as possible, no matter what the kidnapper had threatened, but his arms were bound behind him and he had duct tape over his mouth.

It hurt to have his arms pulled back that way. His shoulders were burning, but there was nothing he could do. The tape over his mouth was sticky, and it smelled like oil. He couldn't move his lips or open his mouth or swallow his saliva properly.

Worst was that he couldn't get anyone's attention. He couldn't save Misty.

Warm tears traced his cheeks and moistened Misty's pillow.

By morning, when his parents finally found him, she was long gone.

1

TORTURING THE NEWBIES

I T WAS THE first Saturday night in June. Tranquility, New York, is far enough north that the warm evening breezes over the lake still felt new and intoxicating. Why folks needed further intoxication I do not know, but the Battened Hatch was hopping. Everyone was in high spirits.

Shortly after 8 p.m., Brent Davis and his wife, Susan, took seats at the beautifully carved wooden bar.

"Hey, Avalon," Brent said. He was of British heritage and wore a long-sleeved button-down shirt, sleeves rolled up, the quintessential newspaper editor. His beard was trimmed and comfortably salt-and-pepper, his glasses wire-rimmed. "Throw me a Stella and a white wine for the wife."

I smiled at Susan. "Chardonnay?" I asked.

"Perfect." She nodded.

"When did you get back from LA?" I queried Brent as I poured. "How's the film shaping up?"

"Got home a few hours ago," he responded, a spark behind his eyes. He was producing a documentary on the town's golden-era movie stars, Pepper Porter and Sally Allison, which had some unexpected new plot twists, due to a recent murder investigation. It now looked to be a humdinger, as Pepper might have said. "It'll be a challenge to finish it in time for the Tranquility Film Festival in August."

"Can't wait to see it!" I responded truthfully. Sally Allison was one of my favorite movie stars of all time. Not to mention, my current landlord.

"Thanks for your help," Brent added, lifting his glass.

"Hope there are no upcoming giant news stories to split your attention."

Brent was also the editor-in-chief of the local newspaper.

"It's Tranquility. I think we're safe," he said.

The ding of new drink orders came to the bar from the POS on the restaurant floor. I exchanged an eyeroll with Marta, my teal-haired bartender-in-waiting, as the paper continued to scroll. Our new waiter, Davros, shrugged at us from the mid-floor machine.

Olympic medalist Brian Eddings was holding court tonight, and the liquor was flowing. Brian wasn't the only Olympian who frequented the Battened Hatch. Gillian Petrakov, a former bronze medalist in figure skating, sat at the bar even now, her blonde hair in a bun, fitted pink sweater set embracing her still-taut figure, next to her partner, Callie (non-skater, brown hair, ran a nonprofit).

"Brian is torturing the Newbies again." Gillian smiled.

Tranquility is one of two places in the United States where athletes can train for winter sports year-round. Brian lived locally. I met him when he turned up here at the Scottish tavern shortly after I came to town. You knew when he was in the room—as did everyone in town, apparently—and they started arriving in groups to join his instant party.

"The Newbies?" I asked.

"Bobsledding is a unique sport," Gillian said. "Take figure skating—you have to train for decades. But bobsledders—all you have to be is strong, fast, and able to jump. Every year, Olympic scouts head for colleges to entice track stars and even shot-putters to come and try out for Olympic bobsled team."

"Really?" I asked, wiping down the bar. "Does it ever work out?"

"Yep, there have been times when a college kid shows up in June and has competed in the next Winter Olympics!"

As she said that, a tall man walked into the bar from the door to MacTavish's Seaside Cottage, the hotel that housed us. It was a sprawling, hundred-year-old establishment that was not seaside (though lakeside) and had no cottages. There was, however, a Mac-Tavish.

The newcomer was European-American, maybe six feet, short brown hair, trim, and wearing a gray polo tucked into gray slacks. His eyes scanned the place and he smiled, as if entertaining memories from his past. I turned, ready to ask if he wanted to be seated, when he saw the group at the back of the room. His smile vanished. He turned on his heel and walked out.

Alrighty, then. I turned my attention back to Gillian. "So how does Brian torture them?"

"He's not their coach, obviously. He competed in luge. But he can't resist so many freaked-out, naïve athletes. They've been living like monks in Olympic housing for the past three weeks. As soon as they're allowed out, he brings them here and buys them beer. They—and their coaches—won't be happy tomorrow morning!"

"So why do they keep letting him do it?"

"Good question." Gillian sipped her drink. "The truth is monks don't make very good bobsledders, but the coaches can't be seen to be condoning this behavior. But—whew—the kids gotta get this energy out somehow! Brian's like a father figure... but father figures aren't always the best influences!"

"Tell me about it."

A huge whoop went up. I looked up—to find the previously full tables suddenly emptied of athletes and their adult beverages.

"What the... ?"

The door to the smoker's porch was open. Another group cry went up, followed by a loud splash.

Marta followed me to the open door. And there, on the smoker's porch, Brian Eddings had built himself a luge. He'd put two square tables together with another four-top on it. He'd added a sturdy wooden chair with arms on top of that table. He'd appropriated all my tablecloth clips to attach a long tablecloth to the wooden chair, again to the lower table, and then to the front of the lower level to jerry-rig a mini-luge run. Seriously. One prospective Olympian stood on the top table, holding the chair solid while two others held the cloth taut lower down. Two young men had already careened down and off into the lake. Another was climbing the rickety contraption even now, holding a bussing tray to ride on his journey.

"Baron McNulty for the win!" crowed the young man, throwing himself onto the slanted tablecloth, sliding off the porch and into the lake.

"Dear God, Brian, what are you doing?" I asked. "MacTavish's insurance does not cover reckless porch slides!"

"Aw, lassie," he said, in an affected voice purposely reminiscent of Glenn, the owner of MacTavish's.

The next young man at the top of the climb pushed off, and hurled down into the lake.

"Back inside! Everyone!" I instructed. "Free buffalo wings. On the house."

That did it. A different kind of whoop and the portion of young men who had little interest in killing themselves jumping off metal chairs headed back in.

Marta and I dismantled the furniture sculpture and stood for a moment. I have no doubt she was joining me to silently pay respects to my predecessor who had died on this very porch.

The rest of the night slid past quickly, as busy pub nights do. At midnight, a minibus pulled up to return Olympic hopefuls to their apartments at the training facility. Shortly thereafter, a trio of young women left, helping their friend walk between them. They'd each had one drink, and I wondered if their affected friend had an intolerance or allergy. Or if she'd simply downed all three drinks herself.

Brian Eddings stayed to help Manuela, the bus-person, clear, as his group's tables were in shambles. Brian's face and chin were square, with an indent in the bulb of his nose, as if someone has pressed a fingerprint to it. His hair was blonde and close-cropped, although Olympic photos of him showed it longer and unruly. His eyes were alert, brimming with intelligence and mischief. Living in Tranquility, you hear pretty quickly that life after being an

Olympian—medalist or not—is rough going for many athletes. I appreciated that Brian was willing to be a bit wild but truly thoughtful at the same time.

I closed out the POS and came back as Manuela and Brian finished separating the now-cleaned tables.

"Thanks, Manuela," I said.

"Good night," she replied and headed out.

"Sorry if we made more work," said Brian, eyes flashing. "But it's a rip."

"A rip?"

"Rip-roaring time!"

He was so pleased as he said it, I couldn't help but laugh. At least no one had broken their neck on his jerry-rigged luge. As we worked together, I noticed that he wasn't inebriated in the least. He said he didn't drink, and he stuck to it.

"Good night," he said. As he passed, he crushed a bill into my hand. "For the extra trouble," he said. "And the wings."

I'd comped the wings, figuring they'd be cheaper for MacTavish's than the bad publicity of a future Olympian breaking his neck luging off the smoker's porch.

"Night," I replied, following, turning out the lights. As I locked the door behind him, I glanced at the tip. It was a one-hundred-dollar bill.

That was, allegedly, the last time anyone saw Brian Eddings alive.

TORTURING THE NEWBIES

Ingredients

Sour mix
Seltzer
Lime

Method

Add 2 ounces of sour mix to a glass with ice.
Top with seltzer.
Add lime for garnish.
Sip all night and be proud of yourself in the morning.

2

LIGHT OF DAY

MARTA ARRIVED AT the Battened Hatch the next morning half an hour before the state police did. She had gone to the 9 a.m. service at her father's church so she could get to work early. The Reverend Tim Layton was not thrilled about his daughter working on Sunday. He was not thrilled she worked in a bar. There were very few things about Marta about which he was thrilled, which was too bad, because she was one of the good ones.

"Okay, you up for this?" I asked her. She still had white streaks through her teal hair, and I was only slightly surprised she hadn't cycled to another shade. Marta had been a waitress during Joseph's tenure as bartender. She was a senior in high school and had recently turned eighteen, so I'd started training her as barback and bartender. Today was her first day in charge.

"Yes," she said, but something seemed off.

"You're confident?" I asked. She and I both loved the tavern, which was officially named That Ship Has Sailed but called the Battened Hatch by those in the know—okay, by everybody. The nickname was on the menus. The place was atmospheric and mysterious, the walls dark wood with a Scottish flare. The wooden bar was long and hand-carved with matching back bar, also hand-carved with bottle stands lit from below. I'd fallen in love at first sight.

"Oh, yes," Marta said. "Ready to cast off and set sail, Skipper."

"What is it, then?" I asked more quietly. "Another hard night?"

She gave me a wry smile and nodded.

"We're going to talk about this," I said. "Tomorrow."

She nodded. I'd said that before. This time, I told myself, I meant it.

"I'd better get going," I said. "Call if there's any problem."

As I spoke, the door from the hotel lobby banged open—and when I say "banged," I reference the retort by a shotgun. In walked three state police officers, two in uniform and one, whom I assumed to be an inspector, in a suit and tie.

"Avalon Nash," bellowed the one in the suit. He was a white guy, just under six feet tall, who walked with the presence and authority of a bull.

"Yes. What's up?" I asked. All I could think about was that I needed to leave, and soon, to get to my other gig for the day. Certainly, they wouldn't send state police if something had happened to a family member back in Los Angeles, or in New York City. Would they?

I went and stood next to Marta behind the bar, putting the wooden structure between us, like a Johnny Carson desk.

"Inspector Gerald Mason. I need to ask you a few questions."

"Sure," I said. "But it needs to be quick. I have to get to a job."

"I thought this was your job," he said.

"It is. I also bartend private events. Today is a private event."

"Yeah? Where?"

"What questions can I answer for you?" I responded. "And where is Inspector Spaulding?"

Mike Spaulding and I had worked together to solve the murder of my predecessor.

"I was out of town during that murder investigation," said Inspector Mason, as if reading my thoughts. Like he was the top tier and we'd been slumming with him gone. In his voice, I read an unwelcome authoritarian tone, dismissive of other, lesser mortals. I tried to tell myself it was how this guy felt about everyone; it had nothing to do with Mike Spaulding being Black and Joe Mason being white.

I gave myself a silent pep talk in which I acknowledged my

extreme dislike for authoritarian men. At the same time, I knew the way to handle them was to disregard this, pretend to be going along with them and then manage a hasty exit.

"What brings you here this fine day?" I asked. *Sound sincere.*

"You know Brian Eddings?"

"Sure. Everyone knows Brian."

"When did you see him last?"

"He was here last night, with a group of Olympic hopefuls."

"And everything seemed all right?"

"Yes. Brian was being Brian. All normal."

"What do you mean by 'being Brian'?"

"He was holding court. Telling stories. Being the center of attention."

"Did he drink a lot?"

"Why are you asking me these things?"

There was a pause, and a slight shifting among the three officers.

One of the uniformed officers, a tall man with thick brown hair, four inches taller than Inspector Mason, said, "Ma'am, Brian Eddings is deceased. He was found in his apartment early this morning."

Both Marta and I gasped.

"You had no idea?" Mason again.

"Of course not. How could we?" I asked. "What happened?"

"We were hoping you could shed some light on that. Who did Mr. Eddings leave with?"

"No one. He stayed to help clean up last night. He left alone."

"Was he intoxicated?"

"No. He doesn't drink."

This came as a surprise. Mason raised an eyebrow. "Oh. An alcy?" His voice dripped distain.

Stay calm. Perky. You can do this.

"He doesn't drink. Were there... signs of violence?" I asked.

"We'd prefer not to say too much at this time. Can you give me a list of who was here with him?"

I shook my head. "I really can't. These kids are new in town. I'd never seen any of them before. They left together in a small Olympic bus before Brian departed."

"What time was that?"

"Bus left at twelve thirty? Brian would have left here shortly after one."

"He helped you straighten? Is that normal? You're friends?"

"No. There were a lot of people in his party. They put tables together. Like that. He's a good bar patron. He tips well. Drinks soda water and sour mix. That's the entirety of my bartender knowledge of the man."

"Tips well?"

"Gave her a hundred-dollar bill last night," Marta piped up. I'd given her half this morning with the other half saved for Manuela.

Shit, Marta.

That stopped everyone cold. "He gave you that kind of tip, for serving soda water?"

"Yup," I said.

Marta cursed under her breath.

"He gave you a hundred dollars, and you didn't leave with him. You didn't go back to his apartment?"

"I don't even know where his apartment is."

"You didn't take him into the back room?"

The worse this got, the calmer I had to stay. The boat to the party left in thirty minutes, with or without me on it. And, from past experience, I knew if I said as much to Inspector Mason, he'd make sure I missed it. Just 'cause.

I motioned to the CCTV camera above the bar and to another in the hallway that led to the restrooms and storerooms.

"Not for a minute," I said. "Help yourself to the video. Listen. Mr. Eddings was fine when he left here. Also on video. I will be around to answer any other questions you may think of. In the meantime, I have to head over to my job."

"Which is..."

"Event bartending."

"Yeah, you said that. Where?"

"The birthday bash for the Cavalleros family."

"Well, excuse us," said Inspector Mason. "By all means." He swept his arm, as if ushering me out.

I looked at Marta, grabbed my bartending kit and carry bag, and took the opportunity to get the heck out of there.

LIGHT OF DAY

Truffled Bleu Cheese Dirty Martini

Ingredients

> 2 ½ oz Lake Placid Spirits 46 Peaks vodka
> Dash of olive juice
> Dash of truffle oil
> Ice
> Crispy bacon
> Bleu cheese stuffed olives

Method

> In cocktail shaker combine vodka, olive juice, truffle oil,
> and ice.
> Shake ingredients together.
> Strain over martini glass.
Garnish with crispy bacon and bleu cheese stuffed olives.

3

BIRTHDAY BLISS

Tranquility on a summer Sunday morning still leads me to believe in the possibility of an old-fashioned, small-town, happy existence.

Aside from the murders, of course.

I rode my bike down Main Street, passing small businesses as they opened, proprietors arriving, keys in hand. Verses of a hymn sung in four-part harmony escaped the opened windows of Tim Layton's large Gothic church.

I tried to reconcile this with the thought that Brian Eddings was dead.

He had been very, very alive last night. Luging off the smoker's porch. Buying people drinks but making sure there was a bus to safely get the athletes home. I was aching to know how he died. Was it murder? If so, who would have that much motive?

I checked my watch and pedaled harder, on my way to the Cavalleros Family Birthday Bash. When I'd been asked to bartend for the party, I'd been clueless. However, when I mentioned it to Marta, her eyes had nearly glowed. "Say yes!" she'd immediately demanded.

I was quickly informed the Cavalleroses are a family of billionaires who autumn, winter, and spring all around the world, but they *summer* at Lake Tranquility. In fact, there is a colony of bill/millionaires on the southwest shore of the large lake, which is in Serenity, the next town over. The most notable thing about this colony is that there are no roads to that side of the lake. It is only reachable by boat and (needless to say) invitation.

The season opens each June with the Cavalleros' Birthday Bash, as three of the Cavalleroses have birthdays clustered within days of each other. It is the invitation of the summer, and dozens of folks who normally never get to "cross the lake" are invited to join those who motorboat over at will.

The opportunity to work the Cavalleros party is apparently impossible to come by, as the same chef runs their household every summer, and his roster of servers, suppliers, and bartenders is fixed, diminished only by death or departure. I had no idea how I'd been invited to join the team.

Neither, apparently, did their longtime bartender, Ray.

He was nearing seventy (best guess) and had a slight limp and a pronounced attitude. His blonde hair was shaved close to his head, and his gray eyes flashed.

"Who do you know?" was his opening line.

He'd undoubtedly watched me lock my bike to a No Parking sign and run to leap onto the servers' boat as it was leaving the dock.

"Excuse me?"

"I'm Ray. The Cavalleros' bartender. You're the new assistant. Who got you the job?"

The context was obviously, "Because *I* sure didn't."

"I don't know. Any. Of the Cavalleros family."

"You are a bartender?"

"At the Battened Hatch. MacTavish's."

"That's Joseph's beat. Was Joseph's beat. Oh."

"Yeah, sorry."

"What the hell is going on in this town?" he asked.

"Another murder last night, did you hear?" asked a twenty-something male server in black pants, white shirt, and black vest with an untied black bow tie lounging around his neck.

"Eddings?" asked Ray.

"Yeah," replied the young man with wavy dark hair.

Conversations ceased and the other servers, all much younger than Ray, started edging his way. "Brian Eddings?"

"How d'ya know it was murder? What did you hear?" Questions overlapped.

The server said, "My friend lives in the apartment across the hall from him. At like two in the morning, he heard a scream, and when he went to his door, he saw Eddings's girlfriend leaving his apartment. She was freaked out, crying, and carrying a bat."

"A bat?" I asked. The inspector hadn't mentioned anything about Brian's head being bashed in. Holy smokes. This town was a bit crazy.

That was obviously the only information the curly haired waiter could add, so everyone returned to their various groups to continue gossiping.

Except Ray, who was eyeing me up and down. "Where's your bag?"

I held up my bartending bag. It held all my tools, bar mats, extra rags, and a couple of flavored simple syrups I'd made in the kitchen of what used to be the Breezy, just for fun.

"Your clothes are in there?"

I was wearing a short black dress, rather formfitting, that was my usual uniform for upscale do's. "Nope," I said, indicating my dress-clad self. "This is it."

"Did they not talk to you when they hired you?" he asked.

"Not much, no."

He turned and stalked (as much as his limp allowed him to) toward the front of the boat.

The boat began to slow. The servers turned in anticipation as we approached the shore.

Back in Los Angeles, I'd attended my share of shindigs with my mother or at the homes of friends whose parents were successful in "the industry." Their homes were not shabby. But nothing compared to the awe dealt by arriving at the Cavalleros family mansion for the first time.

The dwelling rose from the forest floor like a pop-up book setting for a fairy-tale ball. It was four stories, made of local stone. Both the main floor and the floor above were two stories tall, with floor-to-ceiling windows. The third floor had towers on either end with balconies around the tops. A wide terrace stretched the length of the house; from it a triple staircase curtsied to the ground. Tall windows from the house's great room served as doors to the outside. They stood open, with white sheers dancing in the breeze off the water.

A full chamber orchestra was setting up on one end of the patio.

We pulled into one of four slips in the covered boathouse, where house staff waited to take our supplies. As soon as we disembarked, our captain backed the boat out and took off.

The industrial kitchen was bigger than the square footage of my cottage, and it was bustling. There were two full walls of stovetops and ovens and two center rows of stainless-steel countertops, dotted with sinks every ten feet or so. I followed Ray past the obsessed sous-chefs toward a room to the side that had banks of refrigerators and freezers. From there, we took bins labeled "bar."

Ray explained there would be one full bar inside and another out on the patio. There would be two other drink stations which served soft drinks and a premade strawberry champagne punch, staffed by normal servers. He himself began to sort the liquors, mixers, fruits, and other flavor ingredients. He assigned me the getting and distributing of the drinkware to the bars.

"After that, you can start on the garnishes, Alon."

Lucky me. "Yes, sir. And it's Avalon."

"Like I have enough of my life left to use three-syllable names."

He pointed me to a butler's pantry, where staff was doling out china, crystal, and cutlery. Why rent for a party when you can buy?

Yay, being very rich.

I took one of the carts marked "bar," deciding to set up inside first.

I walked into the great room, and, looking up, I gasped, overwhelmed. The tall ceilings, the never-ending windows flooded with midday light, the crème-colored walls, and the elaborate staircases curving softly on each side of the space were stunning. The back half of the room was four stories tall. I walked through with my cart, gazing up, jaw dropped. It was fabulous.

I left the glassware at my station and allowed myself to walk the space, turning at intervals. Huge, colorful canvasses lured one up the staircases. The paintings must have been seven by ten feet, at least. I even thought I recognized some. These people had the means to acquire famous pieces.

A man in casual black trousers with a press that would have amazed Guttenberg and a short-sleeved shirt appeared from the side hall. His hair was silvering, his complexion tanned. It was his posture that tipped me off that he was, in fact, Señor Planton Cavalleros. I hurried to my station and began loading the crystal bar glasses.

He went through the room, smiling, talking to each worker who was setting up.

"You're new," he said to me. "Welcome."

"Thank you," I said.

"We hope our guests enjoy themselves, but we hope the staff does, too."

"I'm certain I will," I said. I'm not much for smiling on command, but the guy seemed sincere.

Through the afternoon, Ray and I got the four stations set up, instructed the servers who'd be with the soft drinks and punch, and distributed the ingredients to the full bars. Tonight's specialty drink was the Blueberry Birthday Bliss, which included blueberry vodka, blueberry syrup, frozen blueberries, and lemon-lime drink. Apparently, the daughter, Dani, loved blueberries.

When we had finally finished setting up, half an hour before the first guests were due to arrive, I sneaked away to freshen up and walk the grounds.

The view of Lake Tranquility was breathtaking. One could overdose on endorphins living in this place. I took a turn into a wooded copse and came out to an inlet on the other side. I was about to head back when I looked more carefully across the bay—and saw another mansion. Or what was left of one.

This one was white stone with a blue roof. The windows and doors were arched; there was a marble terrace that ran the length of the house, which went on and on. It must have the square footage of a small town. A large swimming pool, complete with slides and waterfalls, overlooked the lake. I couldn't tell if the deep blue was indicative of standing water or a heavy pool cover.

The house sat dark and silent. More silent than the Gatsby house when Gatsby wasn't home. Maybe after Gatsby was dead. (Retroactive spoiler alert. Sorry.)

"Yeah, it was somethin' crazy, wasn't it?" a voice behind me asked.

I turned to find the curlyhaired waiter, Jerome, from my boat, e-cig dangling from his lips. He was the one who knew about the old girlfriend leaving Brian Eddings's death scene.

"What's the story of that place?" I asked.

"You don't know? That's the murder mansion," he said, letting a sinister quality drip into his voice. "Edison Hall."

At my blank look, he continued. "Where Misty Edison was kidnapped from and later killed. So I guess it isn't technically a murder mansion. A kidnapped-from-and-later-murdered mansion."

"I haven't heard about it."

"Like that girl... Elizabeth Smart. Misty Edison was kidnapped from her bedroom. They tied up her little brother and duct-taped his mouth and got clean away. Huge search parties. Finally, a week later, a hiker saw a coyote taking off with her arm and hand—they found her torn clothes. The family never recovered. Left the area. Never came back."

"Yikes," I said.

"Yeah. Crazy town," Jerome said, with pride. Then, "Better get back. One screwup and Cavalleros, bye bye—" He made the universal sign for beheading, along with cutting sound effects. "Folks will start arriving soon."

It was late afternoon. The party officially started at four and went until midnight.

"You're manning the outside station," Ray said as I turned up, my rose-colored lipstick refreshed.

"Okay," I said, and grabbed a couple more bottles of Cava, Spain's version of Champagne. "Jerome told me about the mansion next door."

Ray stopped and thought. "Oh, yeah. Hadn't thought about that for a while. Odd thing—Brian Eddings was dating that girl when she was kidnapped. I knew the Eddings. Brian helped out at the woodshop sometimes. He never seemed the same after she turned up dead."

"Few people would be the same."

"I always thought he channeled his grief into sports. That's how he became an Olympian. Not exactly from an Olympic-style family. Not friendly, his dad. Both boys had a hard go of it. His older brother Frank graduated high school and hightailed it out of here. But Brian, gotta give him credit. He worked his ass off to make it where he did."

"Brian Eddings grew up around here?"

"Born and died, I guess."

Guests started arriving by boat at 4:02, and the stream didn't stop. The outside bar was breezier, being so close to the water. Fortunately, the weather cooperated. I was busy enough that time whisked quickly toward evening. When I looked up again, it was to see the great room filled with guests, thick-haired men laughing with ectomorphic women in glittering short gowns and sparkling bracelets.

I thought by now I recognized most of the denizens of Tranquility. Apparently not. Or perhaps these were the Summer People, along with Mansion People from neighboring environs. A chief enjoyment of mine is observing people, and for this night, I chose the host family.

The Cavalleros family—patriarch, Planton; matriarch, Alise;

grown daughter, Dani; and son, Tomás—knew how to host. They spread out and worked the room. As the evening progressed, Dani and Tomás felt freer to hang out with their twenty-something friends. Just after the supper buffet was put out, I noticed Tomás was thrilled by the arrival of a young couple who were obviously old friends of his. He and the young man hugged, and he threw his arm around the fellow. The new arrival's girlfriend trotted alongside.

I lost track, until the three of them arrived at my station.

"I hear you have the Kripta," said Tomás.

Usually, this would wrest my concentration immediately to the Spanish sparkling wine loved for its oaky palate and Roman-style amphora bottle, which had to be stored on its side. But I didn't care about the Cava.

Now that they stood before me, there was no getting around the fact that Tomás' newly arrived friend was Philip Young, attending with his girlfriend, Rachel Hunt. Philip had nearly been killed six weeks ago during a murder investigation in which he and I had been involved. This was the first time I'd seen him out and about.

Philip and I were friends, though I was sure his girlfriend, Rachel, didn't like me. Likely she's brilliant, but I honestly didn't want to know. It was bad enough that she was distressingly good-looking. The red cocktail dress she wore hugged her in all the right places. She probably wasn't even wearing Spanx. Rachel's skin was the color of dark wave-kissed sand, and her black hair was styled in corkscrew curls. Good for her for going natural. Good for him for liking Black girls with natural hair.

My own straight blonde hair, though streaked with a patina of golds, browns, and reds, came from my maternal Swedish line. My mother's thick mane is aggressively blonde, combed through with whiter strands as she ages. Not that she's old. In fact, Mother is one of those people who aren't defined by their looks: she defines herself and it's all her looks can do to keep up.

Me, I'm blonde. End of story.

Philip grinned at me. "This is my friend Avalon," he said to Tomás.

Tomás gave the most charming, mega-watt smile I'd ever seen. "Philip tells me you're not only one hell of a bartender, you save people's lives on the side."

So that was how I got the gig.

"Something like that. How do you two know each other?" I asked.

"Didn't he tell you?" Tomás replied. "We studied together at the École des Beaux-Arts. He obviously outshone me. You saw his damn painting hanging inside."

I looked over Tomás's shoulder to the huge canvas on the right side of the indoor staircase. *That's* why the style looked familiar. It was Philip's.

I looked at Philip before I could disguise my frank amazement—half amazed that kazillionaires had a painting of Philip's very prominently displayed in their mansion, half that kazillionaires had likely paid a pretty penny for the honor. The third half was utter astonishment at the talent displayed.

I'd first become friends with Philip when all I knew about him was that he painted the interior halls and rooms of MacTavish's Seaside Cottage, where I worked. It was a surprise when I found out he had a studio and was a serious artist, but that didn't make me like him more; we were already pals. Same when I discovered his grandfather was a famous painter from India and his grandmother was an American movie star.

Maybe I liked him *a little* more when I saw him at the gym with his shirt off. Partly because, as a melanin-challenged individual, I am envious of people who have gingerbread-colored skin year-round, and partly... okay, mostly because... well, he worked out.

"No, he didn't tell me," I said nonchalantly to the young host. "Here's your Kripta. Enjoy."

I handed Tomás the beautiful bottle, gave Philip three flutes, and the trio melted back into the crowd. As they left, Rachel gave me a smile I read as slightly smug. At least, my smile would have been, were I in her position.

The evening flew by. I love bartending because I'm a Class A Voyeur. I enjoy collecting people's stories. It has helped deepen my superpower, which is that I'm a great listener. I'm also good at reading situations and body language. Observing that party was like going to the drive-in movies and watching all the screens simultaneously.

Dessert buffets were removed at 10 p.m., and the bars closed at 11:00. Ray was efficient at closing both our stations. A professional cleaning service would arrive in the morning, so our only job was stashing the liquor. There was a servers' boat leaving at 11:30 and Ray had every intention of being on it. I considered joining him, but there would be boats every twenty minutes until 1 a.m., and I was still jazzed.

I headed back through the copse of trees. From the water's edge, I saw lights far across the lake where houses and condos formed private property and exclusive clubs. But the remains of the mansion across the inlet lay silent and dark. As clouds floated past, light from the gibbous moon occasionally rimmed silver chimneys on the roof.

A crude bench had been formed near me by placing either side of a long plank atop rocks of similar size. I sat and continued to gaze.

Did the original family still own the house, and the property? They must. Had it been purchased, the investor would certainly have either repaired or razed the dwelling.

History was littered with tales of wealthy clans beset by tragedy. But to lose your daughter, your only daughter…

"Sad, isn't it?"

Philip sat beside me and stretched his long legs. He was lean and 6' 2".

"Unutterably."

"That's what I love about you."

I looked at him.

"No 'yep' or 'nope' from you."

"You haven't met my mother."

"I'd like to."

"Some year," I said. "Where's Rachel?"

"She's got an early morning presentation at work. Already headed back over."

"Ah. How are you feeling? You're up to being out and about?"

"Yeah. I've learned to take it easy when I get tired."

"And you're feeling okay now?"

"Yeah. Just watched a movie of Dani's time in Galapagos. I've been sitting a while, which means I have reserved enough energy to go over to the Edison's. Wanna go?"

"The Edison's?"

He nodded across the inlet.

"For real? How would we get there?"

"Tomás and Dani keep a canoe hidden beneath their old playhouse."

The small structure was well-camouflaged behind trees and bushes. I wouldn't have noticed it. "You sure you're feeling up to it?"

"It's a ten-minute paddle. Across a still lake."

"Sure."

The "playhouse" was a small cottage on a raised platform. A peek through the window showed a full-size table and chairs as well as cushioned benches. I couldn't see a lot in the dark. "So, what's the difference between a playhouse and a guest cottage?" I asked. The place seemed extravagant.

"No running water."

We went around the side and pulled a light canoe out from under the small structure, which we carried easily down to the water. "What happens if we get caught?" I asked.

"Seriously? Who's going to catch us? If we see a boat coming, we'll be long gone before they arrive. Tomás, Dani, and I used to go all the time."

We clambered into the boat and shoved off.

BLUEBERRY BIRTHDAY BLISS

Ingredients

 1 ½ oz blueberry vodka
 1 oz blueberry syrup
 ¼ cup frozen blueberries
 Lemon-lime soda

Method

Pour blueberry vodka into a Collins glass with ice.
Add blueberry syrup, stir until mixed.
Add frozen blueberries (small ones are best) and top with
a lemon-lime soda such as Sprite.
Enjoy!

4

MURDER MANSION

WIND AND WATER were both still, leaving stars swirling both above and below the boat. The air was fresh with lilac, and frogs on the shore sounded like a banjo trio.

We paddled gently but made good time.

The house got spookier as we got closer. It was impossible not to look at it without adding an overlay of music, laughter, and splashes in the marble pool.

"They all really walked out of here and never came back?"

"So I've heard. It was twenty years ago. Back then, the adults didn't tell the whole story to little kids like me—though we knew something bad had happened. For several months, it seemed all the grown-ups abruptly stopped talking when a child approached. The Cavalleros children were young then, too. After what happened to the Edisons, Planton made sure their house is alarmed so well, if you're staying over you have to be careful which bathroom you go to so you don't set off the motion detector."

"I can understand why."

We thunked back onto land and pulled the canoe up onto the grass and flipped it over behind a log, oars underneath.

Philip led me back to a set of wooden stairs climbing the berm on the side of the house. We reached the top and I stepped back into the shadows. "Whoa," I said. The view down to the terrace was breathtaking. The pool had been topped with a (now sagging and algae-prone) heavy blue cover that matched the blue of the shingles and shutters and set off the white of the marble. I would have loved to experience a party here.

"Did the Cavalleros family know the Edisons very well?"

"Not really. Misty babysat Dani and Tomás sometimes, but she and her brother were older. I think Misty was sixteen and Davy was seven when she was taken. Dani and Tomás were a toddler and an infant. Come on."

He led me around the corner of the house, toward the kitchen wing. There was a *porte cochere*—a covered porch—above the delivery entrance. Philip surprised me by climbing onto the railing. He then made use of two heavy bolts to climb the wooden pillar and ascend to the top, where there was a walk-out porch from the bedroom above.

"Aha!" he said. A moment later, a rope ladder with wooden rungs was slung over the top.

"I'm supposed to climb this thing?"

"This is the only way in, to the best of my knowledge."

I yanked on the ladder: it held. I climbed the swaying rope to the upper porch, and he pulled the ladder up after me. The door to the inside bedroom had a lock with raised numbers, awaiting a code. Apparently, Philip knew it.

I looked at him, questioningly. "Dani, Tomás, and I installed it," he said with a shrug.

If it remained undiscovered this long, the place must be deserted, indeed.

We entered the house, closing and locking the door behind us. The shadowed bedroom was large, with a fireplace. "This was for the maid," he said. Apparently, even the staff gets rooms with a view in a place like this.

Together we moved into the hallway. Philip grabbed my hand and led me along. "Service wing," he said. "Kitchen, laundry, etc." Finally, "Okay." We'd come to a white door. "Close your eyes."

He opened the door and led me through; then he put my hand on a railing as we ascended. When we stopped, he turned me around, put both my hands on a railing in front of me and said, "Now."

"Whoa."

I'd been in mansions of entertainment-industry types who worked with my mother. But nothing like this. He'd brought me up to a third-floor landing, from which stairs poured down on either side, their wrought-iron railings curving and dancing, shaped with ivy and roses.

In the midst of the ceiling above was a chandelier that would stun even the Phantom of the Opera. From there, the room expanded, eventually reaching huge doors that would have opened and vanished, leaving the entire lake wall open to the terrace.

I was shocked to find the whole place still filled with furniture. They didn't seem to have taken a thing.

"Holy smokes."

"In their defense, this wasn't just their summer house. They lived here all year around."

"It's really something."

"Come on. I'll show you the family's quarters. It's practically another house."

He took my hand and led me down to the second-floor landing, then across to a door on the opposite side. He opened it, and we stepped through. This room lacked floor-to-ceiling windows, thus was darker. Philip pulled the door closed behind us and we stood a moment, letting our eyes adjust.

We were in another living room. Although it had a second-floor walkway, the room beneath us was more comfortable than grand. There were overstuffed sofas and wing chairs. The television above the fireplace was smaller than I would have expected.

"It's not their main TV," said Philip, following my gaze. "In fact, not even close."

We continued down to the main room, then headed for the kitchen. "Steps down to the family room through there," he said. "Stairs to the family bedrooms that way. There are also back stairs to the bedrooms from here."

It was almost pitch black in the kitchen, since the only windows looked out into the woods. He took my hand again to lead me to tall seats at the breakfast bar when he stepped on something—a lone shoe, it turned out—and tripped. He didn't catch himself. He went down.

He lay on the floor and gave a low moan.

"Philip, what? Are you all right?"

"I..." and he gasped. "I twisted somehow."

"Your wound?"

He nodded. "I was already thinking climbing the porch had been a bad idea," he admitted.

"Should I go get someone? Call an ambulance?"

"No. Just give me a minute."

He lay there, and I sat beside him in companionable silence.

"I can see why you guys found it fun to come over here," I finally said. "You and Tomás were at the École des Beaux-Arts together?"

"Yes. We shared a flat."

"The painting of yours they have... it's wonderful."

"You think?"

"I know."

He took a deep breath and pushed himself into a sitting position.

"Should we head back?" I asked.

"Yeah."

I stood and offered him my hands. He took them and I pulled him up, but it threw me off balance. I took a step back, and he fell against me.

Then he kissed me.

I was surprised. But not so surprised that I didn't kiss him back.

It was wonderful. The taste of Cava still lingered on his lips.

He stood straighter as the kiss continued and put his hand out to balance us against the granite breakfast bar. I didn't think anything. I just let myself experience a welling of happiness that I hadn't felt for a long time.

So it took me a minute to realize someone was weeping.

Somewhere in the empty house, someone was weeping.

MURDER MANSION MARTINI

Ingredients

2 oz Krupnik or other honey liqueur
1 ½ oz of sour mix
Hot jalapeño jelly
Lemon or lime for twist

SOUR MIX

Method

For sour mix, put two cups of water and two cups of granulated sugar into a saucepan. Heat until sugar dissolves. When cool, add 1 ½ ounces of lemon juice and 1 ½ ounces of lime juice.

COCKTAIL

Method

Put ice into cocktail shaker.
Add Krupnik and sour mix to shaker. Then add a small dollop of jalapeño jelly to taste. (Remember to use a spoon, and don't touch it to your hands or mouth.)
Shake until smooth, around six seconds.
Pour into small martini glass.
Cut a strip of the citrus you've chosen. Twist it over drink and use for garnish.

5
THROUGH THE DARKNESS

"DO YOU HEAR that?" Philip whispered, instantly alert.
"Yes," I answered.

He offered me his hand, and I took it. Together we stepped gingerly through the darkness, inching together to the base of the back steps to the bedrooms.

The crying seemed louder.

We headed up, as silently as possible, glad that the steps were carpeted. I tried not to think of the two possibilities: someone else was in the house... or not.

We paused at the first landing. "These must be the kids' bedrooms," he said.

The mournful sound carried. Our hands were sweaty as we continued down the wide hallway. As we reached the first open door, the sound stopped. Abruptly.

I didn't think it had come from that room, but we went in.

The furniture was heavy and expensive, the décor mid-seventies—the French provincial side, not the lava lamp side. Draperies and bed linens were well-chosen and matching. But there was nothing personal in the room. It was likely a guest room, with an attached bath. No one there. Philip also opened the closet doors. Dark, hanging bedspreads, extra pillows. Nothing else.

He went out into the hall and continued to the next room. The door was only open a crack. Philip pushed it open and it swung on a silent axis.

He stepped inside. "This must have been it," he said. "Misty's room. She was kidnapped from here."

I let him enter first. Again, no signs of life.

Misty's room featured a large bathroom with a jacuzzi tub and shower. I hung back when Philip threw open her closet door. Nothing moved. He shone in the flashlight from his cell. The closet was a walk-in, nearly the size of my current bedroom. There were still clothes.

"This is so awful," I said. "It's so sad."

Emboldened, he went over to the French doors that lead to her balcony. We peered through. I could see sitting here on a balmy night or fending off a young Romeo. How did the kidnappers get up? How did they get Misty down?

A large oak was close enough to climb, but still, my guess was some kind of ladder.

"You've never been up here?" I asked.

"No. Never had reason to. Even as kids, we were being... respectful, I guess." Philip sat on the bed. "I don't hear the crying anymore, do you? Give me a minute to catch my breath."

"Sorry," I said to any spirit that might remain. "We're just catching our breath."

"Should we check the rest of the hall?"

"I... don't think we're going to find anyone," I said. I didn't add that I wouldn't *want* to find anyone. Alive, or formerly so.

Philip, who normally wasn't the kind to give up on these things, said, "I think I'd best get back to the Cavalleros.'"

"Your injury still hurts?"

He nodded. I tried not to seem overly concerned about his wound reopening, but I didn't want to be responsible for nearly killing him, twice.

I helped him down the stairs. We went out one of the sliding glass doors, leaving it unlocked behind us. I hated not leaving things secured, but there was no way he could climb down from the balcony in his condition.

I rowed back. It was slow going, even the part with him walking on level ground back to the house. The party was long over and all but a few workers had gone. I got Philip into the hands of the hosts and made it onto the last boat.

Back across the lake, I unlocked my bicycle and headed home, thinking these last two had been strange days, indeed.

I had no idea.

THROUGH THE DARKNESS

Hibiscus Margarita

Ingredients

1 ½ oz One with Life organic tequila (or white tequila of your choice)
1 oz homemade sour mix (or store bought)
½ oz triple sec (or any orange liquor of your choice)
1 oz homemade hibiscus tea simple syrup
Ice
Candied hibiscus flower for garnish (Wild Hibiscus Flower Co. has the best candied hibiscus.)

HIBISCUS SIMPLE SYRUP

Ingredients

1/4 cup of dried hibiscus loose flower
1/4 cup of granulated sugar
1/2 cup of water

Method

In medium saucepan on low heat, add dried hibiscus flower, sugar, and water.
Simmer on low heat until sugar is dissolved and water has turned a bright-pink color, approximately 10 minutes.
Take off heat and let cool.
Strain liquid through a small mesh strainer to clean flower from simple syrup.

COCKTAIL

Method

In cocktail shaker, add ice, tequila, orange liquor, hibiscus simple syrup, and sour mix.
Shake until ingredients are blended and you have a nice frothy consistency.
Pour contents of shaker into rocks glass.
Add candied hibiscus flower on top for garnish.
Sip and enjoy!

6

PERSON OF INTEREST

I WOKE UP thinking about ghosts. Had we heard one the night before? Was it the spirit of young Misty, come back to her deserted house, weeping for the life and people she'd once loved? The sound had been chilling and heartbreaking.

In my past life, back in Los Angeles, it wasn't that I didn't believe in ghosts, I simply didn't think about them much—while erring on the side of common sense. However, here in Tranquility, Marta, my barback/assistant manager confided that she saw them often. I trusted Marta as much as I trust anybody in this world. If I have one point of complete confidence in myself, it's in my ability to read people's trustworthiness. I can say with certainty that I would put my life in Marta's hands, because, in fact, I had, two months ago when confronting a murderer.

Marta confessed her supernatural problem when she started losing sleep. She admitted she'd told her father, a conservative Christian pastor, when she was younger, but he was so horrified, she'd quickly walked back on her assertions. They hadn't mentioned it since. Her mother was dead—but not among her visitors. That had been my promise to her: to try to find someone she could talk to with more knowledge of these things.

Which led me to the only other person I knew would be good for the job—the pastor of St. Barnabas Episcopal Church, Hannah Bricksford.

I squeezed some orange juice and went outside in pajama pants and t-shirt to sit on the small flagstone patio. My rented cottage was on a hidden property just beyond the center of Tranquility. The acreage contained a stream and waterfall; the burble of the running water was soothing to me and to the sparrows who were tending to newly hatched eggs. I had no idea when I rented this place that Philip had grown up here, or that his grandmother, who owned the property and the lodge across the stream from me, was a screen star in the "golden age" of Hollywood.

Philip.

The kiss.

What the hell was that?

We hadn't talked about it afterwards, not a word. In the absence of explanation, I could only assume he was coming to his senses and falling deeply, madly, passionately in love with me. And I would doggone believe that until it was proven otherwise.

I got out my phone and texted: *You all right?*

It would be just my luck that he'd fall in love with me and imme-diately die of sepsis.

There was a minute before the answer came: *Yeah. Thanks.*

Well. That was about as romantic as humanly possible.

I got dressed and decided to head for Hannah's. I promised Marta yesterday I would try to find her some help or advice. I took a breath and texted her: *Hey, you around? Could I stop in and ask you a question?*

The answer came quickly. *Sure. Want lunch?*

I didn't respond. Her overtures of friendship made me crazy.

Not crazy. Threatened. She seemed to think we could be friends, as co-Anne of Green Gables friends of the heart.

And we could, if it wasn't for her profession. Thanks to my father, I had no interest in organized religion. I hated him and hated his religion. There. I said it. I'd gone to him once, looking for com-fort, and he'd told me my beloved friend had gone to hell. I was done with religion and with him.

I didn't know why Hannah wouldn't give up on me and let us remain arms-length acquaintances. She thought I was great. I wanted her to stop it.

As I rode my bike across the bridge and out onto the main road through town, it occurred to me I might need to break down and buy myself a car.

Meanwhile, the day was clear, humidity low, temperature in the low 70s, and on my blue bicycle, on tree-shaded streets, I was about as far from the smog and traffic of Los Angeles as I could be.

It was Monday, my day off, and Hannah's, too, so I headed for her house rather than her church office. The two buildings were on adjacent properties, but not connected, so I went up her private drive. The house was built in the 1960s, one story with lots of glass. It would be at home in Los Angeles with a pool out back and a view of the Hollywood sign. The driveway was circular, with the intention of holding many cars when she entertained the church committees. As I rode up the sloping drive, the front door opened and Hannah appeared, along with a white woman maybe in her mid thirties. The woman was twig-like, wearing loose clothes and heavy eyeliner. Her dyed blonde hair was combed to one side and pinned. It looked like it had been styled in a hurry.

As I put down my kickstand, Hannah gave the woman a hug. Then she saw me and waved. The woman at the door turned anxiously to see who was coming.

"Hi, Avalon," Hannah said. "This is Robyn."

I recognized Robyn from the Battened Hatch, but she wasn't a regular, and I couldn't place her beyond that.

"Hi," the woman murmured. She turned and walked along a small sidewalk toward the church parking lot, where she'd parked her white Impala.

She opened the car with the key—physically putting the key into the lock, it was that old—sat down, and put her head down on the steering wheel. Then she sat up, wiped away tears, and started the engine.

Hannah and I looked at each other. "Brian Eddings's girlfriend."

"Ahhh. The one with the bat."

Hannah looked at me quizzically and we went inside. She led the way to the kitchen and opened the fridge. "I hope you don't mind that I didn't cook. It's hard to commit to it when Avantika makes the world's best curried chicken."

I would never complain about being served anything from the Cardamom Café, and Hannah knew it. She arranged our plates and headed for the Florida room, a glassed-in patio behind the living room. A rectangular garden surrounded by a stone wall was visible out the back. Bursts of hydrangeas in Wedgewood blue and pinkish purple were coming into bloom and a pair of bluebirds had claimed a three-story birdhouse. I imagined it would be a comfy place in the winter to sit inside and watch the snow fall.

Hannah set down our plates and gave us each a napkin rolled around utensils. Water glasses and white wine were set out. We sat. She said a brief blessing, and we both reached for the wine.

"So," she said. "How did you hear about the bat?"

"What? Oh. I was working the Cavalleros party last night. On the way over, people were discussing Brian Eddings. One of the waiters knows Brian's across-the-hall neighbor. The neighbor apparently heard a scream and opened his door in time to see Robyn leaving Brian's apartment, crying and with a baseball bat. Or so it was passed along to me, third hand."

"Darn." Hannah's face clouded. Her face was perfectly oval, and she didn't wear bangs because, well, why? Her brown eyes were large and framed by dark eyebrows; she had a sturdy nose and rose-colored lips that fell naturally into a smile. I knew her father was Black—and as famous in his profession as my mother is in hers—and she was so light-skinned she could pass for white, or frankly, any combination she wanted.

In any case, she wasn't smiling now. "The police came to question Robyn, and she's sure everyone in town knows she was there and hates her since Brian was so beloved."

"He was larger than life, that's certain," I said. "But being there isn't the same as killing someone. And the police questioned me, too, so she can join the club." I took a bite. "She didn't kill him, did she?"

"No. No! She went to talk to him, and he was already dead when she got there." Hannah punctuated the air with her fork.

"Robyn brought a bat?"

"Well, yes."

"But Brian's head wasn't bashed in."

"Not at all. He was sitting up in bed and his eyes were open, so she even talked to him for a minute before she noticed something wasn't right."

"Yikes. That's awful. Why didn't she call an ambulance?"

"She could tell he was dead. And, he was her guy. She'd been talking to him for a while. When she realized, she freaked."

"And there was a nonviolent reason for the bat?"

"It's kind of complicated. She wasn't sure people would understand. But she didn't come to me in confidence, as a minister, so I guess I can talk about it."

"Well, then, why did she come?"

"She came because she was afraid she'd be arrested."

"Yeah? Why come to you about that?"

"Because she heard I listen when people are afraid the... officials... aren't being fair. Also, because I help run the local justice fund, which means I can put my hands on bail money to make sure poor people aren't stuck in prison for lack of bail. She was getting my number, just in case."

"So you're a good choice when you're allowed one phone call? I'll remember that. Good to know. And the bat?"

Hannah sighed. "She's known Brian for a very long time. They grew up here, in Tranquility. They were friends in high school, and even dated when they were young. But then Brian met Misty Eddington and that was that. Even after Misty died, it seemed Brian had moved on. So, last year when Robyn ran into Brian at a St. Paul's parish retreat, they spent time together and started dating. But he has ... anger-management issues, as they say."

"Wow. I never saw any sign of that. In fact, Brian seemed talented at keeping situations in hand."

"From what I can tell, it's one of those situations where the person is usually triggered in intimate situations, with the people he's closest to. Brian never actually hit Robyn, but he threatened to. Then he broke up with her. He said he couldn't be with anyone, because he'd inherited the Eddings family curse. He wanted to leave her before his anger got the better of him and he hurt her. She was crushed. After a week, she went to his apartment with a baseball bat to basically say, 'I don't care, I love you. If I need to, I'll defend myself with a baseball bat, and you'll learn pretty quick not to let your anger win.'"

"But he was dead."

"Yep."

"Did she see any signs of foul play?"

"No. She said, oddly, the door was slightly ajar. He never left his door open. So she thought someone must have gotten there before she did."

"Someone who, unlike her, didn't scream so that the neighbors would open their doors."

"Apparently."

"The funeral will be at St. Paul's?"

"Yes. Brian was Catholic. There will be a funeral Mass on Wednesday, a memorial service at one of the Olympic venues for those who want to pay their respects later in the week. That one will be televised. More wine?"

"Thanks."

"So. What's up? You didn't come over to discuss Brian Eddings."

"True." I took the last bite of curried chicken and cleaned the plate with my last piece of naan. "I know you must hear lots of strange things."

"To put it mildly."

I took a swig of the Chardonnay. "You know Marta, who works at Battened Hatch with me..."

"Sure. Tim Layton's daughter."

"Well. She has a problem. Or, a challenge."

"I'm all ears."

"She says she sees ghosts. Dead people. It used to be just now and then, but now she sees them a lot. Not all floaty, but like they're real people, standing there like you or me. She doesn't know what to do. When she told her dad, he shut her down. She's having trouble sleeping. I said I'd see if I could figure out how to help."

Hannah tore off a piece of bread and chewed thoughtfully. Was she going to suggest psychotherapy? An exorcist?

"You know, I think I might know someone," she said. "Let me make a phone call. Not being able to sleep is a terrible thing. Poor kid."

"I'd appreciate it."

"Coffee or tea?" She stood and picked up her plate. As she did, I heard the bright notes of "Hedwig's Theme" drift from the other room.

I nodded permission for her to go and answer her phone. I picked up my plate and our silverware and followed behind.

"Okay, I'm on it," she said into the phone. "Don't say anything until your lawyer gets there. Nothing. Take a breath. We'll get through this."

She hung up and looked at me with eyes of apology. "I've got to go call a lawyer," she said. "Robyn's been taken in as a person of interest."

We walked out together. "Thanks for lunch," I said as she headed for the Rolodex in her church office. I claimed my bike.

"I'll let you know what I find out for Marta," she said.

"Thanks."

Even though it was my day off, I decided to head to MacTavish's to pick up my check and make certain things were left in tip-top shape though I hadn't been in.

Mrs. Rumple, the head of human resources, was on the phone in her office off a back hall, but she picked up my envelope and waved it like a hanky toward a departing ship. I stepped in and grabbed it, giving her a nod of gratitude.

Out in the hall, I nearly smashed into Glenn MacTavish, the owner of all the odd wondrousness that was MacTavish's Seaside Cottage as well as That Ship Has Sailed.

"Lassie!" he said. "Glad to see ya before I set sail."

"Set sail?"

"Yes. I'm making a pilgrimage to the home country."

"Scotland?" I asked, as if the question wasn't answered by the full tartan regalia he was wearing. He was born and raised here in Lake Tranquility. His father did indeed have Scottish heritage, but, from what I'd been told, not a whisper of a brogue.

"Going to meet the family," he said. "I did the DNA test and found clans! Mostly in Argyll and Aberdeenshire. Going to take a trip before the insanity of the Tranquility Film Festival is upon us."

"Congratulations," I said. He'd always wanted to find blood family. "When is the new chef for the Breezy arriving?"

The Breezy was lakeside dining for the tourist crowd, while the Battened Hatch was a pub more attractive to the local trade. Chef Paul, a stubborn cook and friend to no one, had recently been sent in search of greener pastures.

"I've found a fabulous new chef," he said. "Angelica Dormor. I'll be gone for two weeks. She'll start when I get back. Meantime, we just keep breakfast and lunch trades going—"

"For the tourists," we answered together.

"Chef Angelica will start mid-June to be up and running by the Festival in August."

"Sounds like a plan," I said. It would be nice not to share a kitchen with someone as openly hostile as Chef Paul.

"It'll get busier here this week than I planned on," he said. "Town will be swamped with press and mourners for the Olympic fellow. Hotel is full up. Tavern will likely be busy, too. You can handle it."

It was a statement rather than a question.

"Yes, sir. Marta is being a big help. She oversaw the place yesterday when I was out."

"Ah, yes. You were..."

"Working the Cavalleros party."

"Really? Ray still there?"

"Oh, yes. You know him?"

"He came around here, looking for work, this was many years ago. We didn't have a position, and even if we did, I wouldn't have hired him. I heard the Cavalleroses were looking for a bartender, so I sent him their way. I'm kind of surprised it's worked out this long."

"He didn't seem like a real... people person."

"He's not. But I think he's able to put enough aside during the summers that he can go live in his cabin the rest of the year."

"Is the cabin near here?"

"Sure." The hotel manager had appeared and was seeking his attention.

"May your trip be all you hope it will be," I said. "Take pictures of the clan."

"Aye, lassie. Aye," he said, and moved away.

A brief survey of the Battened Hatch proved that Marta had done a fine job. It was ready to open the next day.

On my way home, I paused at the uphill road that led toward Philip's craftsman cottage. Pinning my courage to the sticking place, I walked the bike up the steep incline until I reached the level street where Philip lived. I hopped on the bike. I didn't do more than turn the last corner when I saw a red Mazda in his driveway.

Rachel's car.

I backed out of sight around the corner and headed for home.

PERSON OF INTEREST

Rapberry Lime Coconut Mojito

Ingredients

Fresh raspberries
2 wedges fresh lime
Fresh mint leaves
2 oz kraft (or your favorite) rum
1 ½ oz Malibu
Coconut La Croix

Method

Put raspberries into shaker. Muddle.
Add the juice of two wedges of lime
Add a handful of mint leaves
Muddle until fragrant.
Put ice into cocktail shaker.
Add rum.
Add Malibu.
Shake until mixed, around six seconds.
Put ice into Collins glass. Pour mixture into glass.
Top with coconut La Croix.
Serve and enjoy!

7

BAPTIST MORTIFICATION

"Where are we going?" Marta asked.

The two of us sat squashed in back of the Prius, which I'd called white, only to be corrected to "blizzard pearl." It was Hannah's new used car and she was proud.

"I don't know," I replied. "All I know is Hannah called late last night and said she'd found someone who wanted to talk to you, and today is our chance."

We both faced front, pondering our mysterious fate. Marta wasn't comfortable going with Hannah without me, so we set an appointment in the early morning so Marta could get to school—fortunately, there was some sort of junior testing, and graduating seniors got to come in on a delay. Hannah, being Hannah, was also giving a parishioner a lift to outpatient physical therapy at the local hospital. Xavier was short and muscled and chatted merrily with Hannah in Spanish in the front seat.

"You don't think she's taking me to a psychologist, do you?"

"No. She's not like that."

"Or, like, an exorcist?"

"Marta, no! If she was, I would get you out of there, taking Lucifer with us."

She looked horrified.

"It was a joke." Dear God, she was skittish.

"Did I tell you that after the Cavalleros party, I went over to the old Edison house?" I asked, attempting to distract her.

This piqued her interest. "No. By yourself?"

Tricky question. Marta was a gifted painter, and Philip gave her lessons. She had a crush on him. Philip was a person on whom it was easy to crush.

"No, with a friend from the party. And, you know what?"

Was I going there?

"What?"

"I think we heard a ghost."

I went there.

"How so?" She was suspicious.

"We'd been there a while when we heard weeping. Like it was coming from the walls. It was so *sad*."

She studied me. "You don't think I'm crazy?"

"I didn't say that. But not because of the ghost thing."

She managed a small smile.

We pulled up to the outpatient door of the hospital, and Xavier got out. He squared his shoulders and steeled himself.

"Estoy rezando por ti," said Hannah. He entered the door that said Outpatient Testing. She rolled up the car window. "Okay. On to the next adventure."

There's a special purple haze in the mountains just after sunrise, with gray-blue afternotes. The drive on the two-lane road leading away from Tranquility was awe-inspiring. Not inspiring enough to get me up at this ungodly hour to experience it when I didn't have to, but stirring, just the same.

We drove on for twenty minutes, taking small roads I'd never travelled. We finally arrived at the entrance to a road that ran up a sloping hillside, adorned at the top by a church with a bell tower in Italianate style. Around it, inside a walled complex, sat other square buildings with butter-orange arched outside passageways. It looked for all the world like we'd somehow landed in Florence, or the Tuscan countryside. Completing the illusion, neat rows of grapes climbed the hillside. The sign above us proclaimed, "Vineyard de las Hermanas del Felice Corazón." On the side of the entryway was a sign that said they'd open this afternoon at 4 p.m.

Hannah made a final check of the GPS on her phone and headed up the mountain. At the top, we drove through tall arches into a large cobbled courtyard, perhaps half an acre, surrounded by the buildings we'd seen from below. A wide stone fountain burbled in the center. There were parking spots across from the church, in front of a large sign that said Gift Shop, surrounded by purple grapes.

Hannah got out of the car. Marta and I followed suit.

A knot of a half dozen nuns exited the copper-colored door of the stone church. They wore denim vests over white collared shirts and denim skirts which fell just below their knees, white stockings, and sensible shoes. A navy-blue headscarf completed the outfit. One of them, a petite woman who looked Latina, saw us. She took leave of the others and headed in our direction.

"She's a *nun*," Marta whispered, drenched in Baptist mortification.

Hannah stood straight as she arrived. "Sister Maria Luisa?" she asked.

"You must be the Reverend Bricksford," she said, offering her hand.

"Hannah," she said, shaking it warmly. "Thank you for seeing us."

Sister Maria Luisa turned to us. "And you're Marta? I hear you have an unusual gift."

"I... guess."

"I was about to walk the back path to check the vineyards one more time," she said. "Why don't you walk with me?"

Marta couldn't very well say no, since we'd come for that purpose. Sister Maria Luisa looped her arm through Marta's and the two headed for an arched door in the back wall.

"Well. This is unexpected," I said.

"Yeah," Hannah replied. "Stuff usually is."

"I didn't know this convent was here. What do they sell?"

"Wines and wine accoutrements," she said. "And these really fabulous chocolate champagne corks with sparkling wine inside."

I was suddenly sorry we wouldn't be there during business hours.

"Could we?" I nodded toward the path Marta and the sister had taken. "I'd like to see where they go," I said.

Hannah nodded. We headed for the arched door. She pulled out her cellphone and pushed in numbers as we went. I heard a tinny ring, then it went to someone's voicemail, with the pre-programmed, "518... is not available. Please leave a message after the beep."

The view from the doorway was magnificent. Tranquility is nestled in the Adirondacks, a range of beautiful mountains, coated with stately deciduous trees and pines that brushed the sky, shining lakes peppered in the valleys that rested between the hills. The view from the convent was enriched by orderly rows of grape vines planted all the way down the hill. We could see Sister Maria Luisa and Marta starting down the path.

There was a tiled terrace with white iron tables by a low stone wall. We found a small table and sat.

Hannah hit "redial," eliciting the same ring and the same message.

"I can't get ahold of Robyn," she said. "Would you mind if I make another call?"

"Sure."

She stood and paced the terrace. This call was answered, and she talked for a while.

"That was the lawyer," she said. "He was with Robyn when she was questioned yesterday afternoon. They didn't have enough evidence to hold her, so he and Robyn left state police headquarters around four thirty. She works at Adams' Microbrewery and was afraid she'd be late for work if she went home, so he dropped her there. She said not to worry; she often walked or Ubered home after work."

Hannah was still troubled, but less so. I said, "You do realize that if you work the late shift, chances are good you're not going to be up at eight in the morning to answer the phone."

"That makes sense." She slipped her phone into her purse. "Wanna see a movie this week?"

"Sure? I mean, I probably can't when the Battened Hatch is open. It sounds like Tranquility is going to have an influx of Olympians and press."

"Oh. Of course.."

We both sat gazing over the landscape. I thought about Brian Eddings, and how I wished I'd gotten to know him better when I'd had the chance.

The police still hadn't released the circumstances surrounding his death. I wondered where Inspector Mike Spaulding was, and if I could pry any information out of him.

Marta and Sister Maria Luisa had settled on a bench about halfway down the hill. They talked for another twenty minutes, heads leaned together, before they headed back up.

We thanked the sister and got back into Hannah's car. Marta sat alone in the backseat. None of us spoke on the ride into town.

To my surprise, Brent Davis was one of the first customers when we opened. He sat at the bar and ordered a croque monsieur, one of the faster sandwiches.

"What was that you said about hoping there were no major news stories?" he asked.

"Sorry if I jinxed it," I replied. "How are you managing the film editing and the investigative journalism?"

"By not sleeping," he muttered.

"Say... does the newspaper have any old files on the Misty Edison case?"

"I'm sure we do," he said. "That's a blast from the past. What brings it up?"

"I heard Misty was dating Brian Eddings when she was kidnapped. That he channeled his grief into sports."

"Hmm. Interesting angle," he said.

"Could I stop by and take a look sometime?"

"Sure. Obviously, we're a little busy, but I'll have our summer intern pull the old articles."

"Thanks."

"On the condition that if you solve another murder, you'll give us the inside scoop."

"Sure. Need anything else?" I asked.

The pub was beginning to fill up with people I didn't recognize, many of them middle-aged but in great shape. Former Olympians was my guess.

Marta seemed distracted when she arrived. At one point, I found her in the hall that led to the storeroom and restrooms, her thoughts far away.

"Listen, how did things go with the sister this morning?"

"Good," she said.

"Everything all right?"

"Yes."

Apparently, she wasn't ready for an in-depth conversation. "Great. Let's move some more bubbly into the wine fridge. It seems to be a popular item this week."

"Will do."

It turned out to be an exhausting night, especially since I'd been up so early. Later, as I got ready for bed, I tried not to think about the fact that the next day was the local wake for Brian, then crowds would only grow larger between the private funeral and the international memorial service on Friday. What a time for Glenn to be away in Scotland finding his roots.

Still, this kind of challenge I could handle.

I thought only one more time about the unexpected kiss. Then, I fell straight into a sound sleep.

The next day, Wednesday, I awoke earlier than usual. I made some Constant Comment tea in a blue bone-china mug with a graceful phoenix rising on two sides. Plates, cups, and dishes came with the place. Many were china, mostly very art deco, made in the original period. When this was a guest cottage for the larger lodge, people must have been very careful not to break anything. Most sets were intact. Savoring scents of orange and clove, I sauntered to the picture window. The cottage sat across from Sally's "rustic" lodge, separated by a running brook with a waterfall that fell into a pond below. A curved wooden bridge connected me to the lodge, an expansive lawn, and the lane out.

Down in front of the waterfall and the pond was a carved white bench.

Someone was sitting on it.

I moved closer to see, then returned to the kitchen and poured steaming water over a teabag in a second blue phoenix mug and went outside. I walked across the footbridge, and around the small waterfall.

I sat next to Hannah on the bench and handed her the mug of tea.

She said, "Robyn's dead."

Then she leaned her head on my shoulder and began to cry.

BAPTIST MORTIFICATION

Ingredients

1 ½ oz vanilla vodka
½ oz amaretto
1 oz Coco Real or other cream of coconut
3 oz heavy cream
Ice
Chocolate syrup

Method

Put vodka, amaretto, Coco Real, heavy cream, and ice
into blender. Blend until ice is crushed into drink,
approximately 2 minutes.
Drizzle martini glass with chocolate syrup. Pour drink
into glass.
Drizzle top with chocolate syrup, add whipped cream.
For a naked Baptist, leave off whipped crème.

8

CLOSED CASKET

"I'M SO SORRY," I said. "What happened?"

She let herself cry. Then we were quiet. Finally, she sat straight. "She was struck by a car walking home from work around 1 a.m. A jogger found her body in a ditch yesterday afternoon. Blunt force. Like an automobile force."

"Dear God. So she was already dead when you were trying to call her from the convent."

"Yes."

"Did you have a feeling about it?"

"I was worried."

"Do they think it was an accident?"

"They're not saying. If so, what a coincidence, huh? Brian's girlfriend dead two days after he is?"

"Yeah. Pretty strange."

"In any case, it was either murder or a hit-and-run. Someone knew they hit her, and just left her there."

"That's awful."

"The lawyer said the police are scouring the area for cars taken to body shops."

"Or hidden in a garage."

"Do you think someone blamed her for Brian's death?"

"I hope not. I don't know."

"Hannah, I'm so sorry. You helped in every way you could."

"She was halfway between the restaurant and her house. She was nearly home."

"How did you find out?"

"Her lawyer called me." She sighed. "I'd better go. I was working out when I got the call. Left my car down on the street. Hope it's okay I came up."

"Of course."

We stood at the same time. I hugged her at the lane and we went our separate ways.

Brian's wake was scheduled from 11 to 2 and then 4 to 6. I decided to stop in to pay my respects on the early side and open the Battened Hatch at noon. I headed down to the pub to put up a sign to that effect. My black bartender's garb was oddly appropriate for nearly any situation.

The wake was at McCready's, a funeral parlor located in a three-story Victorian house on a short road just off Main Street. It had a black mansard roof with scalloped black shingles, a wide front porch, and a porte cochere, so caskets could be carried out even in inclement weather. Unlike the mansion from *Psycho*, the white paint was fresh, and flowers bloomed in profusion in two front flower beds, as well as in large clay pots on the porch. I was glad I'd come early. The place was already comfortably full. I planned to leave before "comfortably" went missing.

Two of the McCready sons, dressed in bespoke black suits, greeted people at the door. We were instructed to sign in at the electronic guest book on an open laptop. Thick burgundy-and-gold Persian carpets ran the length of the hallways and muffled sound. To the right, I was told, was a parlor with punch and a video of some of Brian's most memorable moments.

To the left was Brian, should I care to pay my respects.

I signed in at the guestbook and hesitated only briefly. If passing Brian's coffin and giving my condolences to his family was the price of getting to leave, put me in line.

Folding padded brown chairs were set up, facing the front of the long room. I couldn't see the coffin because of the line of people moving past, but I could see large sprays of gladioluses and flags representing the United States, the Knights of Columbus, and the Olympics. There was also a large photo of Brian looking straight into the camera and laughing, as well as one of him, substantially younger, standing on the top middle of the medalists' podium proudly wearing his gold.

The line of mourners moved slowly against the far wall. I went to find the end.

There, I made a happy discovery. Brent Davis was in line ahead of me.

"Hey, Avalon," he said.

"Hi," I said. "So much for no big news happening so you can work on the documentary."

"So you've heard about Robyn?"

"Yes," I answered. "Horrible." We waited a respectful moment. "Weird that she and Brian dated recently, and also back when they were kids."

"I've been told that. They both grew up here. Lived close to each other, in a Tranquility-manner of speaking. Their houses were off different roads, but not far from each other through the woods."

"Ah. Handy for teenage lovers."

"If they were. I think they were pretty young when they were sweethearts. Somehow both the Eddings boys moved up and out. But Robyn kind of stayed put. Literally. In the same house, even after her mom had to move into assisted living."

"So what gave Brian the confidence to start dating a rich kid like Misty? And to pursue an Olympic goal?"

"Good questions. How do some people leave their childhoods behind? How do they use hardship to propel themselves?"

We'd been inching forward as we talked and were soon in view of the casket. It was solid and walnut-brown, and closed, with a white cloth with the five interlacing Olympic rings on top. I breathed a sigh of relief. I didn't really want to see Brian's corpse.

Did I mention I'm going to be cremated?

"Closed casket," I said. "Do you know why? Was he not...presentable? I heard the bat thing wasn't true."

"The police haven't said anything," Brent said. "Except that a statement will be forthcoming."

Now we were shuffling along in front of the casket. There was an honor guard of four Knights of Columbus, and a pedestal with his gold medal in a plexiglass case. Right in front of the casket was a kneeler in case you wanted to say a prayer.

Brent kneeled briefly, but I stayed standing and bowed my head respectfully. I figured Brian's fate was sealed one way or the other without my input.

At the end of the coffin stood our local Catholic priest, Father Collum, and a short, wiry white man in a navy-blue suit. He had curly brown hair and a long, weathered face that still showed the remains of freckles. He was taking everyone's hand in both of his and thanking them for coming.

"Who's that?" I asked Brent quietly.

"Brian's brother, Frank. Moved away. Lives in Mobile, I think."

"Are their parents alive?"

"Father died years ago. Mother is homebound."

"Ah."

"How did you hear there was no bashing?" Brent asked.

"The day before she died, Robyn talked to Reverend Bricksford. She said as much."

"Hannah told you this?"

"Yes. She said Robyn didn't come to her for counseling but for help with the inquest about Brian, so Hannah felt she could share the information. The bat had something to do with abuse in the past; I'm not sure of whom or by whom. Hannah could tell you."

We reached Frank Eddings. When I offered my hand, he took it between both of his and looked me straight in the eyes. I hadn't realized until that moment how seldom people do that with each other, and the effect was intense. His eyes were brown and piercing.

"Did you know Brian?" he asked.

"Not well," I murmured. Knowing Brian's non-alcoholic drink of choice didn't really count.

"Thank you for coming," he said.

"So sorry for your loss," I said. I meant it, but it sounded hollow, what people say on television cop shows.

Brent stayed and chatted with Frank a little longer.

The line of mourners moved from the casket straight across the hall into the parlor, where soft music played. Someone had chosen the soundtrack to "Chariots of Fire" for the occasion. A table was set up with a pink lemonade punch and almond cookies. Unusual, but it seemed everyone wanted to donate something. A flat-screen television on the wall ran an edited loop of photos of Brian, as well as some television interviews before and after luge events.

"I'm going to say hello to some folks, then head back to the office," said Brent.

"No rest for the wicked," I said.

"Or the newspaper editor," he responded.

"It seems kind of fitting that Brian was dating Robyn again," I said.

"I hope it didn't seal her fate," Brent said. He moved away, greeting folks as he passed.

The table below the video screen displayed one childhood photo of Brian, his parents, and brother, taken for a directory by the local Catholic Church. The photo was in black and white. The mother, with tall hair and pointed glass frames, sat in front with her husband beside her. Young Frank stood in back and younger Brian stood in front. The mother had her hands protectively around Brian. The father's hands were on the mother's shoulders. Either it wasn't a warm and fuzzy group or the photographer had positioned them so unnaturally that their discomfort shone through. Frank looked straight at the camera. Brian looked in that general direction, but off to the side of the photographer. The mother's smile was muted; the father's was aggressive.

Hmm.

I picked up a cup of punch and moved to the back of the room, planning to become inconspicuous enough that no one would notice when I left. While I lolled, my people-watching tendencies took over. One man caught my attention. He wore an Olympic pin and stood next to a petite brunette. He was shaking hands with the knot of people around him, not able to keep a smile from his face at seeing old friends and, perhaps, teammates. The wife was willowy, dark-haired and bred to be gracious. They had a boy with them, of six or seven. Why did the man look familiar? Was it simply that he was an Olympic medalist and I'd seen photos in the paper or on TV?

I leaned back against the wall, only to discover I wasn't alone. Another woman leaned unobtrusively beside me. I glanced at her. She also held a cup of punch, also as a cover. She brought the plastic cup to her lips a couple of times but didn't drink.

"Hi," I said. "Sad occasion."

"Indeed."

"Avalon Nash," I said, casually. "Bartender."

"Isabella Richards. Reporter."

I turned to her. She was shorter than I, maybe 5'5", and striking with a bob of copper hair and bright-green eyes.

"Olympic beat."

"Ah."

"Have you ever ridden a luge or in a bobsled?" she asked.

"No," I said. Have you?"

"No. I'm wondering what gives it the appeal."

"I'm not an expert, but my guess is speed. You can do it, you know. Ride a bobsled or a luge, outside of town near the Olympic complex. A trained sledder goes with you on the bobsled, but I think they have a modified luge you can do on your own."

"Really?" she said, perking up. "I would like to know what it feels like."

"It would add an authenticity to your story that other reporters wouldn't have, that's for sure."

"That's true. Where do you bartend?"

"At That Ship Has Sailed in MacTavish's. The pub is commonly called the Battened Hatch."

"Ah. Any interest in going luging with me?" asked Isabella.

"Maybe."

"Well, listen, if you would do it, or find out any more information, would you let me know?"

"Sure. Where are you staying?"

"Everything in Tranquility was booked, so I'm in Plattsburgh. But here, let me text you my cell number."

We exchanged numbers in case I suddenly felt like luging.

Sure, that was going to happen. The improbability of it almost made me giggle.

I looked around, wondering if there was anyone else I needed to say hi to. More folks were filtering in from the coffin room all the time. I felt I'd done my bit.

I drank the lemonade in three gulps and went to put the cup into the trash. When I looked back to say good bye to Isabella, she was already gone. Taking this as a good omen, I headed for the side door. As I passed the hall door, I glanced in toward the casket again. The brother saw me. He held up a "wait" finger, and headed my way, leaving the good cleric to greet folks all on his own.

"Hi," he said, his voice low. "Sorry to bother you, but did I hear you say you know another clergy person in town? One who isn't Catholic?"

When would he have heard that? "Why?"

"I'm just... there were some things Brian requested that aren't exactly kosher for Catholics. I'd like to enlist some help. Nothing untoward, of course." His smile was lopsided, as if he wasn't used to it, and his teeth had not been whitened in a while.

"Reverend Bricksford?" I asked.

"She's not Catholic?"

"She's a female minister. So, no. She's at St. Barnabas Episcopal Church, here in town. Number's in the paper. She's easy to find."

"Thanks. And thanks for helping me slip out. Nature is calling."

"Again, sorry for your loss."

He was gone before I finished the sentence.

I sauntered past the restrooms and out the back door. It was suddenly easy to breathe again.

I headed for the Battened Hatch, where I knew I'd feel at home. Alive, and at home.

CLOSED CASKET

Blueberry Margarita

Ingredients

1 ½ oz Espolón tequila blanco
1 oz fresh blueberry juice
1 wedge fresh lime
1 ½ oz homemade or store-bought sour mix
½ oz triple sec or any orange liqueur of your choice
½ oz simple syrup (important to use if you make homemade sour mix)
Ice
Salt or sugar for rim of glass

Method

Fill cocktail shaker with ice and combine tequila,
orange liqueur, fresh blueberry juice, sour mix, and simple
syrup.
Shake ingredients together.
Take lime wedge and wipe around the rim of rocks glass.
Put salt or sugar on small plate. Dip rocks glass onto plate
until rim is covered.
Pour contents of shaker into rocks glass. Sip and enjoy!

9

LATE NIGHT

MUCH TO MY surprise, my first customer was Mike Spaulding, the state police inspector I'd worked with to solve the last murder in Tranquility. He was dressed in chinos and an ecru polo that looked good against his dark skin. He sat down at the bar. "Hit me with my usual," he said.

His eyes looked sad.

"I have no idea what your usual is," I said.

"Me, neither. I was hoping you'd help me figure it out."

"All right. I do have a new simple syrup I've been saving. Let me whip something up. Where have you been?" I asked as I worked. "And what's going on in this town?"

"I've been away. And I have no idea what's going on. I'm not working this case."

"I'd assume they'd have everybody working this case."

"It's Mason's case, not mine."

"Yeah. And how is a civilian supposed to talk to Mason? He's so full of himself, he can only see the story he's already made up." I realized too late I was talking to one of Mason's fellow members of the highway patrol, not just a friend come drinking. "Sorry," I said. "I overspoke."

He laughed. "You did. But you weren't wrong."

"Can I tell you if there's stuff going on that seems worth checking out?"

"No. If you become aware of such 'stuff,' call Brad Innisford. He's Mason's second-in-command on this case." Mike took out his offi-

69

cial highway patrolman card and wrote a name and number on the back.

"Okay. Thanks."

By late afternoon, the place was teeming. Marta came running in fifteen minutes late, which wasn't like her at all, but she jumped straight into the fray. Our new waiter, Davros, also took the crowd as a challenge.

At suppertime, Gillian Petrakov, the former Olympic skater, and her wife, Julie, came and sat at the bar. I was pleased to see them. Gillian was my ticket to the inside scoop on all things Olympian. Now in her forties, she was still tiny and always wore her hair up as though she might be called on to do a triple axel at any moment.

As I gave them menus, I happened to glance at the door as the man who had seemed familiar to me at the wake walked in, minus his wife and child. Perhaps it was seeing him come in the same door, but I was able to place him as the man who'd come into the bar on Saturday night when Brian was holding court with the young bobsledders. The man had seen Brian—or something unexpected—and turned on his heel and left.

Well. He certainly wasn't in danger of running into Brian tonight.

I turned back to Gillian. "I ran into a reporter today. She wants to try luging to find out what the thrill is. Do you know if the track is open? I know tourists can do a modified version."

"I don't know," she said. "But I know who does. Jeff, over here," she summoned.

The man who'd been in on Saturday night saw her and headed in our direction. I gasped, caught myself, and smiled at the newcomer.

"Gillian! Julie! So good to see you. Sad occasion."

"It is. Very sad. Nice you could make it back for the service."

He nodded.

"This is Avalon, our favorite barkeep. Avalon, this is Jeff Harris, another fine Olympic medalist in luge." We shook hands across the bar. "Avalon knows a reporter who wants to luge so she can write about you speed-thrill types. Is the tourist course open?"

"Naw, it's usually closed by June."

My relief was palpable. "I'll let her know."

Gillian cocked her head. "You don't happen to know anyone who could help out?"

Jeff was maybe 5'11", sturdy but not carrying an extra pound. It was clear he still worked out and would look fine in one of those form-hugging luge suits.

"Well, if you put it that way. I could probably break away from the family tomorrow before breakfast. How early is this reporter up?"

"That's kind of you," I said. "I'll ask."

I grabbed my phone and texted the number Isabella had programmed in.

The ding of a return message came more quickly than I expected. "She said sure. The earlier the better."

"Okay, then," said Jeff. "Meet me at the Olympic complex at seven."

"Thanks!" Isabella texted back. "You're coming, too?"

Which was funny, because as I read it, Jeff said, "You're coming, too?" to me.

Seven a.m.? Are you crazy?

"I'll... watch."

"Okay," Jeff said, as if it was a joke we were all in on. "You can *watch*."

As the POS machine dinged the next order of drinks from the floor, Jeff gave a snapped salute and headed back to find his tribe.

"So, he medaled, also?" I asked Gillian.

"Yep. One silver and two bronze."

"Wow. So many talented people! But Brian got gold, right?"

"Yes. And it didn't escape Jeff's notice. If it wasn't for Brian, Jeff would have been a gold medalist the year he silvered."

Another friend, who also looked like a figure skater, stood

behind the two women, waiting to order a drink. "You're not going to mention that Brian was the bane of Jeff's existence? That Brian finally had it and beat him up? That Jeff had a restraining order?"

Our end of the bar suddenly got quiet.

"Well, there's that," said Gillian.

"Good thing Jeff wasn't in town Saturday night," continued the newcomer.

"I'm sure he has an alibi," said Gillian.

I said not a word.

The rest of the night was crazy busy. I could only imagine what it would be like between now and the funeral on Friday. Not to mention the televised memorial service on Sunday.

We closed at eleven on the dot. Davros, Marta, and Manuela had worked steadily to keep things cleared. By eleven thirty, everything was tidy. Manuela and Davros headed out.

I turned off the lights, then saw Marta standing by the door to the smoker's porch, looking over the lake.

"You ready?" I asked.

"What? Yeah. Sure," she said. But she didn't move.

"Want to sit for a minute?" I asked.

"Yeah. Maybe."

"How about on the porch?"

We opened the door to the soft breeze and went out to sit in the two brown Adirondack chairs. The moment I sank into the chair, I felt every one of my exhausted muscles collapse with relief. I wondered briefly if I could sleep there.

From our vantage point, I could see golden orbs of cabin lights around the rim of the lake, the far ones looking like fairy lights.

"So," I said, "Have you heard about Jeff Harris, who allegedly had a thing against Brian?"

Marta looked surprised. "Yeah."

"That Jeff would have taken the gold if it wasn't for Brian, that he always came in second? Or third? Or fifth?"

"Oh," said Marta. "Okay." Her shoulders relaxed.

"Why? Did you hear something different?"

"Yeah, but it was probably local gossip." I gave her a "you'd better spill it" version of a side eye.

"I overheard someone talking to my dad once. You hear a lot when you live in a parsonage."

"I bet."

"They said they thought Jeff's son, Milo... looks an awful lot like Brian."

Well. That's more interesting than medal envy.

We both sat. If Mike Spaulding were the detective working the case, I'd tell him this, and that I'd seen Jeff in town the night Brian died. However, to an unknown detective, it would probably sound like... gossip. Or have more weight than it should.

"You want to talk about the nun?" I asked.

"I'd never met a nun before," Marta said. "She wasn't so bad."

"Yeah? What did she say? Was it helpful?"

"It was. She said... I was a sensitive. She's one, too. She said it's a gift."

"You haven't always felt that way."

"I know. She said the important thing is to be in charge of your gift. First, find out what kind of sensitive you are. Some people see things, some feel things, some smell things, some know things—just know them without being told. She said I should keep a notebook with me, and mark down what experiences I have, and at what time of day."

"That makes sense. You usually see things, right? See people?"

"Yes. But sometimes I know things. Sister Maria Louisa also said I can decide to accept having the experiences or not. And when to have them. She tells the dead people who come to her that they can't come in her room at night. And they listen. They want her to see them, so they do what she says." Marta smiled. "She says she even told one spirit, 'It's late. Come back at nine a.m.,' and he did!"

Spirits who could tell time. Nothing surprised me anymore.

"Does what she said ring true to you?"

"I think so. She said if I'm not ready to help them, or if I decide I never want to, I can make that decision, too."

"That must be quite a relief."

"It is. I thought maybe I was the only one who had these things happen. Or that there was something wrong with me. Or something evil happening. It's a relief to have someone to talk to."

"Have you told… them… to leave you alone at night?"

"Yes. And it's worked. So far."

"Wow. Okay. Speaking of bed, you've got school and I've got luging, so we'd better get going."

Marta didn't move.

"Is there something else?"

"Yes," she said. "But it isn't about the nun."

I settled back in my chair, fully aware each settle would make it that much harder to get up.

"Today was senior skip day. My friend Dawson's dad has a boat and Dawson wanted to go out on Lake Serenity."

"Yeah?"

"So we ended up going over… to the Edison mansion."

"Interesting. Did anyone see you?"

"I don't think so. We parked the boat at the next dock over, which didn't seem to be active, and walked through the woods. The sliding door by the pool was open.

Yeah, it was. Oops.

"I'd never been there before. It was… mansion-y."

"It is indeed."

"Dawson was freaked out, so he stayed by the doors to the pool. But I remembered what you'd said about hearing crying in the family quarters."

"Did you go?"

"Yeah. I was curious."

"Did you hear crying?"

"Sort of?"

"Did you leave without anybody seeing you coming or going?"

"Yes. That's how I ended up getting here late. Sorry."

"Did you see any ghosts?" Was that the point of her story? Or, was there more? I had a thought. "Did you see Misty?"

Marta was startled. "How did you know?"

"Did she communicate anything?"

Now my barback seemed uncomfortable. What was protocol for telling the secrets of ghosts?

"She told me the name Jane. I think it must be another girl who went missing around the same time Misty did. Jane was murdered, but no one missed her. I guess it seemed unfair. Unfinished business, maybe?"

"Jane. Do we have any hints or clues as to her last name?"

Marta shook her head.

"Is that all, or do you have any other interesting pieces of news?"

"That's it," she said, sounding relieved. "That's it. Good-night."

And she left me sitting there, wondering how or why one went about looking for a girl no one knew was dead.

LATE NIGHT

Purple Pisco

Ingredients

1 bottle Peruvian pisco (Pisco Portón, Barsol Pisco, Macchu Pisco)
1 pound dried Peruvian purple corn
16 cups of water
3-5 cloves (depending how much spice you would like to have in the juice)
2-3 whole cinnamon sticks (same as above)
1 whole pineapple: cleaned and cut into slices leaving the outside skin on and removing the center of the pineapple)
1 cup raw, white, or granulated sugar
½ - 1 cup of lime juice, fresh-squeezed is preferred
Secret ingredient: 2 cans garbanzo beans (use the liquid only; beans will not be used at all in this cocktail). Aquafaba (bean juice) creates a nice frothy consistency when mixing and shaking cocktail and is also a vegan supplement instead of egg whites or a premade sour mix. However sour mix may be used in place of lime juice and garbanzo bean juice to create the citrus flavors and also for viscosity and frothy texture.
1 green apple sliced very thin (preserve in additional lime juice to stop apples from browning until you compose the cocktail)

CHICHA

Method

Use a large pot (like making soup).

Add: water, dried loose purple corn, cinnamon, clove, and sliced pineapple chunks.

Bring to a boil and then down to a simmer for about an hour, or up to two hours. Keep an eye on the pineapple until they turn a nice deep magenta color.

Make sure to stir the pot occasionally. You may need to add additional water as some may evaporate. It's important not to rush this process. After the pineapple has turned magenta, remove from heat and pull pineapple out with cooking tongs and proper kitchen hand wear, making sure not to burn your hands.

After removing pineapple, add the cup of sugar to the warm liquid, stirring gently. Let cool down to room temperature.

After Chicha is cooled, strain liquid through a stainless steel mesh strainer to remove the corn, cinnamon and clove. Chicha is finished.

COCKTAIL

Method

Fill cocktail shaker with ice. Add:
1 ½ oz desired pisco
3 to 4 oz Chicha Morada
½ oz fresh lime juice
½ oz garbanzo bean juice
Shake all ingredients together to make sure cocktail is cold and has a nice magenta color and nice froth.
Pour contents of shaker into rocks glass.
Garnish cocktail with piece of magenta pineapple, fresh apple slices, and fresh cinnamon stick.

10
EARLY MORNING

"Wow. I had no idea this was back here," Isabella said at six thirty the next morning.

I was running late and asked her to meet me on the bench across the waterfall from my cottage. She was dressed in a white long-sleeve tee with the image of a woman's profile and blowing hair, as well as straight-leg blue jeans. She carried a blue jacket (cotton, not denim), looking every inch the professional journalist about to go luging.

"You know Tranquility?"

"I only meant, you wouldn't suspect this lovely property was back here, given the small lane from the street. Where's the place you wanted to grab coffee?"

I'd spent my trip between the bar and my bed the evening before cursing myself for agreeing to this debacle. This morning, I gave in to the "it is what it is" philosophy. Six thirty and six forty-five are basically the same painful time, but six thirty allows fifteen minutes to get coffee and a roll at the Cardamom Café. Isabella kept her rental car running while I ran in to claim our order.

"You're sure you want to do this?" I asked Isabella, as we headed out of town.

"Covering the Olympics gives you a respect for sports, that's for certain. There aren't many I can experience. I don't have the ankle strength or training for figure skating, and I'd certainly break my neck on the ski jumps. Most Olympic sports don't have a watered-down version you can try."

"Curling?"

She laughed. "Somehow I don't think the thrill would be quite the same."

While the Olympics were a large part of the culture of our town, I'd never been to the Bobsled and Luge Complex, even though it was less than six miles out of town.

Isabella drove along the two-lane mountain roads, a roaring creek beside us and sky-touching purple/magenta mountains ahead. I sipped my cinnamon chai latte. Should I tell her what I knew about Jeff? Or, as a reporter on the Olympic beat, did she know far more about him and his relationship with Brian than I?

"What's the focus of your story?"

"Sorry?"

I'd pulled her from a reverie. "I know it's about Brian and his death. But, what's the focus? His Olympic story? How his death has affected the town? If there are suspicions?"

"Suspicions?"

"About how he died."

"Oh. Are there?"

"There probably will be, until the cause of death is released. And then there's the murder of his girlfriend, Robyn."

"They were together?"

"She hoped they were."

"Is this it?"

Isabella slowed the car, and together we looked at the large sign. The red arrow indicated this was, indeed, the spot. Mountain peaks jostled each other for position in the background.

There were only three other cars in the lot. One was a sedan, one a Jeep, and one was a huge black Chevy Silverado pickup. We pulled into a spot near the entrance, where Jeff was waving.

"All right," he said after we joined him. "Looks like we can make this happen. I was able to pull a few strings. Margot is the manager—she was coming in early today anyway. And Russ here runs both the skeleton and the bobsled for non-pros." Russ was my height, around 5' 7", with red hair cut short, but inching toward curly. He seemed halfway between enthusiastic that Jeff was here and annoyed to come in so early.

"Let's do it." Jeff rubbed his hands together. The same intensity that drove him to an Olympic medal now drove us toward our morning activities.

"Russell suggests you skeleton first," Jeff said. His jaw was strong, his chin square.

"What's 'skeleton'?" I asked.

"It's too dangerous to have folks who haven't trained do luge—taking the turns and steering a careening sled, while lying on your back. You can get much the same thrill from the skeleton. Basically the same, but on your stomach."

"Like sledding when you were a kid," Isabella said.

"If you used to sled at thirty miles per hour. The full track will send you about sixty miles an hour. Needless to say, if you don't know what you're doing and you move incorrectly, very bad things can happen."

"I imagine very bad things can happen at thirty miles per hour," I said.

"You'll get the idea of the thrill," Jeff said. "Only imagine it twice as fast."

"Okay," the reporter answered.

"Who's going first?"

It took me a minute to realize he'd put me into the equation. "I'm not going. I'm here for moral support."

"Let's do it." Isabella was into this experience now, with a singular focus. Russell motioned us to the track to the left of the entrance. We climbed the steps together, veering off halfway up, where the signs led us to the skeleton track. Apparently, what kept you at only thirty miles an hour was starting halfway down the track.

The day had been warming up down in town, but the wind, even at this low height, made it chilly out here. Isabella put on her jacket and buttoned it. She pulled her shoulder-length copper hair back into a ponytail. "Ready."

Russell got out a "sled"—it seemed to me more like a piece of rectangular cardboard on wheels. I expected one of my companions to complain that I wasn't game to break my neck. Thank God Jeff didn't know I'd spotted him coming into the bar the night Brian was killed. One slight thing to make you off center... not that I was going to do it, I comforted myself.

Russell showed Isabella how to position herself to successfully navigate the track. Abruptly, Jeff said, "I'm sure you'd feel better if you saw someone do it."

Without waiting for an answer, he took the sled Russell held, put it onto the track, dove onto it, and disappeared down and around the corner.

"Well," said Russell, surprised, "that's how you do it."

He took the next sled. No sooner had he put it in place than Isabella maneuvered herself onto it. Russell let go and she, too, disappeared in a *whoosh!* of skeleton-speed, hurtling down the track.

Russell and I stood and looked at each other.

"Jeff said you all wanted to bobsled, too."

He took off walking back down the steps and I followed, feeling quite the chaperone.

We met Jeff and Isabella at the bottom of the track, still catching their breath. Each of their faces had an endorphin glow, and each wore wonky smiles.

"Can we do it again?" asked Isabella.

"We only have Russ for a short while—and I've promised to take my family to breakfast," Jeff said. "Let's bobsled."

We fell into line behind Russ, hiking over, then climbing the stairs toward the other track.

At the top, Russ distributed helmets of black and yellow to Isabella and Jeff. He then offered me a helmet. "You've got to ride this time," he said to me. "It would be silly to leave you up here."

"And we can use more weight in the sled," agreed Jeff.

"Come *on*," whispered Isabella, as she put on her helmet.

Jeff and Russell brought the bobsled from the side and positioned it on the track. It looked like a small rocket with seats, and without a back. "I'll drive, you're brakeman," Jeff said to Russ. He climbed into the front of the car. Isabella positioned herself behind him.

Darn. Russell was right. I'd feel silly climbing stairs all the way down to catch up with them after they'd been waiting for a good while.

I took the helmet offered and plunked it onto my head. It was lighter than I expected. How hard could this be? I only needed to sit between Isabella and Russ for a blink of an eye and it would be done. I put down the visor and sat behind Isabella.

Without further fanfare, Russell grabbed the handles on the back of the sled and started running. He jumped on behind me.

We hurtled down the track. Turn, straight, turn, at a speed that took us sideways halfway up the wall. Holy shit.

I thought it would feel like seconds. It felt like it never ended. There were more turns at faster speeds. And faster. When we finally reached the flat ending stretch, the brake went on and the sled began slowing. Jeff steered it off the speed track and onto the landing track.

We all climbed out and thanked Russ, handing back our helmets. I knew it would be best to go along, so I echoed Isabella's happy gratitude and tried to fake her breathless wonder while I fought to regain my landlegs.

"Got what you need to make the story more authentic?" Jeff asked, as we took leave of Margo and headed for the parking lot, where Jeff walked us to Isabella's rental car.

"Yes. It will help a lot," she said. "Thanks for taking time to set this up. Can I contact you if I have any questions?"

"Sure," he said. He took a card out of his wallet and handed it to her. "You know, I think there's one more Olympic experience that might be helpful. Want to do the zip line off K120?"

"Well, sure. But... how? It doesn't open for a couple of hours and I hear you have to have reservations in advance."

Jeff chortled. "Same for what we just did. Give me a minute."

He reappeared five minutes later, with Russ in tow. I wondered how much he was tipping the young man.

"Margo was able to connect with the manager over there. And Russ. Let's go."

We dispersed to our vehicles.

Jeff had the black pickup, and he squealed out of the lot quickly, Russ's red Jeep Patriot on his tail.

"Turning into a great morning!" Isabella said as we fell in line.

"What's K120?" I asked.

"I assume that's it."

I bent down slightly to look through the windshield. We were on the road heading toward the Olympic ski jumps. There were two of them. They weren't built into a mountain to mask their height, they were on man-made stilts and, from our vantage point, looked like toothpicks trying to reach the gods.

Which never ends well.

"Holy smokes."

"I know. I can't believe people ski down those things and jump off!"

"I can't believe the idea entered someone's head in the first place."

We pulled into another parking lot. I looked up the steep incline before us. Sitting at the top, the taller of the two jumps was twelve stories tall at a crazy steep angle. K120. Three zip-line cables came down from the tallest of the jumps onto a raised landing platform

Isabella was out of the car, striding toward Jeff.

"Good?" he asked.

Russ joined us as we headed forward.

We pulled in past a large sign announcing it was the Olympic Jumping Complex. A lodge-like structure sat at the front of the large parking lot, where tickets were sold. It was not yet open. Still, we climbed a series of wide wooden steps toward it and then then took a right, skirting the lodge and grounds. Apparently, a ticket to K120 included a gondola ride up the mountain. Sadly, they weren't running yet. The four of us stood at the bottom of a thin, steep staircase. Surely, we weren't...

We were.

All I could think was, if I make it to the top, I will not need to exercise my legs for a month. Or six.

Unfortunately, Jeff went first. Did I mention he was still in near-Olympic shape? Russ followed close behind, also barely winded. He likely jogged these stairs on an ongoing basis.

Isabella wasn't quite as fast, but she was motivated to get to the zip line. My only motivation was: don't look like an idiot.

We finally crested the hill behind an operator's cabin, and headed straight forward.

Proximity to K120 made it no less imposing. The narrow rectangular building that shot up from the ground looked every inch of its twelve stories. I'm not afraid of heights, normally, but looking up to try to see the top was dizzying.

An avuncular man saw us approach and joined us as we entered the small lobby. "Hey, Jeff," he said.

"Hey, Roger."

"Don't tell anyone. I don't want word getting out I opened it for you."

Jeff gave a brief salute.

Roger had the elevator door open. He stepped inside and turned a key in the operating panel.

Jeff, Isabella, and Russ walked in. I hung back.

"I'll wait down here," I said.

Jeff gave a heavy sigh, with strong "this is getting old" undertones. "Don't you work in town? Don't people ever ask you what it's like to go up K120? Even if you don't want to do the zip line, ride the elevator. That usually costs money and has lines. This is your chance!"

Isabella turned to me with her most pleading look yet.

I *was* curious about the view from the top. I could always ride the elevator back down with Russ.

The elevator was glass-enclosed and the climb was truly spectacular. Isabella and I stood shoulder to shoulder awed by the expansive view of the surrounding mountains, the large burbling creek that ran for miles, the soft green of new leaves budding on the deciduous trees among towering pines.

The elevator went slowly, to give paying riders their money's worth.

At the top, we got off and Jeff led the way up to the enclosed viewing platform, from which you could watch skiers take the jump in wintertime.

"The run isn't open very often. When skilled ski jumpers hear it is, they make a beeline," Jeff explained.

"Why? I'd assume it would be open all winter long," I asked.

"To be in working order, there has to be soft powdered snow. They can create snow, but one or two days of fifty-degree weather, or one rain shower, and that's it. All the work for naught. You'd think we're far enough north. Global warming strikes again."

He turned and led us out and down a flight of stairs and around the corner to the zipline loading dock. The platform was out in the open air. Three sides had tall wooden fencing. One side was open to the large launching platform.

Russ had pulled the first three zip chairs into place on the three cables. The chairs were constructed of a seat surrounded by a strong canvas lattice back and sides.

Still, when you stepped off the platform, there was nothing but air. For twelve stories.

No thanks. Not even curious.

As Russ began to secure Isabella into her seat, I turned and walked back to the elevator. There was no need to make any statement or have any arguments.

The elevator car was gone. I looked up to the floor above. The shaft was empty.

I looked down but could not see far enough to spot the car. I pushed the call button. There was no response. No gears springing into action, no cables shortening or lengthening.

I headed back to the launching deck.

"Hey, Russ," I said. "When will the elevator be back?"

"Not for a while. They're loading in some new equipment."

My jaw dropped. "I told you I was going back down."

Russ looked confused. "Jeff said the three of you were zip-lining."

"No."

I stared at Jeff, who stood near his canvas chair.

"You knew we would talk you into it," he said.

No. No, I did not know that.

As I said, I'm not usually afraid of heights. But I must have had dreams in which I was stuck on an open platform, high in the sky, without control over whether I fell or not. Or maybe I'd dreamed that I had fallen. In any case, I tumbled fast and far into a feeling of horror.

My breathing accelerated as the all-encompassing fear clothed me like a weighted blanket. I knew it was a panic attack. But a rational one. I had no control. There was no way down. My heartbeat quickened as well. I would fall from here. I would die.

I couldn't look over the fencing or even stand near it. I went and sat in the corner next to the structural wall.

Rational or not, my mind and body firmly believed that control of the situation had been taken from me. I couldn't stop myself from falling to my death.

Russ was strapping Jeff into his zip chair. At least Russ had the decency to look chagrined.

"I'll go back down in the elevator with you," I said.

"I have to stay up and run the practice goes," he said. "We always send the zip lines down five times empty before we open."

Did Jeff somehow know my suspicions? Did he know I could place him in town at the time of Brian's death? How perfect was this? How much had he paid Russ? One slight nick in the lattice, one belt that wasn't tight… Russ telling the cops, "I don't know what happened! Usually we test the lines, but Jeff was in a hurry…"

I couldn't stay up here. Irrationally now, I fully believed this structure made from Pick-Up Stix would tumble at the least gust of wind, collapsing with Russ and me on it.

The other two were buckled into their chairs.

"This is the only way down," Russ said, grasping the third chair.

I gasped and gasped, trying to pull in enough oxygen.

I couldn't get into that chair.

Yet I couldn't stay up here, waiting to die.

Seriously. The tower would fall or the platform would give way, or I would simply throw myself off to be done with it.

Such is the logic of panic.

"The elevator. How long?"

"An hour. Or you zip and you're down in three minutes," said Jeff. Who'd planned this.

I closed my eyes. The tower creaked and swayed beneath me. I couldn't wait an hour.

Perhaps if I rode the zip line but closed my eyes.

Perhaps Jeff hadn't paid Russ enough. Perhaps I could get Russ on my side.

I stood up. I held on to the top of the fence and made my way to the chair.

"Don't do it, Russ," I said. "Tell me. Honestly. What's wrong with my chair?"

"What? Nothing!"

"Jeff was in town the night Brian Eddings was killed," I said. "I saw him. If something happens to me…"

"What?" Russ asked again.

"What do you mean?" Jeff asked.

"Nothing is wrong with your chair. I promise!" Russ pulled the straps across the open front of the chair after I'd climbed aboard, having decided I'd rather die quickly than by inches.

"Brian and Jeff were enemies," I said to Russ, who would be the surviving witness. "Jeff even had a restraining order!"

"What?" said Russ

"What?" said Isabella.

"What the f—" started Jeff.

Russ was back by the operating stand. He pushed the button to send the three of us off.

Then the platform was no longer beneath us.

Nothing but air. Twelve stories of nothing but air.

We plunged.

We broke through air, hurtling toward Earth. Hurtling. Falling. Rushing.

Slowing.

Then someone grabbed my chair. The person undid the straps.

I pushed myself forward.

My legs didn't hold. I fell to the platform.

Jeff stalked to stand above me. He was furious. "What the bloody hell was that?"

I was furious, too. Shaking, but furious. I pointed up to the top of the zip line.

"What the bloody hell was *that*?"

"You basically told that freaking kid that I killed Brian!"

"Didn't you?" I asked. There were two other people present who could testify, should Jeff murder me here and now. Whoever disengaged us from the zip chairs had moved back to the edge of the platform away from us, but Isabella had moved closer, I assumed, both to hear and to protect me, should that be necessary. "You did have a restraining order against him. He stole your gold. You were enemies."

Jeff gave me his best incredulous look. "Nobody kills someone for taking their gold! The slopes would be littered!"

"Your son," I said, still gasping. "Folks say he looks a lot like Brian."

"Hell," he said. "Bloody hell."

Jeff grabbed my arm and jerked me to my feet. He then pulled me to and down the steps to the parking lot. Isabella, the reporter, trotted along. Once on the cement of the parking lot, he stopped and thought. He knew who Isabella was, and why she was there.

He made a decision. My legs barely worked, but I was able to stay upright as he dragged me to that hulking huge pickup of his. He pushed the fob and the doors clicked unlocked. He opened the door to the second row and basically lifted me up onto the camel-colored bench seat. He climbed in, nearly on top of me, and slammed the door shut behind us.

Then Jeff grabbed me by both arms and pushed his long face close to mine. "What have you done?" he demanded. "I could kill you. Right here. I could kill you."

EARLY MORNING

Ingredients

> 6 oz sparkling white wine
> ½ oz of elderflower liquor
> 1 oz of honeydew puree
> Fresh honeydew puree

Method

> Cut honeydew in half and remove seeds, then cut off the outside of skin of melon. Dice the remaining flesh of the fruit into small pieces and put into food processor to make a nice silky honeydew puree. Set aside some chunks of honeydew for garnish.

COCKTAIL

Method

> This drink is served in a wine glass or Collins glass over ice.
> Stir ingredients together. (Do not toss or shake as sparkling wine will create a fizzing effect.)
> Garnish with fresh honeydew on a skewer, and add fresh honey or a small piece of fresh honeycomb on top of honeydew.

11
NOT ONE SOUL

T HE TRUCK CAB door opened behind Jeff.

"What are you two talking about in here?" Isabella asked, climbing in and closing the door.

She had her cell phone out. She snapped a photo of the two of us, then pressed record.

Jeff groaned, and let himself fall backwards against the leather. "Turn that damn thing off," he said.

"Yeah?" she asked.

"Look," Jeff said to me. "Let's not have any misunderstandings. What I said to you, just now, it was a figure of speech. I was mad. I am mad. But I haven't killed anybody. Ever."

"What did you say to her?" asked Isabella.

"Turn it off. Please."

Isabella looked at me. I nodded. She complied with his request.

"Who else have you said that to... about our son... about Milo?"

"No one. Not a soul."

"But people are talking? How did you hear that?" he continued.

Through Marta, overhearing at the parsonage.

"From someone who heard it long ago... who isn't spreading it around."

Jeff said, "The Alpine Express is open. Let's get a cup of tea and sort this out before it gets out of hand."

He opened the cab door. I was relieved to be out of the vehicle and back in public.

He waved us toward the lodge-themed restaurant as he dug out his phone and called someone.

Isabella and I walked over. The Alpine Express was inside the wooden lodge at the base of the jumps. Inside were tall ceilings and chandeliers made of antlers. You ordered from a walk-up counter and they'd deliver it to the wooden table of your choice. We bought tea and went to sit in the corner.

Jeff came in, ordered a coffee, and sat. He stared at me. "I don't even know who you are."

"I'm the bartender at That Ship Has Sailed. You stopped in on Saturday night, saw Jeff, and left."

"Oh. That. I saw all the Olympic hopefuls and I had no inclination or patience. I'm not Brian." He smoothed back his hair. "I'm not Brian."

He paused, gathering his thoughts.

"There was a time when we were both young bucks, and stupid, and drinking... when I would get all up in Brian's grill because I knew I could provoke him. When he drank, he was easily provoked. It was simple and it was fun. At least I thought so back then. Until, finally, we got into a fight over a woman, and he broke my arm. Put me out of training for nearly two months! Everybody was saying I should get a restraining order... and I did. As a show. I knew Brian never meant to hurt me that badly. He had apologized and I knew he meant it. We had both let it get out of hand."

Jeff stopped. He used his sleeve to wipe unexpected moisture from his eyes. He turned to Isabella. "I know you're a reporter, but this is off the record. Completely."

She nodded. "Completely off the record."

"Nobody knows this. It's none of their business. But to stop rumors in their tracks, if it's not too late... when I met my wife, Charlotte, there was an immediate attraction between us. Passion. All-encompassing. But neither of us were good at relationships. We both had baggage. One thing about me... I can't father children. I knew it. I didn't tell her, because I knew she wanted kids. I figured if it got serious, we'd work it out.

"But we fought hard and we loved hard. We broke up. We got

back together. That was back when Brian and I were going at it. So of course, to make me mad, she flirted with Brian. She was gorgeous, and a good flirt. Brian basically didn't stand a chance. We broke up after an especially bad fight and next thing I knew, she was with Brian.

"I saw my part in our problems clearly, and I started counselling. Started unwrapping some of my coils. Realized I still loved her... and that, damn it, I also liked Brian. If we could ever stop fighting, we'd be close. We were very alike. But not the same. I wasn't Brian. No one was Brian.

"Around Christmastime that year, after Brian and Charlotte had been together four months or so, Brian asked to meet me in private. He said Charlotte still loved me. That she talked about me all the time. That she'd started seeing a shrink, also. Brian knew he and Charlotte weren't a good match, and he suspected Charlotte wanted to break up with him but didn't know how to. She felt she needed to stay because they'd just found out she was pregnant."

Jeff took a long swig of coffee. I guessed he wished it was whiskey.

"Brian told me he could never marry and have a family. He asked if I would take Charlotte back if that's what she wanted. The child would be ours. He would help out financially if we ever needed it, but...

"It was actually the best gift anyone's ever given us. Brian Eddings gave me my wife and my family. I have nothing but gratitude to the man. In the end, I would've taken a bullet for the guy."

We sat, considering.

"In fact, I stopped in Tranquility to talk to him, to see if he'd be willing to donate sperm to give Milo a little brother or sister."

"I heard he was a good guy," Isabella finally said. "And it sounds like you ended up being good friends."

"We did."

"Did he say why he wasn't cut out for marriage or children?"

"No, never did. It could have been his temperament or his priorities. But I think... I think he never got over that Misty girl he was dating. The one who got kidnapped. Thought he was bad luck, somehow."

He sipped his coffee. "Can I count on you not to go talking this around? For Charlotte and Milo's sake..."

I made the motion of locking my lips and throwing away the key.

"I apologize for thinking you would change your mind about zip-lining."

"Okay. Never make me do it again."

This time, he held up three fingers. "Scout's honor. Now if you don't mind, I am going to join my family for breakfast."

Once he'd left, Isabella and I headed back toward Tranquility. I had stopped trembling but was in that awkward weakened state when your adrenaline has subsided, not leaving much in its wake.

As we neared Main Street, I saw, tucked just off the thoroughfare, the local newspaper office. I had a sudden urge to talk to Brent Davis. "Can you let me off here?"

Annabelle nodded. "Sure."

She took the left and I got out. "Thanks," she said. "Quite a morning."

"Yes, indeed."

She headed off in her rented Kia.

Lights were on in the office. Despite everything that had already happened, it was only 8:35 a.m. I walked up the wooden porch steps. A bell jingled as I pushed the old wooden door open. In fact, the whole place smelled of wood and consternation. It was like walking into the 1940s, which I was more than ready to do. A journalistic-looking woman in her mid-forties sat at a computer. (Darn! A typewriter would have been perfect.) She wore black slacks and shirt, her hair mostly pulled back into a large barrette.

"Hi," I said. "Is Brent here?"

"He should—" she started, when the door opened behind me.

"Avalon!" Brent entered in his newspaper uniform of chinos and a blue button-down. He carried a cardboard cupholder with two fancy coffees covered with whipped cream. "We've got a Keurig," he said, "but strange times call for strange drinks."

He handed the second one to the woman at the computer and they air-toasted.

"To what do I owe this honor?"

Why was I there? I wasn't a hundred percent sure I trusted Jeff, but he'd seemed sincere and I didn't want to talk about him only minutes after promising I wouldn't.

"I have an odd question. Back when Misty was kidnapped, was there another missing person? A young woman named Jane?"

The question surprised him. "Not that I recall. Do you know how old Jane would have been?"

"Not sure. Around Misty's age, possibly?"

"What brought this up?"

Oh, a ghost told my barback. "Someone... possibly connected to the case mentioned something. That no one had noticed Jane had also gone missing."

"Interesting. We don't have the staff to follow up right now." He waved his arm to encompass himself and the woman typing away. "But a last name would help. Maybe you could look through the high school yearbooks around that time? They have them at the local library."

"Good idea," I said. "Good place to start."

"Let me know if you come up with anything."

"I will. Any further leads on who killed Robyn?"

"No. Word is out for any car that has damage to the right front. Nothing yet. Poor woman."

"If it was someone passing through, one would assume the car just kept going and we'll never find it," I mused.

"First, it's harder than you think to hide or fix a car with human blood or bones on it, unless you're a well-connected mobster. Second, it seems a mighty big coincidence that Brian Eddy's girlfriend is killed within days of the death of Brian himself. It seems likely there's some connection."

"We only need to figure out who, and why."

"Exactly. Tell me if you do."

"Well, I'll let you get back to it," I said, and walked back out into the twenty-first century.

I walked down to the sidewalk and realized I had no car and no bike. It was about a forty-minute walk across town to my magical glade. I could make it by 9:40, possibly grab breakfast at the Cardamom Café—that small roll had worn off several hair-raising events ago—and take a nap to get me through my shift at the Battened Hatch.

Tranquility has distinct Jekyll and Hyde attributes. The sleepy town the residents know and love becomes a completely different place when swollen with tourists or Olympians. There is basically one main street—Main Street—and it was where everyone shopped, ate, and hung out. Even now, throngs were gathering to give Brian Eddings a proper send-off, and it was hard to keep up my pace on the sidewalk. I paused to study the posters for the upcoming Tranquility Film Festival in front of the movie theater, so it was 9:45 when I made it to Avantika's, which was nearly at the turn to my place.

The Cardamom Café was where the locals congregated, as well as a few visitors who had the inside scoop. There was a counter in the back where you ordered, and a room off to the side where you could eat, read the paper, check in with your neighbors. The white walls were hung with paintings and photographs by local artists.

As advertised, the homey place smelled of cardamom, along with coffee and cinnamon.

Three people were ahead of me, but the line moved quickly. "Good morning," I said to Avantika.

"Weren't you already in this morning?" she asked with a smile.

"It's been a long day since then. I'll have a curried banana wrap with coconut and almond, and a Masala chai."

"That's more like it," she said. "Your usual."

"Yep."

"For here or to go?"

"To go."

"Funny you came back this morning," she said, clipping my order to the spinner for the kitchen. "Since you were here earlier, someone came in looking for you."

"Really? Who?"

"Didn't recognize him. He wasn't from here. Tall. Good-looking"

I stood rooted to the spot. *Who's found me?*

"Could you tell if he was from Los Angeles or from New York?"

She laughed at the question. "My American accent radar isn't quite that good."

"What did you tell him?"

"I said you came in now and then. Hope that was all right."

"Sure."

"He left a phone number. Would you like it?"

"Sure."

She handed me a torn-off page from an order book. I paid and stepped aside. It held a scribbled first name, phone number, and a short note.

I read it.

Damn. My days of running from the past were over. My past had caught up. As it always does.

Now what?

Now I would take a nap. And figure out my next step.

I took a step backwards into the dining room. It was a little late for many of the regulars, but I saw one familiar face: Hannah Bricksford. She sat by herself at a table under a painting of Philip's, this one in sweeping strokes of primary colors. Hannah looked haggard, as if she hadn't slept in years.

A young man pushed past me, Aedan, a local youth who was known to have a crush on any female who was kind to him. Which meant, of course, that he had a fetish for Hannah. Without thinking, I made a beeline for the empty chair at her table, reaching it moments before Aedan did. "Sorry," I said to him brightly. "Have to talk to the reverend."

He looked unhappy but went and found a place elsewhere.

"Unless you two were…"

Hannah looked at me, then looked at Aedan. She simply shook her head. She was not herself. She sat in front of an untouched wrap and an unsipped tea.

"Mind if I sit?" I asked.

Again, the head shake.

"May I say you look awful?"

"Do I?"

"When was the last time you slept?"

"Can't sleep. Phone keeps ringing. And Robyn…"

My wrap was ready. "Hold that thought."

I grabbed it and returned. "Look," I said. "I was up before sanity this morning, too. I'm heading back to my place to sleep for a couple of hours. I have a guest bedroom and also a comfy couch in the living room. Come with me. Turn off your phone. Disappear and sleep for a couple of hours."

"What?" she asked.

I repeated my offer.

"Maybe. What time is it?" She checked. "Thing is, I have to go…"

"Have to go where?"

"I promised Robyn's mother I'd go to her place and get a dress to bring to the funeral home. Robyn's burial dress." Hannah looked up. "Would you come with me?"

"Not until I take a nap. If you come take one, too, maybe I will."

"Really?" She perked up, but still looked like death on holiday. She was wearing loose-fitting clothing, a gray sweatshirt and sweatpants. Like she'd gone to the gym but hadn't worked out.

"You also have to eat." I nodded to her plate. "We're both going to sit here and eat our wraps, then we'll rest, then we'll figure out the rest of our lives."

"Okay."

She seemed grateful for the instruction. I again thought how hard it must be to always be the one being there for everyone else.

Hannah ate half her wrap in the time it took me to inhale both my wrap and drink. Which were marvelous, by the way, and filled with life-sustaining properties.

She picked up her gym bag and we walked together from the café, where Aedan sat, with his puppy-dog eyes, watching us go. We turned right when the roads split and fairly soon started up the nondescript lane past the old brick house that sat like a sentry and back up to my place.

Hannah chose the family room couch. She sat, said, "We'd better set an alarm," put her legs up and was sound asleep. I covered her with a light blanket and went to my bedroom where, somehow, I accomplished the same feat.

I awakened two hours later, before my alarm went off, oddly rested. There was something soothing about having someone else in the house. I peeked in on Hannah, snoring blissfully, and went back to the kitchen.

I put on the tea kettle. There aren't many things in this world I'd say I truly love, but I truly love my little kitchen. It is cheerful with white furniture, blue accents and tablecloth, and white cabinets that looked like they were installed in the 1940s. Which they were. The appliances were new, but the rest of the house looked like it had been styled by a Hollywood set designer. Which it was. "English country cottage" was the request and they'd accomplished it wonderfully well. They had also designed the larger lodge across the stream with "Sally Goes to the Country" as their mandate. Hers was built from full logs. Mine, formerly her guest house, was painted white wood, accented with outside gardens and a terrace.

The terrace was where I went with my tea.

I pulled out the piece of paper Avantika had given me and once again studied its contents.

"Reggie" was scrawled next to a phone number with a 719 area code, which was Colorado.

Underneath it said, "Call me. Mormor is ill."

Reggie was my cousin. Mormor was my grandmother.

How had he found me?

I grew up in Los Angeles, where my mother was a successful actor and comedian. I never liked the atmosphere much. When a good friend died of an overdose, I had to get away. The only thing I knew to do was to head for my ancestral home in Brooklyn, New York, where part of Mom's family still resided.

Life had other plans. I'd gone for a drink while changing trains in Tranquility, turning up in time to be present when the much beloved bartender at the Battened Hatch was murdered. A bartender myself, I was offered his job, and I took it. I wanted to start fresh. I sent my cell phone to Montreal by itself on a train. Which had almost gotten Philip killed, but that's not my point here.

The point was that fresh start. I ditched my past and started a new life here, which I loved. I know you can't run forever from emotional baggage, but I was giving it a try and enjoying the results.

Yet somehow Reggie found me. I sat sipping my tea and listening to the burble of the brook in front of the cottage as it came to the small waterfall and leapt into the pond beneath.

What to do?

Mormor was sick. Her name was Alice, and she was the family matriarch, a tall, willowy woman, the first American-born daughter of a family who'd immigrated from Sweden in the late 1800s. Her parents, Elsa and Eric, arrived separately from the old country and met at the Swedish Covenant Church in Brooklyn, where they married. Elsa, my maternal great-grandmother came from aristocracy; her new husband, Eric, was from farmer stock. Perhaps because of this, her father provided the down payment on a brownstone as a wedding gift—then the young couple was on its own. After their children dispersed, moving to Nashville and Chicago, the great-grandparents kept the house. Eventually, Alice, my Mormor, moved back with her family and it continued to be the gathering place for the family and all the cousins.

Mormor and Morfar (Mother's mother and Mother's father) put a great emphasis on education and every one of their children had a college degree, as did most of their grandchildren. There was one abstention—me. I'd started at NYU, gone home on break and started bartending, and never looked back. Or went back.

Yes, here I was, their own granddaughter, nothing but a high school graduate and happy bartender. With a dead addict best friend.

I had been happy to stop here, an eight-hour train ride short of arriving at their brownstone.

"Hi," came Hannah's voice from behind me. She stood with her hands around a blue and white mug from which steam and the scent of orange spices arose.

"Hi," I said. "You look much better. And it's not just the collar."

She must have had her work clothes in the gym bag. She now wore a black shirt, black jacket, black skirt, pantyhose, black flats, and the aforementioned white priest's dog collar.

She laughed. "Thanks."

I motioned to the other chair at the table and she sat. "You've got a special hideaway back here."

"I lucked out. Right place, right time. Then again, you probably wouldn't call it luck."

"Maybe not. But it is a great place." We fell into a companionable silence. "Who is Reggie?"

Avantika's note was laying on the table.

"My cousin."

She lifted an eyebrow.

"My grandmother is apparently very ill. Reggie came to find me."

"How did he track you down?"

"I don't know."

"Where does your grandmother live?"

"Brooklyn."

"Brooklyn isn't far. Are you going to go?"

"I don't know."

"Are you her only grandchild?"

"There are twelve others."

"Oh. That's a bit less pressure. Believe me. I'm an only child and my dad is wanting me to join him for vacation in Aspen after Christmas."

"Yeah? You going to go?"

"I don't know."

We smiled at each other.

"Families can be tricky." I said.

"That's putting it mildly."

I'd known Hannah for a while before discovering that her father was Samuel Bricksford, a well-known Black civil rights leader and stirring minister. Hannah, though an only child, seemed happy tucked away here in Tranquility, pastoring a comparatively small congregation.

"How come Robyn's mom asked you to get her dress? She doesn't go to your church, does she? I thought they were Catholic."

"I was the person who was visiting at the time the funeral parlor called. So she asked me."

"Her mom is in a nursing home?"

"Yes. She's widowed and has advanced Parkinson's. Robyn was an only child."

"I'm sorry. That must be hard for her."

"Unbearably."

I fought with myself. I had no obligation. My rational mind listed a dozen reasons I could still back out. Yet...

"Would you like me to go with you?"

NOT ONE SOUL

Blood Orange Margarita

Ingredients

1 ½ oz of preferred white tequila
½ oz orange liquor
2 oz fresh blood orange juice
Juice of half fresh-squeezed lime
Sugar and dried sage for rimming

Method

Dip rocks glass in fresh lime juice and dip into a sugar and dried sage mixture.
Add other ingredients to shaker. Shake together to create a nice frothy texture and pour in rocks glass over ice.
This is a great winter cocktail as blood oranges are in season and the juice can be fresh. You can also buy blood orange juice in some gourmet grocery stores.

12

THROUGH THE WOODS

BARTENDERS AND PRIESTS have a lot in common, I believe, at least in the counseling department. To do our jobs effectively, we must be good listeners as well as handy with the advice and with a remedy to make folks feel better when they leave us. That, and we both wear a lot of black.

Hannah picked me up at MacTavish's after I rode my bike over and stashed it as after-work transportation. She put Robyn's address into her GPS. We headed out of town and made a hard left on the road that passed Adams' Microbrewery, where Robyn had worked. We took another right and a left, turning onto a smaller road that led up into wooded hills.

The road was rough tar, not recently paved, with no side or center lines painted. A couple of one-lane tributaries branched off. When Robyn's lawyer offered to pick her up from work, she'd told him she could walk home as it was only two miles. The GPS claimed closer to three.

There was no obvious spot to mark where Robyn was hit and thrown into the ditch. I couldn't even tell which side of the road she was walking on. The location and nature of the road seemed to remove the possibility the hit-and-run was caused by a tourist hurrying through town. The fact that there were no streetlights, and tall trees created an overhead canopy did raise the possibility someone was speeding and simply didn't see her in the dark.

But if that was the case, the person would have stopped. Right?

Robyn's house had a half-circle drive. We missed the first turn, but the rural delivery mailbox alerted us to the second. Unpaved stone crunched as we climbed. Hannah stopped in between Robyn's old Impala and the walk to the front door. Maybe five hundred feet of berm, covered by trees and brush shielded the house from the road below.

"Okay," Hannah said. "Let's do this."

The house was a one-story mid-century ranch, painted brown. Hannah picked up the welcome mat, which actually said WEL-COME, and found the key. She opened the door and we both paused on the threshold.

It's funny how a death automatically turns a home into a shrine. It's no longer simply a dirty glass in the sink, it's your last drink of iced tea, the last place you set down the remote, the hamper of laundry that held the final shirts with your perspiration.

Even though Robyn had grown up here and her mother lived here until a couple of years before, it wasn't one of those preserved time capsules the guys from *Queer Eye* would need to come fix. There was a flat screen television, and the cabinets and appliances in the kitchen were all fairly new. What I guessed were once wood-paneled walls were now smooth painted sheet rock. It wouldn't need much when the real estate agents descended to gussy it up to put it on the market. Brian could have done worse than to marry his childhood sweetheart and move in.

Hannah bowed her head briefly, then took in the living room front entry. Her phone buzzed with a text.

"It's from Robyn's mother," she said. "I texted that I was here and her aide answered with a list of some items she'd like me to bring her before things start getting cataloged."

"A long list?"

"No, not at all."

"Would you mind if I waited outside?"

"Sure."

The woods surrounding the house were old growth, tall trees with crowns that kept sunlight from the forest floor, which meant there wasn't a lot of scrub and undergrowth. It wouldn't be hard to get back and forth from the Eddings' house when Robyn and Brian were kids.

I wondered where the Eddings' house was. Miraculously, I had cell service, so I went on Google Earth, where I could see glimpses of Robyn's roof through the trees, and another cleared backyard which marked the next house. It would have been a couple of miles by road, but it was a straight shot through the woods. A ten-minute walk, if that.

Text me when you're done, I sent Hannah.

Will do, she replied.

It didn't take much looking to find the remains of an old path leading from Robyn's backyard. The ground was covered with dead leaves, which swirled gently as I walked. Why I wanted to see Brian's childhood home, I cannot tell you, but I continued on, tracking my little footprints as they appeared on my phone.

I came upon the woodpile first, very dry wood with spiders, leaves, and a curious chipmunk in between the circular chunks of tree. Beyond it was a metal pole with four spreading arms, and rope like a spider's web running from post to post. It took me a minute to place it as an al fresco clothes dryer.

A single step led up to small back porch. It had once been stained a red-brown but had settled into a mud color with gray-brown boards clearly showing through, and an old metal Weber barbecue grill looked like it hadn't been opened in decades.

As if the decision was made for me, I followed a short path of brick-colored pavers toward the front of the house. The Eddings home had a gravel drive like Robyn's, and a carport, open to the elements except for a corrugated tin roof. There was no car.

Did anyone live here?

One way to find out.

I walked up to the door. It was white, with three small rectangular decorative windows in the top. There was an old storm door, with silver metal on the bottom and a worn but intact screen on the top. To the right was a perfectly round white button.

I pushed it. A tinny two-noted ding-dong sounded from inside. I waited.

"Yes?"

The female voice came from inside.

"Mrs. Eddings?"

"Who is it?"

"It's Avalon Nash. I was a friend of Brian's." An overstatement, but the only good explanation available to me.

"Oh."

"May I come in?"

"I'm not dressed for company."

"It's okay. I'm not dressed for calling."

A short pause, with limited rustling. "All right. The door is unlocked."

A bit of muscle was needed to push the inner door open, as if the wood had expanded and it wasn't often used. I stepped inside a small living room, perhaps 8' by 8'.

Straight in front of me was a large brown recliner currently occupied by Mrs. Eddings. She was a small woman wearing a floral housecoat. There was a side table that included a lamp with a woman's magazine and several pieces of mail next to a silver four-footed walker.

"May I come in? I wanted to say hello."

"You're here, might as well."

I stepped over the threshold and closed the door behind me. It only took a glance to see the entirety of the room: a bookshelf ran the length of the wall to my left, with an opening to a front bedroom. At the corner, a short hall led back to two more bedrooms. At its opening sat a stopped grandfather clock with its weights resting on the clock floor. Across the room was a flat panel 18-inch television with a console beneath, a doorway to the kitchen, and another to the laundry room and exit to the porch.

Above Mrs. Eddings was a rectangular picture of Jesus, wearing the obligatory Catholic crown of thorns with his sacred heart burning through his white robe. Beside it was the old family photo that had been published after Brian's death, when the boys were in the ten to twelve range and the dad was alive.

There were no other photos, which seemed strange. If I had a child who had won Olympic gold, believe me, visitors would know it.

"Who are you again?"

"Avalon Nash, Mrs. Eddings."

"Alma, it's Alma."

"I was with Brian the night before he died. He helped welcome and entertain a new batch of Olympic hopefuls. They had a very good time. When he left the restaurant, he was as happy as I'd ever seen him."

"That's good to know, I guess."

My phone buzzed. *Where are you?*

I answered Hannah: *At the Eddings' home through the back yards. Back in 10.*

"Brian was very much loved," I continued. "Thousands of people are arriving in town to go to the Memorial Service on Sunday. Will you be there?"

"No, he thinks it's best if I don't go."

"But you'll be at the family Mass this afternoon?"

"Yes, he said that'us fine."

Before I could ask who "he" was, the back porch door opened and a male voice called, "Let's get you some lunch before you go."

Alma Eddings smiled. "He takes good care."

No car had arrived. I'm sure my eyes registered my surprise when the tall man who stomped into the room was Ray, the bartender from the Cavalleros Birthday Bash. He wore an open-collared square-cut shirt and carried two brown paper shopping bags. One had a loaf of white bread sticking out the top, the other a roll of paper towels.

He stopped in his tracks. "You. What are you doing here?"

I could have asked him the same thing. I did recall Glenn Mac-

Tavish telling me Ray lived in a cabin and used the Cavalleros money to finance most the rest of the year—which, unless he was paid many times more than I was, would be a sparse year indeed, even though he worked for all the summer months, not one party.

"Paying my respects."

"Who invited you to do that?"

"Ray, she'us with Brian the night he died. She wanted me to know he was happy."

"Okay, then. You've done your bit."

My eyes went again to the old photo of an intact family above her chair. "It was nice to meet you, Mrs. Eddings. I'm sorry about Brian. It must be hard with both your son and your husband gone."

"Her husband? Keep him out of this. Certainly no one misses that son-of-a-bitch!" Ray said with a snort.

"Don't speak ill of the dead," Alma reproved.

"It was a happy day when he fell down the stairs and broke his neck."

Alma's spine straightened. "Ray!" She crossed herself.

"True is true," he said. "I've got some Campbell's soup. I'll heat you some."

"That's nice. Is it time to get ready?"

"Mrs. Eddings," I started, once Ray was in the other room.

"Alma," she said.

"Alma. Wouldn't you like some photos of Brian, with his medals? I could get you some."

"He don't like it," she said.

"All right. Let me know if you change your mind."

Alma beckoned me over. She picked up her small purse on the side table, opened it, and took out her wallet. From inside, she brought out a small, worn photograph with crinkled edges. It was head and shoulders of Brian, grinning, holding his gold metal up to his lips in a proud kiss.

Alma smiled. I smiled.

The smell of barley wafted in from the kitchen.

"I'll let myself out," I said.

A playful breeze was refreshing. I stood for a moment on the small front stoop, looking down the steep drive toward the road, which was hidden from view by a forested hill.

"Hello," said Hannah.

I whirled to find her rounding the side of the house.

"You came?"

"I thought the fresh air would clear my head," she said.

As she did, there came the crunching of a car heading up the gravel drive. Thirty seconds later, a rented silver metallic Nissan Versa appeared and pulled up in front of the house. The driver's door opened and Frank Eddings, Brian's brother whom I'd met at the wake, got out. He looked wiry and thin, even wearing a blue suit.

He looked surprised to see us, then recognition dawned. "You were the one who knows a woman priest," he said to me. Then he looked at Hannah and took in her collar. "Is this?"

She stepped forward, offering a handshake. "Hannah Bricksford," she said.

They shook.

"I'm sorry about Brian. If there's anything I can do."

"Actually, there is," he said. "Actually, there is."

With a sweep of a hand, he invited her around the side of the house. I stood, waiting, trying to remember why he told me he was interested in finding a non-Catholic priest.

She reappeared shortly, and Frank climbed the cement stairs to the front door.

"Let's get going," she said.

Together we walked the pavers around the side of the house and struck out for Robyn's.

"What was that?"

"Apparently Brian has some last wishes, one of which was to have his ashes scattered. Father Collum says Catholics have to have their ashes interred in holy ground—i.e., the Catholic cemetery. Frank wanted to know, if he acquired some of the ashes, would I say a prayer when he scattered them."

"What did you say?"

She shrugged. "I don't know why I wouldn't. Especially if he doesn't tell Collum. I don't need him glowering at me during Chamber of Commerce meetings."

I glanced at my watch as we reached Robyn's back porch, where Hannah had left the bag of items she'd collected. She picked it up as we passed. A glance at my watch assured me I was in plenty of time to open the Battened Hatch.

Together, we rounded the house on the garage side, where Hannah's blizzard pearl Prius sat next to Robyn's white Impala, both vehicles facing forward toward the garage.

Coming from this way meant we approached the Impala from the passenger's side.

We both stopped short.

"Shit," I said.

"Shit," said Hannah.

The Impala's right-hand bumper was crumpled. There was blood and what looked like hair on the casing of the headlight.

Best guess: we'd found the car that hit Robyn.

THROUGH THE WOODS

Early Summer Strawberry Rhubarb Cocktail

Ingredients

> 1 oz of preferred vanilla vodka or regular unflavored
> vodka (vanilla vodka brings the sweetness and the sense
> of comfort and warmth of a strawberry rhubarb pie)
> ½ oz of preferred orange liqueur
> 2 oz of fresh strawberry puree
> 1 oz of fresh-made rhubarb simple syrup
> Orange peel for twist

FRESH STRAWBERRY PUREE

Best to make this cocktail and puree in late spring and
early summer when strawberries are fresh, sweet and
abundant. Remove stems from strawberries and dice into
small pieces and blend in food processor until you have a
silky-smooth consistency.

RHUBARB SIMPLE SYRUP

This rhubarb simple syrup is best made in the late spring
/early summer when rhubarb is also fresh and abundant.
Bring equal part of sugar and water to boil. Add cleaned
and chopped rhubarb to boiling mixture and then lower
temperature on stovetop. Simmer until you have a nice
nape. Let mixture cool and strain with cheese cloth and
pour into desired storage container.

COCKTAIL

Method

Mix and shake all ingredients together creating a nice frothy consistency and serve in a rocks glass. Finish with fresh cut strawberries and an orange twist.

13

ADVENTUROUS MOOD

Inspector Gerald Mason, whom I'd met at the Battened Hatch, was noticeably more respectful to me when I was with the Reverend Bricksford.

"I thought you didn't know Brian Eddings or Robyn Forsyth well?" he asked me.

"She doesn't," Hannah answered. "Avalon is a friend of mine and I asked her to accompany me to get Ms. Forsyth's burial outfit, for moral support."

That was enough to dismiss me, in his book.

We were allowed to leave as the driveway became an active crime scene. They took casts of Hannah's tire treads, to rule hers out in case the perpetrator had been careless enough to drive up and leave tread marks in the gravel and dirt before "borrowing" Robyn's car for his fatal trip. Although, had it been me, I would have parked below and walked up on the grass.

"Well," said Hannah, as we pulled away onto the rural road. "I wasn't expecting that."

"The day has been full of surprises. How do you suppose whoever ran her down got her car keys?"

"They're hanging on a key rack in the kitchen. And the house key is under the mat."

"Indeed it is."

Where I had once been on track to arrive at work in plenty of time to open, by the time Hannah dropped me at the Battened Hatch, I crossed the lobby of MacTavish's Seaside Cottage at a run.

Marta waited outside the interior pub door. I unlocked and pushed the heavy door open, then relocked it from the darkened hall. Inside the restaurant, I turned on the lights and grabbed an apron. Marta grabbed one, too. We had half an hour to set up.

On Marta's second trip from the ice maker in the back hall to the ice freezers behind the bar, I paused, wine bottles in hand to restock the bar. "Say, aren't you graduating from high school very soon? If you have celebrations or graduation activities or simply irresponsible partying to do, just let me know as far in advance as possible."

"Graduation is on the twentieth at two p.m.," she said. "I think I have to go. Dad is going to say the invocation. So I need that day off."

"Of course you have to go. It's your graduation!"

"I'm not so interested in graduation. I'm more interested in having graduated."

I laughed. "I know the feeling. Have you decided on your plans for next year?"

She stopped what she was doing. "Well, yeah," she said.

"And?"

"I want to take a gap year. I really want to go to art school, so I need to save enough money that I can go away and live in a dorm or apartment or whatever."

"I applaud all three decisions. What do you mean when you say 'gap year'? Are you thinking of going somewhere exciting to work? Like Europe?"

"Actually... I was hoping to become a really good bartender. I was hoping to work here. Maybe get more hours."

I smiled. "I can't tell you how relieved I am. That will be no problem. In fact, it will be a big help. What does your dad think of all this?"

It was her turn to laugh. "So, I finally told dad about Sister Maria Luisa and my journal and... everything. That freaked him out so much that when I told him I wanted to go to art school, he looked relieved. Like compared to becoming a certified séance leader, it was a good choice."

"You can become a certified séance leader?"

"No, silly!"

"How am I supposed to know about these things? This is a new area of expertise for me."

"For both of us," she said.

"In the meantime, if you want a vacation, or, like I said, to go do some partying... I've heard Tranquility has quite the party scene."

"My friends and I aren't really into that."

"Who are your friends? I mean, your besties?"

"Like you and Reverend Bricksford?" she asked.

Seriously? For all my studied avoidance, now everyone thought Hannah and I were friends? Damn. As long as they didn't put me into the do-gooder category by association.

"Colin and Lisette, I guess," Marta said. "Lisette is going away to college in the fall, but Colin is going to stay here and work for a year, like I am."

"Colin is only a 'friend'?"

"What? Yes! Gosh, yes!"

And, still horrified by the suggestion, she went to get the final two barrels of ice. Davros sauntered in shortly thereafter, and Manuela. The kitchen crew stood ready to cook. We opened the doors.

By 5 p.m. we were humming. I knew there was that private funeral Mass for Brian at four, but that left the rest of those gathered for his big send-off on Sunday at loose ends and ready to drink. It was shaping up to be a big night for both orders and tips.

The stool-height chairs pulled up to the bar itself stayed occupied. I will note that they are very comfortable with dark wooden carved backs and sides and pleather-covered cushions, the idea being settling in rather than high turnover.

Marta and I worked the bar patrons and made drinks with

Davros and Manuela on the floor. I had asked Manuela if she'd like to try being a waiter instead of a busser and she was happy to give it a go. She was a quick study. Her son, Andy, and his friend Oscar were bussing.

We all had our hands full, which was unusual so early. It's also why I didn't notice when one of the patrons at the bar left and another man took his place. That is, until Marta cocked her head toward the newcomer. "That man asked for you," she said.

I glanced over. Then I nearly dropped the soda gun.

The newcomer was my cousin Reggie.

I knew he was in town, of course. Avantika gave me his note. It wouldn't take long asking around town to find out where I worked.

I looked at Reggie and he smiled.

If the family had to choose someone to find me and reel me back in, there wasn't a better candidate. Not that I had a favorite cousin. I loved them all. But Reggie was my favorite cousin.

He was an only child, as was I. The rest of our multiple first cousins came in family squads of three to five members. They were set in their ways and had shorthands that they somehow shared, family to family.

At reunions and holidays, Reggie and I tended to hang back and watch. With caustic commentary, of course. Besides being the only "onlys," we were also the outsiders. He was half Swedish and half Black, and I came from "unmarried parents," shorthand for not only Mom's sexuality, but the whole LaLa Land weirdness.

Marta shot me a questioning look, and I nodded.

I stood in front of Reg, grabbed the last patron's dirty glass and square cardboard coaster that advertised Ciroc then wiped down the bar with a cloth.

"What'll ya have?"

"What do you suggest?"

"If you like beer, we have some good local brews on tap. If you'd like a mixed drink, we have a special involving cucumber and citron vodka that isn't too sweet. There's another with cucumber and wasabi, if you're in a more adventurous mood."

"Adventurous mood? Well, I'm here, aren't I?"

"Yes. Apparently, you are."

"I'm in an adventurous mood. Should I try the wasabi version, or is that a trick you play on unsuitable suitors?"

"Order wings and celery and fourteen glasses of water and you'll be fine."

"Sold."

"Coming up."

I put in the wings order. As I blended the drink ingredients, I studied Reggie. He wore business casual, a camel-colored sports coat that nearly matched his skin, along with an open-collared green shirt. I couldn't see his trousers, but I'd put money that they had a nice press. He delighted in his pants being well pressed. Even in the darkness of the bar, I could tell his skin was smooth, unblemished, and unwrinkled. As a teen I would have killed for his skin. Now he had a close-cropped mustache and beard, which made him look stately and grown-up. Damn. How was it that we were now grown-up? That we could no longer blame youthful stupidity for our actions?

Reggie did not look like he'd made any stupid decisions lately.

This left me alone in the dubious decision department. I felt abandoned somehow.

I made a quick assessment of the room and decided I could take a minute to talk.

Which didn't mean I knew what to say.

I gave him the drink, two glasses of water, and a plate of celery. "Wings will be along shortly."

He studied the items before him. "This does seem like a drink that comes with its own skull and crossbones."

Reggie looked me straight in the eyes and took a generous sip.

He gave a small cough, took a drink of water and a bite of celery.

He landed on holding the celery like a professor's pointer and took bites as if it was the finest caviar.

"So, what have you been up to lately?" he asked, as if it was a simple question.

I laughed.

"Simpler question: How did you find me? I sent my phone to Montreal!"

"Google alert." He pulled his iPhone from his pocket. On it was a copy of the local paper's article about the catching of the last murderer. I was mentioned only tangentially. Apparently, it was enough.

"This would have alerted you six weeks ago."

"I figured if you wanted us to know where you were, you would alert us yourself."

"What changed?"

His face fell. "Mormor. I didn't say it in the note 'cause it didn't seem the kind of thing you scrawl on an order pad. But she's dying. I thought you'd want to know."

"Oh," I said. "Oh. Thanks."

He put a hand over mine. It was a simple gesture but with it, everything good and warm and accepting and connected about my family washed over me. It all traced back to Mormor and Morfar.

"You're busy," he said. "You seem to be in your element. I'll let you get back to it. I'll finish my drink—ah, and here are the wings. The perfect drink and supper for an adventure. Then I'll be on my way."

"Okay. And Reggie, thanks."

Five drink orders came spitting out together, sent from the POS on the floor. Marta looked at me with wide eyes. I gave her a nod, then a one-minute finger.

I went back to Reggie.

"Where are you heading from here?"

"Back to Brooklyn. The family is gathering. Can I tell them I saw you?"

"Are you driving back tonight?"

"Yes. I'll get in late, but I should avoid any traffic."

"It's a good plan but sounds fairly painful. Would you like to stay over? There's a spare bedroom at my place. You could get a fresh start in the morning."

He considered. Are you sure?"

"Yeah. I get off at eleven if you don't mind waiting. There are some good movies at the Palace you could check out in the meantime. Or, you could not pretend wings were supper and go to have a nice dinner."

"Where would you suggest?"

I recommended some local restaurants that were known for great food.

"You're sure you don't need to hurry back to Brooklyn tonight?" I asked.

"I've been down there for a couple of days already. Had some time with the grandparents. If I leave early tomorrow morning, I should be okay. And you're right, I'd prefer not to drive all that way tonight. I'm beat. And I just had a wasabi thing. So, if you mean it, I will take you up on your offer."

"I mean it. And, Reggie, it's good to see you."

He smiled and offered his martini up in a toast.

As it turned out, Reggie was not the last surprise of the night.

ADVENTUROUS MOOD

Cucumber Wasabi Cocktail

Ingredients

1 1/2 oz Hendrick's Gin
2 oz of fresh cucumber juice, made in juicer. Leave skin on
for darker green, peel for lighter color
1 oz fresh squeezed lemon juice
1 oz distilled or sparking water
1 inch wasabi paste (or 1/4 teaspoon of dried wasabi)
*wasabi is much like horseradish. Depending on your
palate use more or less.
Ice

Method

Put all ingredients into a shaker; add ice.
Shake ingredients together and pour contents of shaker
into Collins glass
Garnish with fresh rose petal, lemon wedge, fresh cucumber slices and some dried wasabi peas for a little crunch.
Cheers!

14

PLOT TWIST

WE KNEW FOR certain Brian's funeral Mass was over when Father Collum, the local Catholic priest, came in. His name suggests a man of Irish extraction, which he is. To me it also suggested a man of a certain age with a rotund, ruddy appearance, which he was not. Father Collum was early thirties, tall, slim, and earnest.

He arrived with his assistant vicar, both of them wearing priest's collars, and two other gentlemen in black suits. The unerring fit of the suits was what placed them for me: they were scions of the funeral parlor owner who had greeted callers as we'd arrived.

They sat at a table for four. Father Collum ordered a Guinness. The others went for craft beer. I guessed they'd order a nice dinner and keep the beers flowing. It was likely as close to a wake as Brian was going to get.

Not long after they arrived, Brent Davis slid onto the stool closest to the door.

"Hey Brent, what can I throw you? A Stella?"

"Naw, I'm headed home. I remembered you asked for info about the Misty Edison kidnapping and I found a clip of a piece about it I wrote a few years back. Thought you might be interested."

He slid a manila folder across the bar. "Ever get a last name on the mystery Jane?"

"Nope," I said. "At least not yet."

"We'll call her Jane Doe, then." We both chuckled. "Let me know if you find out."

"I do have some new information for you," I said. "We found the car that hit Robyn."

"What? By we, you mean…"

"Hannah Bricksford and me."

My mind whirred. The police hadn't told us to keep the information secret. Had they? Inspector Mason wasn't one whose threats could easily be forgotten. Was there any reason I shouldn't be blabbing this? Especially to Brent, the newspaper man?

"Avalon," he said, "I believe I'll have a Stella."

"I'll be back in a sec."

I went to the other end of the bar, where I could step back, and texted Hannah: *Did they say we couldn't tell anyone about Robyn's car?*

Then I helped Marta catch up with the drink orders.

My phone pinged.

I don't think so. We don't want to feed any rumors, though.

No, we don't. So maybe the best thing would be to give a reputable reporter the correct facts, as many as were known?

I trusted Brent and returned to where he was seated.

Once there, I went to the photo gallery on my phone and called up the photo I'd snapped of the Impala's front bumper. It wasn't a pretty picture.

"Holy smokes," said Brent. "Can you tell me how you found it?"

"I went with the Reverend Bricksford to Robyn's house to get a dress to bring to the funeral home. It was in Robyn's driveway. Someone hit her with her own car."

"Well. I wasn't expecting that."

"I know," I said. "Plot twist."

"Can we step out for a minute to talk where it's a little quieter?"

Brent and I went out into the hotel lobby and found a corner. I told him the story, which he recorded on his phone. He asked pertinent questions. I sent him the photo.

"Thanks," he said.

"If you could keep my name—and Hannah's—out of it as much

as possible, I'd appreciate it. Inspector Mason is already not a fan of mine."

"I'll do what I can."

"Not to deal in rumors, but do you have any idea why someone would kill Robyn? You don't really think it was retribution for Brian's death, do you? Robyn told Hannah there was no obvious physical trauma when she found him. That he was sitting up in bed with his eyes open, mouth agog. Kind of like he'd seen a ghost."

Hannah hadn't said that last part, but it seemed appropriate and I admittedly had ghosts on the brain. "If there wasn't physical trauma, if he wasn't hit with a bat, can't the police say so? Why couldn't they quash the rumors about Robyn?"

Brent shook his head. "I asked again earlier today. They said they can't release cause of death until they have toxicology reports back."

"But those take weeks, don't they? And why do they need toxicology? I can tell them exactly what he imbibed that evening!"

"To your knowledge."

"Well, right, to my knowledge."

"And maybe to his knowledge."

That stumped me. "What are you saying? That he ingested something without his knowledge? That he was poisoned?"

"I can't tell you. But to my mind, that's what they weren't saying in their carefully worded statement." Brent said. "And, I agree, quash as many rumors as possible, as soon as possible."

"Thanks for the article about Misty," I said.

"Thanks for the info."

Six more drink orders had arrived during my brief absence, and I leapt into the fray next to Marta. I found it ironic that Brian, who didn't drink, was the source of this free-flowing alcohol.

As we set up the orders, the inside door swung open. I glanced up at the room: all the tables were full. I didn't remember the last time we had a waiting list.

I took a look at the newcomers and my adrenaline surged.

"Hello, Ms. Nash," Jeff Harris said. "You remember my wife, Charlotte?"

I reminded myself that I was on solid ground, firmly on earth, and took a deep breath.

"Darling, this is Avalon Nash, who I spent the morning with."

And Charlotte Harris shot me the nastiest drop dead look I've ever received. It wasn't a side-eye. It was straight on, piercing and heartfelt.

And then it vanished.

Father Collum saw them and waved. He gestured, and the men he was with started to pull chairs over to accommodate the Harrises.

Jeff drew Charlotte to him and they both gave me charming smiles.

Holy shit.

She didn't say a word, and she retracted the look immediately, but I still found myself trembling.

Maybe she didn't like that I'd accused her husband of murder.

Or maybe she had a different version of the peaches-and-cream-and-thanks-for-my-family-Brian story that Jeff had told.

"Okay," I said to Marta, "I'm ready for this day to be over."

We closed the bar at ten but didn't shoo people out until eleven. By then, Reggie had returned. He waited as Marta and I did the final closing. Since I'd be walking home with a companion, I decided to leave my bike for the next night's late return.

Once the sun set, it was sweater weather, even in June. Main Street was more alive than usual for a Thursday night, although the other restaurants and bars were also closing. "Nice town," said Reggie. He put an arm around my shoulders companionably.

"I like it," I said, although even as I said it, I was aware that, besides the occasional Avantika and Philip, the town was very white. Would anyone have a problem with a Black man putting an arm casually around the shoulders of a white woman? Neither of us said anything, but I know we were both on alert.

"How did you end up here?" he asked.

"I was changing trains on my way to the city—to Mormor and Morfar's in Brooklyn, as a matter of fact—when I went for lunch at the Battened Hatch, where I now work. The former bartender was murdered while I was there. No one could leave before the police questioned everybody, but they let me sell drinks. Afterwards, the owner asked if I wanted a job."

"One of the more interesting 'how I got my job' stories I've heard for a while."

"Right? You know me, eschewing the expected."

"Which is exactly what I'd expect. And therefore, the expected."

I laughed. "How about you?"

"Still in Colorado Springs. It's nice. You should come visit."

"At the same law firm? Still specializing in pro bono work?"

He nodded. "Everyone else is busy racking up billables. They're happy to sluff their pro bonos off on me.

"Which is exactly what I'd expect."

"What was it we promised each other as kids? Never to become boring?"

"Yeah. Or predictable."

"Or snooty." He smiled. "I think we're doing okay."

"By those criteria."

"You should always live by your own criteria."

It was a twenty-minute walk home, and I enjoyed all twenty of them. Nothing else could have gotten me out of my head and away from Brian's and Robyn's deaths.

"This is it," I said, as we turned up the hidden lane into my glen.

"What on earth, Avalon?" he asked as the trees cleared and the fairy-tale meadow sat before us. Two tall lamps that looked as if they'd been recently visited by the lamplighter glowed with a flickering flame. "That's my cottage. Across the footbridge."

"Over the waterfall? Wow. You've done it this time. Created your surroundings by force of imagination."

"It feels that way sometimes. You can see why I stayed."

"And that... massive cabin. Whose is that?"

"The lodge? My landlord lives there, but she's in India now with her husband. Did I mention I rent from Sally Allison?"

"You don't mean *the* Sally Allison? She's still alive?"

"And feisty as hell. Well, come on up. It sounds like we could both use a good night's sleep." We headed toward my cottage. "Want to know how much I love you? I'll get up in time to give you breakfast before you leave."

He gave me a full-on bear hug.

"It's great to see you, Avalon."

PLOT TWIST

Ingredients

1 ½ oz Dulce Vida Pineapple Jalapeño tequila
1 oz Godiva White Chocolate liqueur
1 oz coconut cream (like Coco Lopez)
2 oz coconut milk
Fresh-sliced jalapeño (wear kitchen gloves to cut jalapenos; oils from hot peppers can stick on your skin; refrain from touching face, eyes, nose)
Toasted coconut flakes (toast at home on a warm skillet on low heat until coconut flakes turn light brown)
Ice

Method

In cocktail shaker combine tequila, Godiva White Chocolate liqueur coconut cream, coconut milk, and ice.
Shake all ingredients together to get a nice frothy consistency.
Pour into rocks glass.
Add toasted coconut and fresh jalapeños for garnish.

15

STRANGE GIFTS

IT RAINED OVERNIGHT. Tranquility had been in a Camelot pattern as of late, as in, "The rain may never fall till after sundown/ By eight, the morning fog must disappear." I hoped the rest of the verse would hold true: "In short, there's simply not a more congenial spot/For happily ever-aftering."

Reggie was still sound asleep, snoring heartily, and I decided to walk down to the Cardamom Café to acquire my favorite breakfast items to share with him before he left. It was either that or tea and half an orange.

Outside, I smelled the rich earth and heard bluebirds over the pounding of my little waterfall. Carrying a basket with a gingham cloth was all it would take to place me firmly inside a fairy tale.

As usual, the Cardamom was hopping. I recognized many of the clientele, but no one seemed in need of rescuing from Aedan.

My eyes fell to a flyer posted on the wall near the counter. It was for a used Subaru Legacy, 3 years old, silver, 80,000 miles. Inquire for price.

Was I ready?

I still had the money in my account from selling my own vehicle in Los Angeles, and I'd been saving consistently since arriving. It would be great not to have to depend on others to get anywhere outside bicycling distance. And Subarus are all-wheel drive, necessary for winters in upstate New York, or so I've been told.

Still, "inquire for price" was seldom good.

At the front of the line, I ordered one of each of their breakfast items, wanting to make Reggie happy, but not knowing what he'd like. Then I off-handedly said, "So, who's selling the Subaru?"

"Avantika!" Presley, the order-taker, called over his shoulder. "Subaru inquiry!"

I hadn't meant to make that much of a deal out of it.

Avantika came to the counter and Presley pointed me out. She smiled. "Avalon! Are you interested? Step over here." Today she wore a sari of orange and brown. It was one of her working outfits. I'd seen her in some gorgeous saris when she was at important events. This one was nice, and likely easy to clean in case of kitchen mishap.

We made way for the others in line. "Are you serious about buying a car?"

"I need to get one pretty soon. I've been surviving with only a bicycle, but it's not ideal."

"You have only a bicycle?"

I nodded. She laughed and said words I had perhaps dreamed of hearing in my lifetime, but never thought I would: "I realized I needed a bigger car for hauling. I'd like someone to buy this one who'd put it to good use. How does three thousand sound?"

Way under Blue Book value, that's how it sounds. "Are you sure?"

"Would that work for you?"

"Yes. It would."

"It's a good little car. Only three years old."

"I'll take it."

"Perfect. I was hoping it would be in good hands. Do you want to drive it for a few days to see what you think?"

"Unless there's anything really wrong with it, I'll take it."

"Very good! I'll bring it over after the breakfast rush and fill out all the paperwork. You can take it to a mechanic to check it out, and if it's all good—and it is—you can drive straight to the DMV and have a car!"

"All right," I said. "I'm bringing breakfast to my cousin, but I'll go to the bank when he leaves."

"Your cousin who was in the other day?"

"Yes. Thanks for the note."

Reggie was just out of the shower when I returned, perfect timing to put on the kettle and set up our breakfast outside. He loved the food and ate half of several of the crepes, declaring the one with egg, spinach, and brie to be his favorite.

"Will you come back and visit?" I asked, hating to see him go.

"You know I will. Can I tell the others I saw you?"

"Of course. I've written a note for Mormor, if you would be kind enough to read it to her."

"Can I tell them where you are?"

That one gave me more pause. "Maybe say 'upstate'?"

"As you wish."

We smiled together at the *Princess Bride* reference, one of the many shared favorite movies from our childhood.

"I'll be in touch with everyone. Before long." Maybe. As anyone who has a family knows, family can be a *lot*.

Reggie was parked in a public lot off Main Street, and I walked him to his car. I felt a pang as he pulled out and waved into his rearview mirror. I wished we had longer to talk. It was our habit to burrow down to the important stuff eventually. I longed for someone with whom to share the important stuff and wanted to find out what was up with him.

We'd exchanged phone numbers, and I texted *Bye* to be at the top of his list.

On the way home, I stopped in at the local bank where I had my accounts and got a bank check for $3000. Breakfast rush was ending as I stopped into the Cardamom Café and handed Avantika the envelope.

"Come back in an hour," she said. "I won't cash this until you've driven the car and had it checked out."

A mix of emotions followed me back to Cherry Lane. Happiness, sadness, excitement, dread—the latter lurking from the knowledge that Jeff's wife, Charlotte Harris, hated me and that something was behind the recent deaths that I didn't understand.

Excitement from the thought that I'd soon have my own set of wheels.

As I entered the meadow, a new emotion emerged: confusion.

For on the bench in front of the pond, a man was seated. He wore trousers, a button-down shirt and a navy blazer. A few steps closer and I was able to make out who it was: the Reverend Timothy Layton. Marta's dad.

The first time I'd met the good reverend, he'd scared the bejesus out of me. That was even before I started training his daughter to bartend and run a bar. On Sundays.

However, I had learned more about him since then and had come to understand him. A little.

He knew Sally from back when he was a boy. Certainly, he was here to see her.

I decided to take the bull by the horns and walked over to the bench. "Hello, Reverend Layton. Sally is out of town. She'll be back later this week. Shall I tell her you were looking for her?"

He looked up at me. "No. I'm not here to see Sally."

He didn't say anything else. He sat, looking pensive.

"All right. See you soon." I started toward the bridge to my cottage.

"Avalon," he said.

I stopped.

"Could I talk to you for a minute?"

Crap. Crap. Crap. Was he going to ask something about Marta? To fire her from the bar? To make her go to college next year? To become an accountant?

To help me repent of my sins, of which I was certain there were many?

Hesitantly I returned and sat next to him.

"Marta seems happy. In fact, she seems like a new person," he said.

"Really? I'm glad to hear it. Graduating high school is a big deal."

"It's not that. It's not high school. Well, maybe that's a part of it."

"What, then?"

"She says she talked to a nun."

"Oh. Yeah. Sister Maria Luisa."

Now he was fidgeting.

"That this nun told her she had a gift."

"Oh. Yeah. Marta talked with her for a while. Apparently, the sister has the same gift, herself."

"I don't understand."

"I'm with you there. There are many things I don't understand. Seeing dead people is one of them. But Sister Maria Luisa seems like a good person. A person of faith, who seemed to give Marta comfort."

"Were you there? When they talked?"

"Yes and no. Reverend Bricksford and I waited up by the convent. So I didn't hear their conversation."

"Did Marta say anything to you about the theology of this gift?"

"That is a conversation we have never had," I replied truthfully.

"Would it be possible for me to talk to this nun?"

"Hannah knows how to get in touch with her. You could call Hannah."

"No!" he said and sat straight. "I mean, I don't think I should."

"I'm pretty sure the Sister gave Marta her contact info."

"I don't want to ask her. It would get complicated."

"Those are the only ways I can think of to contact her."

He looked at me. Instead of looking intimidating, he looked almost pleading. "Could you find out her number and give it to me?"

"Can I ask why? This is Marta's problem, er, challenge, and it seems she's found a path that's working for her. I'm not sure the sister wants a theological argument. And I don't want to spoil what's helping Marta."

"Neither do I. That's the last thing I want."

"Then, why?"

Now Tim Layton looked truly uncomfortable. "You won't tell Marta?"

"Yes. I promise." I almost added, "Bartender's honor."

"I... I have the same gift. It's haunted me... for a very long time."

I smiled at the use of "haunted." He got it too and shook his head. "Do you think you could get her number?"

"I can ask Hannah if that's what you want."

"It is. I would appreciate it."

"Okay."

I got ready to stand, but realized he was expecting me to do something. Now.

I got out my phone and texted: *Could you give me Sister Maria Luisa's number?*

There was no reply for a couple of minutes. I started, "I can let you know..." when there was a reply. Hannah gave me the number and added *Why?*

I said, "Here it is. Do you want to put it into your phone?"

The Reverend Layton got out his cell and I read the numbers off slowly enough that he could input them as we went along.

"Thank you," he said. "Much appreciated."

We both stood. He held out his hand and I shook it. Then he headed back toward the lane.

Once he was gone, I replied, *Tim Layton wanted it.*

You don't think he's going to give her grief, do you?

I hope not. Apparently he has the same "gift" as Marta.

No kidding. Why didn't he ask me himself?

He can't. He likes you.

What?

He likes you likes you.

What? How do you know?

You wouldn't believe me if I told you. He isn't thrilled about it. But, girl, half the men in this town like you like you.

Yeah, sure. That's why I watch Netflix alone every Friday night.

They're scared.

Then I'm better off with Netflix.

True that. Hey, guess what. I bought a car!

For reals?

Yeah. Going to Plattsburgh to get it registered etc.

To the DMV? I will pray for you.

Thanks.

I smiled and headed to the house to get my stuff. Those prayers, I could use.

STRANGE GIFTS

Gingerbread White Russian

Ingredients

1 ½ oz vodka of your choice
½ oz Kahlua
Ice
2 oz half and half or heavy cream (any milk product of your choice or milk substitute is fine as well)
1 ½ oz gingerbread simple syrup
Cinnamon sugar
Crushed gingerbread cookies
Whipped cream

GINGERBREAD SIMPLE SYRUP

Ingredients

¼ cup honey
4 oz molasses
½ oz of fresh ground ginger
2 cinnamon sticks
1 teaspoon vanilla extract
1 cup water

Method

In medium sauce pan, combine all ingredients.
Simmer on low heat and stir occasionally until ingredients are combined, about 10 minutes.
Remove from heat, let simple syrup cool, and strain through small mesh strainer to remove ginger and cinnamon sticks.

COCKTAIL

Method

In cocktail shaker, add vodka, Kahlua, gingerbread simple
syrup, ice, and milk product of your choice.
Shake ingredients together until you have a nice frothy
consistency.
Add cinnamon sugar to rim of glass.
Pour ingredients from shaker into rimmed glass.
Top with whipped cream and crushed gingerbread cook-
ies for garnish.
Sip and enjoy!

16

MYOB

THE CAR WAS sweet. It had heated seats, satellite radio, found my phone connection immediately, and had a large front screen for the back-up camera so I could know exactly who I was hitting in real time without turning my head. It also had remote start, so I could turn it on from inside my cottage and have it warm up on snowy days.

The car I'd been able to afford in Los Angeles had an endearing growl and windows with real handles to roll them down. And yet I was able to sell it because everyone is desperately in need of a car out there.

But here I was with a nearly new ride, and although it was the beginning of June, I felt in charge and ready for winter.

Did I mention a built in GPS? It took me over beautiful if windy back roads to the local metropolis of Plattsburgh, the last American city before Canada.

Admittedly, Reggie's visit had put me into a pensive mood. I was tired of Los Angeles, tired of everybody being in "the business." I was a certain person when I was out there, the same way I became a certain version of myself when I was in Brooklyn with my family. Both reflected a part of me; neither defined me. I guess I was using this time on my own to mold my true self.

Which was lonely work. I wished there was someone in the car with me to celebrate the moon roof.

I told myself I was doing well on my own, that I wouldn't be feeling this way if Reggie hadn't shown up out of the blue and then left.

I was starting to make friends here. Or at least interesting acquaintances.

Which category did Philip belong in? I had no idea. I was still protecting my heart.

But that kiss...

The DMV in Plattsburgh unexpectedly had a spot for someone to take the written test, which was required when changing licenses from another state to New York. I'd been holding off because any private investigator with a computer can find you once you've got a license with the correct address. Still, I'd been practicing the test online, just in case, and I passed it, missing only questions I thought were pretty shady on the part of New York State. I had my birth certificate and passport with the wrong address but electric bill with the right one, so I was able to get a New York State license, register the vehicle, get new plates, and pay a boatload of tax on the sale.

In other words: done. I had my own car and a local ID. And the whole thing only took three hours! I even took the car to get reinspected and it passed.

To complete the experience, I ate at a chain restaurant, which Plattsburgh has by the dozen, but which Tranquility bans with gusto. The meal involved deep-dish pizza and it was great.

On the return trip, I felt grateful to have had time away to clear my mind. I decided to trust the State Police to do their job and solve the mystery behind the local deaths. I would attempt to mind my own business.

Marta again waited for me by the door to the Battened Hatch.

"You know you don't have to wait," I said. "You have a key."

"Really?" she asked. "It seemed polite to wait for you to open."

"You're assistant manager. Opening is something you do."

She gave a satisfied smile. She used her key to open the door and we both went in, relocking the door behind us until we were ready.

"Have you thought about where you want to go to art school?" I asked as we started our respective opening chores.

"There are a number of good schools," she said, as if quoting a brochure. "But I'm not sure yet what my top picks are. Philip said he'll help me put together a portfolio. He went to the École des Beaux-Arts, but I don't speak French."

"Does Philip speak French?"

"Yeah. And Spanish and Malayalam."

"What's the last one?"

"They speak it in south India where his grandfather lives."

"Got it. Well, I'm already excited about you going to art school."

She smiled. "Me, too. Nervous, but happy. Do we have any drink specials tonight?"

"Yes. It's the MYOB. I'm concocting it right now. It involves whiskey."

"I love how you do that."

"Thanks. I enjoy doing it." In fact, I enjoyed it so much that I made sure the Battened Hatch had a printer at the ready for new specials. On my way through the kitchen, I'd smelled basil and had nicked some. Mixing flavors and liquors calmed me. Tonight, I was ready to mind my own business.

Until around 6 p.m. when Brent Davis came back in. The man with him was compact, well built, white, with short brown cropped hair. His biceps were so pronounced they poured from the shoulders. This was a man who worked out and was sure of himself. Best guess was early thirties. He and Brent sat together at the bar.

"Hey, Avalon."

"Hey, Brent."

"Have you had a chance to read the clip of the old article I gave you?"

"No. Sorry about that. I had an unexpected visitor who wrested my attention."

"I only asked because it was based on an interview I did with Misty Edison's brother, David. And this is David."

"Oh! Hello. Nice to meet you."

"David is a financial advisor who lives in Marin County, California. Avalon here is also from California, although from the southern climes."

David had a sturdy handshake.

"Are you back for the funeral?" I asked.

"Yes," he said. "Brian was one of the few people who was close to Misty at the time she was taken. We sort of formed an odd bond over that, even though he was older than I was, and from a very different family."

"I'm sorry about Brian's passing. And your sister's, of course."

"David isn't aware of anyone named Jane who went missing around that time," Brent said. "I already asked."

"It might be a misunderstood piece of information," I said. "These things happen. How do you like the Bay Area?"

"Very much. Close to San Francisco, but room to spread out."

"And Marin County likely has many folks who can use financial advice."

"Also true."

"You've never thought of returning here?"

"No. My dad died of a heart attack ten years ago. Mom isn't well. When she dies, I can finally sell Brimstone and be really and truly gone from here."

"Brimstone?"

"It was our joke name for the mansion—Misty's and mine. The place is a little over the top."

It was all I could do not to speak up and let him know I'd recently been there and did, indeed, share his opinion.

I took their order and let them get on with their chat.

Toward the end of the evening, the door from the street banged open and four young men entered together. It was clear they'd started drinking before they arrived. They wound their way through the room and ended up at the bar. Two stools were free, and the other two stood adjacent.

One young man on a stool, the de facto leader, saw me and his face lit up. "You were here! The night before Brian died. See, boys, she can tell you! I was with Brian that last night, and we had a hell of a time!"

In fact, the fellow's square face and nearly shaved hair did look familiar.

"That was when you were still trying out for the team. Before they let you go," teased one of his friends.

"Drinks all around, my fine woman," said the leader, not listening. "You do remember me, don't you? Baron McNulty."

Ah. The last one down the porch luge. His clothes had been wet for the rest of the evening.

"Yes, I remember."

"See? I told you. Brian Eddings and me. Like this." He wound two of his fingers together.

"But I thought you said you were afraid Brian was going to turn you in. That he saw you roofie that girl!"

I stopped dead in my tracks.

He roofied someone? In my bar?

Which to do first–punch his lights out, or call the cops?

Instead, I put my cell phone behind the spill mat where he likely couldn't see it and hit "record."

"Yeah? You roofied a girl? Was she cute?"

He was confused by this turn in the questioning.

"Keep your mouth shut, Stevens!" he said. "I didn't roofie anyone. But she was the cutest one. With two other friends."

Shit. The girl whose friends had to help her leave.

"But you were with a bunch of guys from the Olympic village. How were you... going to get together with her?"

"See? It makes no sense," he said. "I didn't do it."

"You said you would have skipped out if you could have gotten her to the lobby. You were going to rent a room. But Eddings saw you."

"I didn't do anything. But if he said I did, if that's why I got cut–"

"Did you drug anyone else's drink? Like Brian's? Were you mad at him?" I asked, nonchalantly but carefully.

"What? No. I didn't do anything. Stevens, shut up. Just shut up. Drinks, my dear madam."

I was trying to think clearly. Had he incriminated himself? Did I have enough evidence to call the cops? Did I want cops coming to the bar, called by the bartender on a patron?

All I knew was I was furious with this guy. Could I take him out to the alley and deck him?

He wasn't from here. He'd been cut from the team. I did have a record of his friend saying he'd roofied someone and he thought Brian Eddings saw him do it. But did that mean anything? Damn.

Likely if the police did come, the friend would backtrack on the accusation and there was no proof.

"I said, drinks, barkeep!"

"You've already been drinking. We're going to close soon. I can't serve you."

"The hell you can't!" Baron McNulty was angry, his voice rising.

"Look. You roofied that young woman. I know who it was. If you don't leave, I'm going to call the police."

"Actually, the police have already been called. They're on the way." I looked up to find Philip coming in the door from the lobby. He lowered his voice and spoke to the four guys, "Officer Shay is on duty tonight, and he lives to rough people up and interrogate them all night before letting them go. If I were you, I'd depart quickly."

The four looked at him, not sure what to do. "Let's just go, McNulty," said the tall one who hadn't said anything during the previous discussions. "Come on, you're leaving in the morning. Let's just go."

"Damn," said McNulty. He knocked a stack of cardboard coasters onto the floor and turned and headed back out with his buddies.

Marta came over to watch them leave. "What was *that*?"

"That idiot roofied a girl the night Brian died. He was here with the Olympic hopefuls. But he's been cut. He isn't happy."

"Hopefully, they hide out in their hotel and leave in the morning," Philip said.

"Are the cops really coming?"

"No. We can call them if you'd like. I thought you just wanted them to go."

"I did. Thanks. I recorded the conversation, but McNulty didn't ever admit to anything."

Marta went back to work. I was still trembling.

"You okay?" Philip asked.

"Yeah. I will be. I'm furious, though."

"You should be. I am, too. Want me to go find that guy and clock him?"

"Clock him?" I smiled. "You've been watching too many old movies."

"Could be true. Want to watch another one tonight? It's probably the best way for you to calm down."

"What do you mean?"

"I'm footloose and fancy-free. Was looking for a friend to watch a movie or two with."

"Really?"

"Yeah."

"Where's Rachel?"

"Not that it matters, but she's in Saratoga. She has a job interview. Actually, a second interview for the same job. Getting serious. She wouldn't mind if you and I watched a movie. She knows we're friends."

She knows we're friends.

That was a loaded statement. But I could use a movie and a glass of wine tonight. With a friend.

"Okay," I said. "Let me close up."

MYOB

Mediterranean Gin Fizz

Ingredients

1 ½ oz Gin Mare
2 oz homemade basil tea
1 ½ oz sour mix
1 ½ oz sparkling water
Ice
Fresh basil leaves
Fresh lemon peel
Kalamata olives
Homemade Basil Tea

Method

In medium saucepan place 5 fresh basil leaves and 2 cups of water on medium heat.
Simmer on low heat for 3-5 minutes.
Remove from heat and bring to room temperature.
Strain liquid through mesh strainer to remove basil leaves.

COCKTAIL

Method

In cocktail shaker add gin, basil tea, ice, and sour mix.
Shake ingredients together.
Pour into Collins glass.
Top with sparkling water and stir.
Add fresh lemon peel, basil leaves, and Kalamata olives for garnish.

Sip and enjoy!

17

WHY NOT?

PHILIP MET ME on the corner of Main Street and Acorn, where the latter led up to his cul-de-sac. He wore shorts and a white crew-neck sweatshirt, which looked great on him. His hair had just enough mousse to make him look impossibly nonchalant. Together, we traversed Main Street, me walking my bike, him walking his Pomeranian, Whistle.

Whistle had stayed with me while Philip was in the hospital, and we were excited to see each other. She danced her greeting and leapt into my arms to lick my face. If every dog was like Whistle... never mind. A new car was enough for now.

"What a putz," Philip said, referring to Baron, the roofie guy.

"I've never been so furious. I guess I'm more protective of the Battened Hatch than I realized. Not to mention, though it's a long shot—what if Brian saw him do it and reamed him out? Brent Davis thinks they're waiting on toxicology to release the cause of Brian's death. He wasn't drinking that night—at least as far as I know, but something is leading the state police to think something unexpected happened."

"Really?"

"According to Brent. If Mike Spaulding was working the case, I would tell him this. I'd tell him every seemingly insignificant piece of information I have, on the small chance it plays into something bigger. But the things I've found out about supporting players sound unimportant. Or maybe passing it on would give it too much importance. I don't know what Inspector Mason would do with information about Jeff Harris, Brian's Olympic rival, for example, unless he brought him in for questioning, which none of us want. It's very frustrating."

"Jeff Harris? Tell me about Jeff Harris."

I trust Philip completely, except in the kissing department, so as we walked, I filled him in on my adventures during the past week. It helped clarify my thinking to go over the information I'd accumulated, which seemed to lead only to further questions and dead ends.

Philip asked pertinent questions.

As we neared Cherry Lane, I finished my recital.

Philip finally spoke. "I'm trying to say something intelligent here, but all I've got is: You zip-lined off K120? Thinking you would die?"

"Yes. I faced my own mortality this week. It wasn't fun. I don't want to do it again for a very long while."

We came to the tall house, now empty, that looked out over the secret entrance to the glen. Philip looked agitated. I stopped. What was it? Was he remembering his own recent brush with mortality?

"Who was he?" he finally asked.

"Who was who?"

"The guy you were with last night. I saw you walking along Main Street with him. He had his arm around you. You looked... chummy."

I studied Philip's face. I saw pain in his eyes, and fear in the tremor of his fingers.

He was jealous.

Seriously. I spent this whole twenty-minute walk talking about murder, and he was biding his time until he could ask who walked me home.

Still, I felt the same unexpected gratification as when I won a school scholarship for oration, when I'd only orated to get a final grade in class, and I'd beaten the puffed-up future lawyers and politicians. It hinted at an innate worthiness I didn't need to fight for.

"Yesterday? That was Reggie."

"It seemed like you knew him pretty well."

"You know how I've been hiding out from my old life? Well, he was the first one who found me. It turns out I'm glad he did."

"Is he still here?"

"No. He left this morning."

"Will he be back?"

"I hope. Someday." Yes, I was being purposely coy. "He left just before I got my new car."

As we emerged into the glen, Sally's lampposts illuminated the vehicle sitting up in the flat lot. As I hoped, it changed the conversation before I had to either tell him I was related to Reggie or flat-out fib.

"You bought a car?"

"Yes. I have joined the ranks of the vehicular elite."

"Around here, it doesn't make you elite. It makes you normal."

"All right. Throw me a bone. I'm excited."

He looked in the windows. "Sweet. Where did you get it?"

"From Avantika."

"Did she give you a good price?"

"And how."

"Man, talk about luck. Right place, right time."

"Well, if 'right place' is down at the Cardamom at breakfast time, I stand a pretty good chance of showing up."

He let Whistle off her leash and she trotted halfway across the bridge to my place.

"Want to come in? I don't have many old movies, but there's got to be something on Netflix."

I wondered if it was odd for him, being invited as a guest into the cottage where he'd grown up.

"I know who does have lots of old movies." He motioned to the lodge. "Gran."

"But she's not here. We can't barge in."

"You forget I'm her beloved grandson."

He showed me the current text conversation on his phone. *Gran, can I watch an old movie at your place?*

With a girl?

Yes.

Don't do anything I wouldn't do.

"You texted her in India?"

"Yes."

"She assumes you mean Rachel." I couldn't believe I said her name and invoked her presence.

"Not necessarily. I said, 'a girl.' She said, 'have some whiskey.'"

"When did she say that? Ah, *Don't do anything I wouldn't do*." In fact, I'd shared really expensive whiskey with Sally.

"Shall we?"

"I will not say you nay."

Philip had a key, so we went into Sally's lodge. It had been designed by a Hollywood set designer back in the 1940s to reflect what Hollywood considered a house in the country. It was built with full-sized logs, had chandeliers made of antlers (I didn't mind after finding out that stags shed theirs every year and you don't have to kill them to acquire a set), and a huge stone fireplace.

Once the lights were blazing, it was a happy place. Sally had a working phonograph and Philip put on the soundtrack from *Why Not?* It was one of Sally's hit musicals.

"So you like Reggie enough to let him put his arm around you while you walk down Main Street?"

"I like you enough to risk my life saving you from a psychopath."

"Well, true..." He smiled. I'd derailed him again. "Okay. Any movie preferences?"

"The music puts me in the mood for *Why Not?*"

"Funny, I was thinking the same thing. Let's make some popcorn. And have a wee dram."

He went to her bar cart and carefully placed two tumblers. He picked up her bottle of Balvenie, Batch 7 Speyside Single Malt. "Can I tempt you?"

"I know you're a favorite grandson, but you do realize this stuff costs $5,000 a bottle?"

"What else would Sally have us pour?"

"Ask me in French."

"What?"

"I'm told you speak French." I didn't mention I took French in high school only because it was the thing to do. Now I can recognize if someone is speaking it, and I can order off almost any menu, but that's about it.

Philip spent the rest of the evening speaking nothing but French. He didn't speak it carefully and politely, like an American showing off. He spoke it casually, in the off-handed way of a native speaker. I was not only impressed, I was entertained.

If we hadn't been giggling before, we were by the second dram of Balvenie. It went well with popcorn, although we each poured a glass of water as well to slake the salt.

The movie was fun. We sat together on the comfortable sofa. And yes, by the end of the movie we had fallen asleep.

I roused myself at the closing credits. I turned off the television and put an afghan over Philip and Whistle, though Whistle climbed out from under it and curled up next to her master. I turned off the lights and went back to my place.

If Philip wanted me sharing breakfast with him, he would have to earn it.

I went to the Cardamom Café the next morning, partly because it's my favorite thing to do, partly to thank Avantika for the car.

She was pleased that I was pleased. She hadn't declared yet, but she was running for mayor against the incumbent Arthur Bristol. I appreciated her political views, but I'm also saying, offering people practically new cars for $3000 will take you a long way.

I ordered my usual and took it back to the glen, where I sat on the white bench beside the waterfall. At around ten, Whistle came running toward me enthusiastically, Philip close behind. He had showered and changed, which led me to believe he kept necessities at Sally's.

"What are you having?" he asked.

"A curried banana wrap with coconut and almond, and a Masala chai."

"Yum. I might have to stop on my way past."

"You're the one who first sent me to the Cardamom. I remain in your debt. Want to sit for a minute?"

"Sure. I've only got one room to finish painting at MacTavish's. I'm not expected until one o'clock today."

He looked at the bench, hesitated, then sat beside me.

"What was the hesitation?" I asked.

"Remembering."

"Oh?"

"Gram used to have a white wrought-iron table and four chairs just over there. It's where she often had afternoon tea. Oh, forget the tea. It's where the yardarm was first crossed, shall we say. And this bench... well, this, to my mind, will always be the spanking bench."

"Oh?"

"My parents were enlightened folk, time-outs and all that. But when something crossed the line and needed to be dealt with in a more memorable manner, my folks always seemed to be away, and the punishment was left to Gran."

"Ah, Sally's spankings."

"You've heard about them?" He was genuinely surprised.

I nodded. Then I purposely remembered my own mother's admonition: *You don't need to tell everything you know.*

"On more than one occasion, I'd come home from elementary school wondering if my parents had heard about my latest transgression, and Gran would be sitting here, waiting for me."

"You were never tempted to run?"

"Oh, I was always tempted to run. But that would have made my fate so much worse."

"She spanked you here? Outside?"

"Right here. A brief discussion before a bare-bottomed thrashing. I was always terrified someone would walk up the road onto the property. Or FedEx would arrive. I suspected her crazy caretaker hid himself and watched whenever he got wind of a punishment."

"Well. That does give me a new appreciation for the bench. Filled with childhood memories, as it were."

"Afterwards, we'd have another discussion. Only once did she find me unrepentant enough that I went back over her knee. That was the end of my snide remarks. In her hearing."

"Yet the two of you are close now? She lets you pour the good Scotch?"

"We were always close. She never held a grudge, and I knew I deserved what I got."

"When was your last spanking?"

"She stopped when I was in elementary school. Although... there was a time in high school when I was thoughtless, maybe worse than thoughtless, and I really hurt someone. Then I had a choice between losing car privileges for two months or one of Gran's spankings."

"You took the spanking?"

"Yeah. Not outside, thank God. So I guess that was the last time. When was your last time?"

Damn. "My mother didn't spank me. Like your parents, up on the latest child psychology."

"So you never had the pleasure?"

"Of being spanked?"

"Yeah."

"I often spent summers at my grandparents' house with my cousins. They had to have more practical ways of keeping us in line. Usually a few whacks with a wooden kitchen spoon."

Changing the subject seemed like a good idea. I said, "Can I ask a question: Why are you still here? In Tranquility. You've been all over the world. Certainly, there are places with more opportunity."

"A painter can work anywhere. And Gran isn't going to be

around much longer. Of course, we've been saying that for a while, and here she is, nearly a hundred."

"So when she goes, you will?"

"I don't know. Maybe."

"Have you heard anything from Rachel? How her interview went?"

"It's tomorrow. She went down a day early to stay with school friends."

"What does she do?"

"She's an event planner, and a good one. Obviously, a place like Saratoga would hold many more opportunities."

"Would you... go with her?"

He looked at me, trying to read the thoughts behind my question.

"I... don't... know. Even Rachel and I haven't discussed it."

"Didn't mean to pry."

"I know. I'd better get going."

"Okay. See you around."

"See you around."

He picked up Whistle's leash and headed down the lane. At the corner, he turned. "I had fun last night."

"Me, too."

And he was off.

What was my problem? Leave it to me to bring his girlfriend crashing into a rather titillating conversation.

But, you know what? He had a damn girlfriend. And I'm nobody's side piece. I couldn't let him flirt so successfully. In fact, I should probably stop him from speaking French. Or offering me drinks.

Damn. Life is hard.

I checked my watch. If I was going to catch a murderer before work, I'd better get to it.

WHY NOT?

Ingredients

1/2 oz Sailor Jerry Rum or your favorite
Poached pears (recipe below)
1 oz of cooking liquid from poached pears
Other cut fruit of choice
Red wine of choice. Recommended: Cabernet, Tempranillo, Rioja

Method

Fill a glass with ice. Recommended: Collins, mason jar or wine glass
Add poached pears and other fruit of choice
Then pour rum, cooking liquid and red wine.
Stir all ingredients together.
Enjoy!

CABERNET POACHED PEARS

Ingredients

3 pears peeled and cut into small cubes.
3 cups Cabernet
1 cup water
1/2 cup of orange juice
1/2 cup ground sugar
1 tbsp ground cinnamon
1 tbsp honey
2 whole clove pieces
Small dash of allspice

Method

In medium saucepan add all ingredients and turn on medium to low heat. Let simmer on low for an hour, until pears have turned a deep dark Cabernet, but still have a little crunch to them. Take off heat and let sit until room temperature. Transfer into a container and place in refrigerator. Making sure to keep the cooking liquid, which will be used in the cocktail. Make a day in advance of making sangria.

18

LOST IN THE NIGHT

THE SKIES WERE overcast, billowing clouds threatening rain, so I grabbed an umbrella along with the manila envelope with Brent's story inside. Then I headed for the public library as he suggested.

Tranquility's public library is on Main Street and has been since it opened in 1886. From the front, it looks like a cute white cottage, which belies the multiple stories and even an annex that lies behind and beneath. The perky librarian pointed me to copies of the local high school yearbooks, which were downstairs in the young adult reading room. I found the yearbook from the year Misty Edison, then a junior, was kidnapped, and flipped to the back. Fortunately, there was an index with students listed alphabetically. Unfortunately, of course, it was by last name, so finding "Jane" meant running through the whole list.

There was a long window seat overlooking Lake Serenity, and I sat there, running my finger along the names.

There were two Janes: Jane Fellows and Jane Rodriguez.

I began finding the pages on which photos of each girl appeared. There were six photos of Jane Fellows, who was a freshman and in a lot of clubs, and only two of Jane Rodriguez, who was a senior. One was her senior photo, and another was of band. She played oboe. There were also candid photos of groups of seniors interspersed with their official senior pictures. I nearly didn't spot her in one, because she was in the background and not identified in the caption. Five kids in the foreground were horsing around the flagpole in front of the school. Jane Rodriguez was minding her own business, sitting on a wall, talking to a young man. A brief read of body language suggested he might be her boyfriend.

The young man was Frank Eddings, Brian's older brother.

Hmm.

Of course, Jane Rodriguez might not be missing at all. She could be happily married and living across the street from where I now sat. The fact that she knew the Eddings family meant nothing. How could I find out if either Jane Fellows or Jane Rodriguez had gone missing?

First, I texted Brent. *Two last names on Janes, Fellows and Rodriguez. Either go missing? I mean, when you have the chance.*

Then I texted my old friend, Inspector Mike Spaulding. He'd told me not to involve him in the Eddings death investigation, but this was about another case altogether. *Sorry to bother you. How might I find out if a young woman named Jane Rodriguez or Jane Fellows went missing twenty years ago?*

Then I opened the envelope given to me by Brent and took out the pages. The story was old enough that they were actual "clips"— i.e., columns of type that had been clipped out. These weren't the clips themselves, they'd been Xeroxed onto full sheets of paper. As promised, it was a story from an interview Brent had done with David Edison ten years earlier. I settled in and began to read.

Given their notoriety—their significance—you might think they were kept in a safe, or a locked cabinet, or in a secure office reserved for a special task force.

But the files for Serenity's most famous unsolved crimes are kept in worn and smudged manila folders on the desk of the inspectors assigned to them. On one desk, the folders are in a box marked "ACTIVE."

At Inspector Curtis Pope's desk a folder sits upright in a wire organizer. A label on the tab reads "EDISON, MELISSA." It's not quite at Pope's eye level, but after you spend a bit of time with this man and learn his habits—his short hair always lightly gelled and carefully parted, his Dockers always creased (even after hours of bending over a bloody body at a crime scene), his coffee cup always placed just so on the State Troopers Fraternal Organization coaster by the phone—you can imagine that the file, in front of his face as it is, is a constant, sickening reminder of a piece of disorder in the universe for which he is responsible.

"There are people who know what happened," Pope says. "Someday someone's going to come forward and this case is going to be closed."

You can't help but wonder who he's trying to convince.

For this special issue, Serenity! Magazine conducted an investigation into the status of the area's major unsolved crimes, which include the 1987 Safeway Armored Truck Heist, which resulted in a $1.2 million dollar loss for Tranquility Lake Bank; the unexplained fire that destroyed Ellsworth Publishing nearly a decade ago; and the hit-and-run death of Rep. Tony Stinzano's wife in 2011 when she was on a morning run. But none of these crimes has captured the imagination of area residents the way the Melissa "Misty" Edison murder has.

Why is this the unsolved crime that's still discussed in whispered conversations over hands of bridge at Serenity Country Club and among the retired farmers who linger over coffee after breakfast at McDonalds?

Because this crime has a witness, and he had vowed to remain silent, at least to the press.

And he did… until Serenity! Magazine published his story ten years ago this month.

"My sister," David Edison began, and then fell silent. And

remained silent. Why would he finally consent to an interview about Misty's kidnapping and murder if he wasn't going to talk about it, I wondered when we finally met. I set my pen beside my reporter's notebook and waited.

"All they found was a hand, you know. Hunters saw a coyote running off with it in its mouth." He stubbed out his cigarette, the third since I had arrived. "Has to be hers. No one's reported a missing hand," he said, not with humor, but with a sense of resignation.

It's easy to understand why a sense of humor could not have survived that night, nor the innocence that would allow one to answer to "Davy," the innocent, childish version of his name he dropped soon after that unimaginable ordeal.

"Misty was the older sister every kid wants," he continued. "She made everything fun. That night Mom and Dad had gone out and she was babysitting, we'd made a tent in the family room and ate barbecue wings while we watched Goonies on TV. Because it was never just babysitting with Misty. It was an adventure. It was special. Everything was."

Though her body has never been found, Misty Edison was declared dead two years after what Pope believes was a botched kidnapping. Anxious about the stalled case, he had reluctantly shared some details of the case when I interviewed Edison, hoping going public might spark a witness's memory or encourage someone to come forward with information. Davy woke around 2 a.m., startled to find himself alone in the fort. Misty wasn't in her sleeping bag.

Edison decided to go to his real bed. When he passed Misty's room upstairs, he was surprised to find the door was slightly ajar. He pushed against it silently and opened it a few inches to see if she was still awake.

Her bed was still made. Hadn't been slept in. One of the French doors to her balcony was open.

"I called for her and I stepped into her room," Edison continued. "It was dark, and I was sleepy, but I knew that room better than my own. I saw some shapes moving and I knew something was wrong. Then a hand came over my mouth I did the first thing I thought of and bit the hand as hard as I could."

Investigators found no signs of forced entry into the house. Edison says his parents always left explicit instructions that the door was to remain locked after they left, and he says his sister always followed instructions. If Det. Pope has theories about how the assailant(s) got into the house, he isn't saying.

"The man slipped his hand around my neck like he wanted to choke me, but he didn't take his other hand off my mouth," Edison remembered. "He threatened to kill Misty and shoot my parents if I made a sound."

Edison sat back and folded his arms. He had agreed to meet me at Tranquility House Restaurant, and every time the door opened, he started and turned to see who was coming or going.

"The thing is, he sounded kind of insane, like he was really ready to kill someone."

Det. Pope's notes from the night say Davy Edison described it as a "rusty sounding voice," but not one he'd heard before. Davy's guess was that the perpetrator wasn't from the area. Pope thinks the voice could be a key in identifying the killer.

"I told him to put me down," Edison continued. "I was trying to act tough. As tough as a seven-year-old can act. And when he relaxed his grip I fell and stepped on his foot and stumbled. When he grabbed me again, he was even

*madder.I felt cold steel against my throat. I cried out, and
the sound must have carried through the open door, because
suddenly I heard another cry. I didn't have to look. I knew it
was her. It was Misty.*

*"'First you, then her,' he said. And that's the last time I saw
her. Then he squeezed my neck. I passed out. And every
day—every minute—I wonder if I'd been able to stay
awake, if Misty would still be alive."*

I finished and sat looking out over Lake Serenity. Misty had been taken from a house not by this lake, but over by Lake Tranquility. The lack of roads made me wonder if David was right—if he had been able to alert someone, could Misty have been found? The abductor had to either cross the lake or go through the woods.

Part of me was glad I hadn't read the article before I met David Edison. I mean, what do you say?

As far as the mysterious Jane, I didn't know how to check on Jane Fellows unless I heard back from Brent or Inspector Spaulding. Jane Rodriguez might be easier. Frank Eddings could know if she'd gone missing, but I didn't know how to get in touch with him. He seemed to like me—at least, as a way reach Hannah.

However, I admitted to myself I wanted an excuse to go back and see Alma Eddings, Brian and Frank's mother. I didn't trust Ray and wanted to make sure he wasn't controlling where she went and who she saw—and even what photos she displayed. Was I inserting myself into a circus whose monkeys weren't mine? Or had I just worked with Ray and had a bad feeling about the situation?

I decided to go before I lost my nerve. If things seemed normal, if she didn't seem under threat, I'd henceforth leave Mrs. Eddings alone.

I headed back to get my new car, buying a half dozen Moose Track cookies from the bakery on my way.

LOST IN THE NIGHT

Apple Mash Old Fashioned

Ingredients

2 oz. bourbon whiskey
1 T apple mash (recipe follows)
Orange
Cocktail cherries

Method

In a rocks glass, add orange and cocktail cherries, usually
luxardo or any dark cherry (note: do not add sugar)
Muddle fruit at bottom of glass
Fill glass with ice
Add bitters of your choice, whiskey, and apple mash
Stir all ingredients together
Add orange slice and cherry for garnish
Enjoy!

APPLE MASH

Ingredients

3 apples sweet and tart peeled and cut into small cubes
1 cup sugar
1/4 tsp ground ginger
1/4 tsp ground all spice
2 tbsp ground cinnamon
Dash ground black pepper
1 small orange cut into slices
Juice of one fresh lemon
1 cup orange juice

3 cups water

Method

Pour all ingredients into medium saucepan. Keep on medium to low heat until apples have become soft, about 35-45 minutes, making sure to stir occasionally. Turn off heat and let sit until room temperature. Pour into container and keep in refrigerator. Retain the cooking liquids as you will use in cocktail.

19
RAINY DAY

B Y THE TIME I turned off the main drag through town, it was misting. I didn't know the direct route to the Eddings', but I wasn't planning to drive up to their house in any case. I didn't want Ray to know I was there.

Instead, I drove up Robyn's driveway. There was no longer any crime-scene tape. I banked on the fact that the person taking tire impressions had already come and gone.

I left the car in the circular part of the driveway, pointing toward the road. Not that I thought I'd need to make a fast getaway, but you can never be too careful. I locked it and pocketed the key. It still wasn't raining, exactly. Instead, it was spitting, big gobfuls of drops occasionally plummeting through the trees, hitting my face or hair whenever I became complacent. Gray clouds gave the forest a fairy-tale feeling, not in a Disney way, more Brothers Grimm. The damp earth smelled of loam. Usually, it's a natural, comforting scent. Today, it seemed a warning.

I reached the Eddings house from the back and used the pavers to circle to the front door. There was no car in the driveway. A glance through the window revealed the television was on; a closer look showed that Alma Eddings was in her lift chair, an afghan of colorful flowered blocks over her lap. Her head had fallen to one side as she nodded off.

I opened the storm door and knocked heavily; then I waited a moment for her to awaken and knocked again. Then I opened the door a couple of inches and said, in a friendly voice, "Alma? It's me, Avalon. I visited the other day. May I come in?"

I was in before she could answer.

She looked up, confused.

"I brought some cookies. I hope you don't mind. They're Moose Track cookies from the Adirondack Baking Company."

This time I noticed the heavy, musty smell that lingered in the air.

"Who're you?"

"Avalon Nash, Mrs. Eddings. I visited the other day. I was at the Battened Hatch with Brian on his last night. I wanted to see how you were, if I could bring you anything."

The confusion hadn't cleared, but she seemed resigned to my entry. I put the cookies on an autumn-leaf plate next to her.

"Thank you. Sorry, I'm not dressed for company. But I appreciate the cookies."

"Do you mind if I sit for a minute?"

There was silence. Clearly, she did mind. I wouldn't stay long. I sat on the couch, which was chair adjacent. I wondered if I dared turn off the television.

"How was the service yesterday?" I asked.

"The service? Oh, the Mass. For Brian. It'us fine."

"I bet Father Collum was happy to see you. Do you get to church often?"

"No. I'm homebound, now."

"Do they come visit often? From the church?"

"No. Why would they? I'm fine. I don't need anything."

"How about company?"

She glared at me. Company was clearly not sought. "I'm fine, dear." *Dear* had the sound of a supreme insult. "Ray brings me every-thing I need."

"He does? Why is that? Is he a good friend?"

"You'd think, if he brings me everything I need."

"Does he live nearby? Last time he came, it didn't seem he had a car."

I'd meant to ask about Jane before getting to Ray, but she'd brought him up.

"His cabin is just over the hill. He buys me groceries whenever he goes to Ivar's Bait and Tackle."

"Ivar's has groceries?"

"A little deli. My needs aren't much."

"Is it Ray who doesn't want you to have photos up of Brian? Of your boys."

Another suspicious look. "No. Why'ould Ray care?"

This wasn't going well. We weren't going to be BFFs. Usually, my story collecting went much more smoothly. "Alma, could I ask you something? Back when the boys were in high school, do you remember a girl named Jane?"

"Jane? You're askin' such strange things."

"Did Frank date a girl named Jane?"

"Jane? Now that I think of it, I guess he did. During their junior year. She run off, though. When they'us seniors. She quit comin' around. I ast once and Frank said her folks said she'd run off. I had thought maybe they'us serious. But she run off."

I noticed that two of Alma's front teeth were missing. It seemed odd, since Brian had lived in town, that she wasn't seen to more carefully.

"I know you'll miss Brian," I said. "It must be hard with your husband and son both gone."

"Never missed my husband," she said.

"How long has he been gone?"

"Long time. Since the boys were in high school. Well, since Frank graduated high school. Brian was still going."

"He fell?"

"If you must know, he'us drunk. Fell down the basement stairs."

"Oh! I am sorry." And I was, about every part of that sentence.

"Can I get you some milk to go with the cookies?"

"No. I'd appreciate if you'd just leave."

"I will, Mrs. Eddings. Sorry to have troubled you. But when he was alive, didn't Brian see to you? Bring you groceries? Take you to the doctor? Will you need someone to do that?"

"I told you, Ray does it! I don't need any doctor! Them boys didn't do a damn thing for me. So stop your sympathies. It won't make no difference that Brian's dead. He was dead to me, anyways."

"Why?" I asked, shocked at such a forthright admission.

"They never forgave me. Neither of 'em. So screw 'em. I'm fine."

I half expected her to throw the cookies back at me, but she eyed them and kept quiet.

"I am very sorry to hear that. Obviously, I'm in the dark on some matters. I don't mean to ask offensive questions. Forgive me. I didn't know. I only came to see if you needed anything or could use any help."

"Well, you came, and now you can go."

"Yes, ma'am, I will. Glad to see you're all right. Hope you enjoy the cookies."

I turned and left, more confused than I'd been when I arrived.

Back in my vehicle, I locked the doors and rested my head on the steering wheel.

One question answered: Alma didn't seem scared of, or intimidated by, Ray.

But what a family Brian and Frank had come from! It kind of made sense that Brian and Robyn would have dated. She was, after all, his girl-next-door. But having been in both their family houses, I'd say that Brian Eddings dating Misty Edison was a huge leap. Of course, Brian had gumption. Not everyone can turn an upbringing by an alcoholic father into Olympic gold.

Misty Edison. I'd been so focused on finding Jane Rodriguez that I hadn't looked at Misty's yearbook photos. Was she a cheerleader? A mean girl? A songbird soprano? Did she play the lead in the annual musical? Her little brother certainly worshipped her. But it's odd how sainthood grows around you, once you're dead.

I drove home and parked, then changed into work clothes. After checking the time, I grabbed an umbrella and headed back to the library.

Misty did have several photo pages listed after her name in the index. I went in order. The first was Math Club, then Honor Society. The photos were black and white, small and grainy, so I didn't take the time to pick her out. She was also in band, playing saxophone. She was not a cheerleader or in the musical *You're a Good Man, Charlie Brown.*

I flipped to her junior picture and was immediately struck by her long, straight blonde hair, large green eyes and dainty nose. She could have been the girl singer in a folk band, or the photo people carried when they went to a plastic surgery consultation.

The questioning in her eyes was startling. She looked like she was both asking for answers and not sure how to act on the answers she had.

I stared at her face. And stared.

Then I went to my phone to see if I got cell service—four bars— and typed in her name, then "images." Soon images came up of Misty, her younger brother, Davy, and one of the whole family. The family photo was an interesting contrast to the Eddings' family photo. The Edison family's photo had not been taken by an itinerant church-directory photographer. The lighting was warm and the family was dressed in upscale casual, as though they'd been interrupted from a brisk game of croquet.

The parents stood behind their progeny, who were seated in front of the center staircase. The mother was behind Davy, who had a wide, enthusiastic face and a broad grin. Mom's hands were on the back of his chair. Dad stood behind Misty, hands firmly on her shoulders. She looked demure. They all had impeccable posture.

I stared at Misty.

Then I put the yearbooks back and went outside.

Holy shit.

I was about to send a text when my phone rang.

My phone never rings. I'm sometimes not sure why they need to make them phones anymore, instead of texting and internet devices.

I was so conditioned to be in hiding that my first impulse was to ditch the phone, which was nonsensical. The second was to stare at the screen, which read, "Reggie."

Finally, I answered.

"Hey, Av," he said.

"Hey, Reg."

"Mormor died today. I thought you'd want to know. She passed in her sleep. The viewing is on Monday and the funeral is on Tuesday. I know everyone would love to have you here, but it's okay if you don't come."

"Oh, I'm sorry. Thanks for letting me know."

"Sure. It didn't seem like something you should text."

"No, you're right. I'm glad you called."

"She's been sleeping, or out of it, since I got back, so it's not like you could have said good bye or anything. I didn't want you to carry that guilt. Plus, she knew you loved her. She lived a long, full life. It was her time. So don't feel bad. The only reason to come this weekend is if you want to be with the family."

"I've got it. Thank you."

"Love you, Av."

"Love you, too."

The call ended.

I knew Mormor's death was coming. I'd expected it. Reggie was right, it was her time.

Yet somehow, the loss of this gutsy woman who'd lived many good decades, who'd raised a singular family, who'd watched times change, was a gut punch that got all entangled with a kidnapped girl, a woman run down, a drunk who fell down stairs, a dead Olympian.

Why was this world so crazy?

How did I think I could make it any better?

My first impulse was to call Hannah. But... everybody called her when there was a death in the family. It would turn me into just one more parishioner type. I didn't want to call Philip. And Marta actually had the night off for pre-graduation things.

If my landlord, Sally, were here, perhaps I'd talk to her. But she wasn't.

I pride myself on being the person who holds it together. Who listens to everyone, yet skates by unscathed.

Why was I about to dissolve into a pool of tears on Main Street?

I swallowed my pride and texted Hannah. *My Mormor died. I don't know why it's hitting me so hard.*

I put my umbrella down, so the rain would soak me. Then I put my hands in my pockets and started walking home.

RAINY DAY

Peach Rum Sangria

This sangria is great for a group. Serve it in a cocktail pitcher.

Ingredients

5 oz Bacardi orange rum
2 cups of white wine (preferably sauvignon blanc)
2 cup of peach juice
Fresh peaches or any stone fruit for garnish cut into small pieces
Ice

Method

In a small cocktail pitcher, combine all ingredients and stir.
In small cocktail glasses add ice and pour sangria.
Add small pieces of fresh peaches and any other fruit for garnish.

20

OVER THE BACKYARD FENCE

A T HOME, I took a hot shower and changed into a different black shirt and slacks, then put on the kettle and sat down at the kitchen table. It was round with a floral cloth that matched the curtains, both provided by Sally's studio's interior designers. Not my style, but I embraced it.

As the electric kettle began to squeal, there was a knock at the back door. I had a moment of kinship with Alma—if I wanted company, I'd invite company.

Looking up, I realized I sort of had. Hannah stood there, carrying a large umbrella featuring women writers.

"Got enough tea for two?" she asked, opening the door.

"Sure. Choose your favorite."

I got down a blue floral mug, and she chose Paris tea. We sat.

"So, tell me about Mormor," she said.

"Look, I'm sorry I texted. I know people bother you with this stuff all the time. I don't want to be yet another local in need of counseling."

She was wearing a light beige sweater and brown skirt. Her low-heeled brown pumps were darker near the bottom where they'd gotten wet. She sat there, staring at me.

Finally, she said, "Is that what you think? That I think of people as a steady line of counselees?"

Well, yeah. But I wasn't going to actually say it.

"First of all, okay, maybe I do feel extra-protective of my parishioners and glad they're in my life and I can be in theirs. I've been trained on how to counsel people, and it's something that gives me a sense of being helpful. I appreciate being trusted.

"But most people aren't my close friends. I had hoped you would be. But I'd about given up."

"Why?"

"No matter how I tried, our friendship was one-sided. I confided in you, and asked you for help, and even came over when I needed to cry. But you never did any of those things. You have a wall up. Oh, you ask me for help for other people, like Marta. But this text, this was the first time you treated me like a friend."

We held each other's gaze.

"It's not just you," I finally said.

"I'm aware. But I think I'm the one who needs you most. It's why I was willing to go out on a limb."

"People needing me is exactly what I'm hiding from."

"I know. Tough luck." We sat. "So, are you going to your grandmother's funeral?"

"I don't think so. I don't know. Probably not."

"Okay."

We sipped.

"Would you tell me about her?"

My first response was to shy away from the question. Somehow, the languid smell of vanilla mixed with spicy citrus in the tea tipped the silence between us from guarded to companionable, and I found I wanted to remember.

"I'm the youngest grandchild. My mom was a surprise after Mormor's other four kids were practically grown. Alice—Mormor—was raised in Brooklyn but moved to Chicago and trained to be a nurse. My grandfather, Arthur, was considered a real catch by the ladies at that time. He was smitten with Alice and even followed her to Chicago. She used to climb out the window of her room in the nurse's dorm to go out with him. The irony was that, to my aristocratic relatives still in Sweden, he was a real step down. She married him anyway—and those relatives turned their backs on her. Apparently, she received a nasty letter from the cousin she'd considered her best friend, which terminated their relationship and broke her heart.

"But Alice was a loving, adventurous woman, and she taught her offspring to be the same. Of course, back then, being educated and adventurous meant going to a religious college and becoming a missionary or teaching in a religious school, which three of her offspring did."

I remembered to whom I was speaking, and added, "Not that there's anything wrong with that."

Hannah laughed out loud.

"My great-grandfather died of a stroke when he was only in his late fifties, and my great-grandmother became ill when she was only in her sixties. Alice and Arthur uprooted their kids and moved back to the family home in Brooklyn to take care of her. Alice found work as a nurse but was sometimes thought to be too opinionated about what the doctors prescribed. She was 'let go' from nursing."

"For speaking up when she thought something wasn't right?"

"Well, no. They couldn't fire her for that. She was fired because she got pregnant. She was fired because of my mom. Turns out women could be fired legally from about any profession for being pregnant. Until 1978."

"Wow. Didn't know."

"Anyway, I'm selfishly glad they moved back to New York. That brownstone in Brooklyn shaped and informed my childhood. When I was little, all us grandkids would visit for a month in the summer. Mormor and I were the ones who would get up early. On Thursdays and Saturdays, before the heat would settle in, we'd walk to the local Farmers Market to buy fresh veggies and cheeses and pastas, whatever looked good. Sometimes, my cousin Reggie would come, but always, it was me and Mormor. Then we'd come home and snap the beans or shell the peas. We'd talk and sometimes, we'd sing. I used to pretend we lived in the country and went out and picked the beans. A funny fantasy, I know, from a fourth generation city slicker.

"Mormor was special. Oh, I know, everyone thinks their grand-mother is special. But she had an air about her. She was kind, and she was unusually... present. She paid attention. She was fully alive, or so it seemed to my ten-year-old self. The analogy I made up at the time was that she was a cashew in a world of peanuts."

"You like cashews?"

"Love cashews."

Hannah smiled.

"Not only was the Engstrom brownstone magical—but next door was the Benton house, where the Benton family had lived since the early 1900s. They were very elegant, all of them. They were Black—upscale Black. Black bourgeoise, which, at the time, was a small, cliquish thing. They belonged to secret societies, and their daughters were debutantes, the whole nine yards. Educated, well-to-do light-skinned Blacks who kept to themselves."

"I'm well acquainted with colorism," said Hannah. "Trust me."

"Well, a hundred years ago, back when my great-grandparents bought their house, most upscale Blacks would have nothing to do with the newly arrived Swedes, whom they thought were dirty, uncouth, and uneducated. Wouldn't let their children play together. And, as I heard it, the Engstroms didn't really know what to do with Black people, either. There weren't many in Sweden.

"At first, the two matriarchs kept a wary distance. My great-grandmother, Elsa, didn't approve of secret societies or drinking, for that matter. Meanwhile, Maybelle Benton wasn't one to care whether she was being judged by Swedish Lutherans or not. May-belle was a New Woman, a suffragette, fighting for women's right to vote. Their whole family was heavily involved in the Civil Rights movement. On the other hand, Elsa had been taught to keep a lovely home and be discreet, not out marching in the streets.

"What saved the day were the pianos. Both women had pianos, and they were against a wall shared by the two brownstones. When the windows were open, you could easily hear the neighbor's concerts. One summer afternoon, after Sunday dinner, both women sat down and started playing hymns. At first, they played over each other. Then, families gathered around each piano, and they began taking turns. This quickly became a Sunday afternoon tradition. Soon pies were traded across the backyard fence. The rest, as they say, is history."

"The two families remained friends?"

"Best friends, through the decades. Those two pianos still sit opposite each other, against the same walls. On the Engstrom side, there's a framed print of a blonde woman in a blue gown at a grand piano. On the Benton side is a framed tinted photograph of Ida B. Wells. I don't know what will happen when one family sells their townhouse, but it will be a sad day. A hundred years of friendship. It's probably surprising that it took as long as it did to wind up with my cousin Reggie."

"He's—"

"Half Engstrom, half Benton. Mormor's two youngest daughters were the wild ones: Elizabeth, who had Reggie, and my own mother, who rebelled by doing stand-up comedy, back when women didn't. She got some traction in New York, then moved to Los Angeles. Mom is one of those ten-year-in-the-making overnight successes. She met my dad, who was a fun, creative guy. They had me. He changed. They broke up. He and I broke up. Mom has never married, and she's now pretty well known for being openly nonbinary. I think Mormor is okay with it—was okay with it—but she said she wished Mom had someone to look out for her."

"Where have I heard that before?" said Hannah. "Your Mormor sounds like a special person. I wish I'd known her."

"You'd have liked her. She, like her mother, was gracious but strong. She not only talked back to doctors, you should have heard her light into anyone who cared to talk behind Reggie's back when we were kids and went with her to the Farmer's Market. And if someone was unfortunate enough to assume dark-skinned Reggie was somehow bothering us, look out."

"I'm sorry. This world, and our culture, is really messed up."

"Yeah. It is."

"Her passing takes with it a big part of my past. She accepted me, unconditionally. Occasionally had strong words about some of my choices, but there was never an ounce of doubt I was her grandkid."

"I'm sorry. Death sucks."

"I never know what's going to come out of your mouth."

"Generally, with friends, I tell the truth."

"Well, death does suck." I looked at my watch. "I'd better get to work. Brian's big memorial service is tomorrow, and the town is packed. And, of all nights, Marta is off at a pre-graduation thing."

"Sounds like a fun night. Shall we walk out together?"

"Sure. And thanks for coming."

"You're welcome," Hannah said.

The rain had stopped, although a mist filtered through the air. "Say, now that we're friends, if you'd ever like to get out of town on your day off, I could use a day or two away from here," Hannah said.

I didn't mean to stiffen, but she read my body language at once.

"Too fast? Okay. Friendship baby steps."

"Baby steps," I agreed.

"Just so you know. In a world of peanuts, I think you're a macadamia nut."

"Thanks. I think."

We both smiled and headed back out to real life.

OVER THE BACKYARD FENCE

Ingredients

1 oz Bacardi orange rum
1 teaspoon Small Town Cultures Orange Zest or an
orange for zesting
San Pelligrino Blood Orange Soda
1/2 oz of Sailor Jerry Spiced Rum

Method

In cocktail shaker add ice, orange rum, and orange zest.
Shake ingredients and pour into rocks glass with ice.
Top with Blood Orange Soda
Add 1/2 oz of Sailor Jerry Spiced Rum as a floater

21

GOLD AND SILVER

Tʜᴇ ᴄʀᴀᴢɪɴᴇss ᴏꜰ the Battened Hatch was exactly what I needed.

The place was packed from the moment we opened. A waitress named Sandy who used to work at the Breezy was back in town, and she agreed to help out for the night. She knew how to work the POS, which, to my mind, is 80 percent of the waiter gig.

Many people who came in knew each other from different sets of "olden days." Since I knew none of them, I worked on mixing drinks as fast as humanly possible.

Shortly after we opened, Inspector Mike Spaulding slid onto a barstool around the corner of the bar farthest from the door. He was in civilian clothing. As an inspector for the state police, that was the norm, but I could tell he was off duty.

"Hey Mike," I said. "The usual?"

"You betcha."

Tonight's "usual" was Gold & Silver and he seemed to like it. I told him to inform me when he found a "usual" he wanted to stick with. Mike had an oval face and brown eyes that hadn't lost a mischievous sparkle. When we'd first met, I suspected he was flirting, and I'd rebuffed him. Mostly because I was running away from relationships and people in general. Also because he was a cop, and I had a deep distrust of the culture. Also because the detective and the civilian crime solver hooking up is a cliché.

"What the hell is this?" he asked of the drink. I gave him the recipe. He laughed.

No, it was a me-running-away-and-being-suspicious-of-police thing. I liked Mike fine now that I knew him.

"So this text you sent. Any more info on Jane?"

"As a matter of fact, I believe the young woman in question was named Jane Rodriguez. I was tipped off that her disappearance was worth looking into. I have it on the best thirdhand authority that she was thought to have skipped town. Only maybe she didn't."

"Can you tell me who gave you this extremely credible information?"

"I really can't."

"That's extremely helpful. Can you at least say whether you think it does or doesn't have anything to do with the Brian Eddings investigation?"

"I don't think so. The only Eddings connection is that Jane apparently dated Frank Eddings, Brian's brother."

"The one who lives in Nevada?"

"Yes. But he's back in town for his brother's funeral Mass and tomorrow's memorial service."

"You can't give me any clue about what brought up Jane Rodriguez?"

"Someone who was around back then suggested it should be looked into."

"This was firsthand?"

"No. Secondhand." Could ghosts be considered *any hand*? "Look, if there's nothing there, don't worry about it."

"I'll see if there's a case file."

"Thanks. Um, anything you can tell me about the Eddings case? Or Robyn's death? Or if there's any proof they're connected?"

"They're acting as if they're not."

"Do you know if Brian was poisoned?"

"I do not."

"Do you know of a bartender named Ray who lives up in a cabin behind Bessel Street?"

"No. Why?"

"I find him suspicious."

Mike laughed. "Oh, I miss you consulting on a case."

"You have to admit my suspicions have proven correct, on occasion."

"I do admit that. Are you going to the memorial service tomorrow?"

"Maybe. I assume there will be a police presence?"

"It's possible that the perpetrator, should there be one, will be in attendance."

"I guess from experience, we know that to be true."

"Indeed."

He held up his glass in a toast salute and I scooted off to catch up on orders.

Sometimes it's fun when you have a fluster of drink orders all come in at once. But when they keep coming and keep coming, it becomes exhausting. By nine thirty, I was shot, with another hour and a half yet to go.

That's when I looked up to see Philip standing in front of the bar. He wore sand-colored pants and a white shirt, open at the collar. He had two days' stubble. He looked purposefully nonchalant and pulled it off damnably well. "Hey," he said.

"Hey."

"Usually, I'd order a drink to show my respect, but I suspect tonight you'd as soon I didn't."

"I'd be fine if you didn't. Unless you want a five-thousand-dollar Scotch and have your Gran's credit card."

He laughed. "Naw, I came in to see if you were free later. Thought you might need to unwind. My friend Tomás is coming home tonight. I'm meeting him to take a boat to his place to hang out and watch a movie. Any interest in joining us?"

"Your friend Tomás, as in Cavalleros?"

"That's the one."

"He doesn't mind you bringing a friend?"

"No. Any friend of mine is a friend of his."

"We don't close until eleven."

"I'm meeting him at eleven thirty. We'd wait for you."

Granted, I do need to unwind after work. "If we don't get there till midnight, what time would we get home?"

"Oh, sorry, didn't make it clear. We'd spend the night and come back in the morning. Were you planning to go to the Eddings memorial?"

I hadn't thought about it before Mike brought it up, but I kind of felt I owed at least that to Brian. One of his very last earthly acts was to hand me a hundred dollars.

"Um, they have enough bedrooms?"

Philip gave me an *are you serious?* look. "The Cavalleros mansion? They have six guest suites. I usually have the wing to myself when I'm there. You'd have your own suite."

I wasn't sure what to do. I was still spinning over Mormor's death. I would be grieving for a long time. Did I want to be with anyone? Or did I want to wallow in sorrow alone?

Wallowing in sorrow alone sure sounded like fun.

"Yes. Yeah, sure. I'll come."

"Great. I'll be back at closing."

"Okay." I went back for more bottles of bubbly; it was selling like crazy tonight. What was I thinking? Was I getting myself into hot water? Philip promised me my own suite. In the Cavalleros mansion. I'd never even been upstairs. It would certainly take my mind off things.

If he hadn't kissed me, I wouldn't be confused.

If I hadn't had such an intense reaction to the kiss, I wouldn't be worried.

My current working theory was, if you have multiple overwhelming emotions all swirling at once, mix them together and throw them into a mansion. Why the hell not?

GOLD AND SILVER

Chicken Bone Broth Hot Toddy

Ingredients

> 4 oz chicken bone broth or chicken stock (with salt; adds more flavor to hot toddy)
> 1 fresh-squeezed lemon
> Dash of crushed black pepper
> Tiny dash of crushed red pepper (omit if you do not like spicy things)
> 1 ½ oz of Belvedere Ginger Zest vodka
> 1 lemon wedge
> 1 carrot stick
> 1 celery stick

Method

> In small saucepan add chicken bone broth or stock, fresh squeezed lemon juice, dash of crushed black pepper, and a tiny sprinkle of crushed red pepper.
> Heat all ingredients up on low heat until warm or at a low simmer.
> Pour warm liquid into snifter glass.
> Add Belvedere Ginger Zest vodka to warm liquid. Stir together gently (remember contents in glass are very hot).
> Add fresh slice lemon to side of glass.
> Add celery and carrot stick inside of glass for garnish.
> Sip slowly and enjoy.

22

COAT OF ARMS

I RODE MY bike home and hopped into Philip's car, slightly disappointed not to find Whistle. Philip explained she got seasick and was parked overnight with his neighbors.

We headed for the town of Serenity, home of Lake Tranquility, and parked in a reserved spot at the marina. Tomás was on one of the Cavalleros's boats and he waved enthusiastically as we approached. He gave a hand to help us onboard, and the pilot took off within moments of us having our feet planted.

There were lights sparsely dispersed on the far shore. I'd been told there were many "camps" surrounding the lake—large compounds of Adirondack-style houses and cabins, some of which had been used as actual camps, more of them Kennedy-style compounds where rich folk gathered their clans during summers.

A breeze made the water slightly choppy. The ride across the lake was ten minutes at full throttle. I'd brought my bartender bag as it held a fresh Doubleclicks t-shirt, which I'd use as pajamas. Philip promised we'd be home tomorrow morning in time to shower and change for the memorial.

Lights were on in the boathouse as we arrived. A couple of household workers waited for the return trip. One was Ray.

He gaped, as surprised to see me as I was to see him.

Then he said, "Ah," as in, "Ah, now I see how you got the job."

The meaning behind his thoughts was not friendly.

I turned away and accepted the deckhand's help to step out and away. As I walked up toward the house with my two compatriots, I admit I did look back over my shoulder to make certain Ray was sailing away. I wouldn't sleep well in a suite by myself knowing he was around.

The kids' wing branched off from the four-story entertaining center of the house. Tomás and his sister had quarters on the third floor. I first assumed it was because "the youngsters" could climb that many stairs, but we took an elevator up, so never mind.

Tomás' bedroom suite included a full living room, done in shades of ecru and brown, with sofas and double chairs. The large original art on the wall featured autumn colors, including golds and burned magenta. I remembered Tomás was at the École des Beaux-Arts with Philip and wondered if any of the pieces were his.

Once we'd chosen a movie, our host didn't even ask, he went into the attached full kitchen and butlers' pantry, made a strawberry punch with the Spanish Cava, Kripta (there was so much of it around I wondered if they either knew the vintners or were the vintners), then put a pizza into a brick pizza oven built into the wall. He and Philip chatted animatedly as he put together a tray of tapas, including meats, cheeses, olives, kumquats, and olive oil, while we were waiting.

At first, I was hesitant around Tomás, but, although he was certainly self-assured, he wasn't snooty or standoffish. He didn't treat me at all like former hired help. Tomás's hair was thicker and longer than Philip's, his skin a shade darker, his eyes were large and brown and flashed fire. If I'd never heard the expression "Latin lover," I might have made it up, just for him. I'm still certain he could successfully romance anyone he put his mind to romancing.

At one point, he and Philip lapsed into Spanish, but they quickly remembered I was there and switched back to English. I imagined they spoke French with each other at school.

Tomás turned off the lights with a remote, keeping small lights on so we could see the food, and started streaming the film.

It was supposed to be scary, but it was mostly silly. We laughed and ate and drank and pretended to scare each other at intervals. If only I could wind down like this after work every night.

For a short while, I almost forgot Mormor died.

When the credits started, Tomás said, "Another? Maybe a short film?"

Philip said, "Naw, I think I'm ready to hit the hay."

Tomás stood and helped me up. "Would it be rude of me to let Philip show you to your quarters? He knows the place as well as I do."

"Of course not," I said. "Thanks for your hospitality. It was fun. Very few people are up late enough to help a bartender unwind."

Why did I say that? Why did I have to remind him I was a member of the working class?

"Oh, I'm early to bed compared to my dad. He's up nearly all night. Part of it is that he does work with his companies around the world. But he also likes being up at night."

"Anyway, thanks."

"Sure. See you in the morning."

I followed Philip out into the long, carpeted hallway.

"Stairs or elevator?" he asked.

I laughed. "Stop talking sexy to me. But stairs are fine."

Back in Los Angeles, I'd often felt uncomfortable in mansions as over-the-top as this one because they were used as status symbols, displays of power, and if you had less power or a smaller mansion, you knew your career was beholding in some way. Whereas here, I wanted nothing from the Cavalleros Family—I didn't even really care if I continued to be a bartender at their parties. So I could recklessly enjoy.

"Come on, then." Philip extended his hand and I took it.

Stairs carpeted with a red and gold crest design curved down at the far end of the hall. "Here, I think you'll like this one," he said, choosing a guest suite overlooking the front of the house. We entered into a smaller version of Tomás' living room. The furniture here was stylish and light blue. "No full kitchen?" I asked.

"Only a wet bar with a fridge and microwave."

"I think I can survive till morning."

We proceeded into the bedroom, which was large, with a four-poster bed and carved headboard. There was a sitting area with a sofa, two wing chairs, and a coffee table, a wooden desk by the window, a flat-panel television and a fireplace with a remote. The windows looked out over the stone terrace and the lake. It was late enough that most lights in town across the water had been extinguished. I could still make out a streetlight by the marina.

"Not that you need it tonight," Philip said, continuing the tour by showing me a walk-in closet. There was enough space that it could be used as a dine-in closet. Off an interior hall was the bathroom, with marble floors and double sink, a rainforest shower, a personal sauna, and a small separate room for the toilet and a large jacuzzi.

"Before you ask, yes, the floors and towel racks are heated."

"Holy smokes," I said. "Do you know how many wells you could dig for communities with no fresh water with the money that bathroom cost?"

"Thirty-two is my guess. Though I will tell you, the Cavalleros family is committed to doing good with their money. They also make sure to pay their workers a living wage."

They paid me well for one night's bartending.

"Whoa. Too bad we leave in the morning. Where's your suite?" I asked.

"Across the hall and down one. If Ray comes in the middle of the night, holler and I'll come running."

"Shit. Why did you have to bring up Ray?"

"Come on. I was kidding."

"Ray could claim to have forgotten something. He could have come back across."

"Really?" Philip asked.

"He could be inside now, waiting for you to leave." I was only half kidding. Horror movies are not best watched before bed.

"Look. Planton makes sure this place is alarmed like the Louvre when he goes to bed."

"But he's still up. How many outside doors are there? And staff, like Ray, probably know a lot of them."

"I'm so sorry I brought him up."

"Now I wish we'd watched a comedy. Or a Hallmark Christmas movie."

"You don't." He laughed. "How about I sleep here. On the sofa. So he'll have to kill me to get to you."

"Aw, geez. Let's both get ready for bed. Then you can come back for a few minutes."

"Deal." He headed to his room. "I'll leave the doors open so I can hear if you scream."

The bathroom had a lovely assortment of soaps and face-wash creams. It also had multiple new toothbrushes and choices of toothpaste. I finished my oblations, changed into my nighttime t-shirt, and ran a brush through my hair.

The t-shirt was longer than some cocktail waitress outfits I'd seen, so I decided it would be okay for mixed company. Still, I hurried to put a backrest behind my pillow and climb underneath the bedcovers before Philip came back.

"Still alive?" he asked as he reentered the room. He wore a pair of pajama pants and no shirt. There was still a square gauze bandage covering his wound, part of it below the waistband of the pants. The muscles of his torso had lost some of their definition during his recovery. I'd first seen him shirtless at the gym, where he used to work out with serious commitment. "Here, let me settle in." He went to the closet to grab a blanket and came to the other side of the bed from where I sat to take a pillow back to the sofa.

"Don't be stupid," I said. "You can just sleep here."

"Really? I promise to stay on my side of the bed. But I'm more than happy to sleep on the first-to-die couch."

"The bed is the size of Lithuania. I'm not sure I'll even know there's anyone else here." Lie. Complete and total.

Philip leapt on top of the covers and stretched out, settling the blanket from the closet over him.

"So. Are we friends?" I asked. I wanted to settle my confusion.

He moved his pillows against the headboard and sat up a little. "I certainly hope so. We've been through a lot together. Don't you think we are?"

I decided there was nothing to be lost by honesty. "You confuse me. Half of me is charmed by your goofy self, and part of me is terrified by the genius of your art."

We sat in silence. "You're charmed by my goofy self?"

"Who isn't? You're a walking goofy charm magnet."

"The genius of my art?"

"Yeah. You're not just good. You're phenomenal. The colors and strokes are masterful. I can see your thoughts and emotions on every canvas. Some explode with joy and others question deeply. If I was Planton, I'd buy every freaking piece in your studio just to grow my fortune in the near future."

"Shit, Avalon."

More silence.

"So, what terrifies you?" he asked.

How truthful were we getting here? "I don't understand why someone with your innate brilliance—I know it's not all innate, I know you also work crazy hard—I don't understand what you see in me. Why you want to be friends."

More silence. Fairly agonizing.

Finally, "You're joking, right?"

"No."

"Avalon. You have... the noblest heart of anyone I've ever met. If I had a coat of arms, I'd want it to say Courage and Compassion, and that's what I see in you. Oh, you're nobody's fool, nor do you suffer fools. But with my own eyes, I've seen you run into a burning room to save Glenn, not to mention running into the basement of a well-armed madman to save me."

"You didn't actually see that."

"True. I was busy bleeding out. But I have it on good authority."

"Courage and compassion," I repeated. "That's kind of your

whole life. Polly. Marta. Joseph. Whistle. And you've vouched for me with the community basically since I arrived, so they accepted me. You pull people together. It's what you do. So that's your character, but you've also got extraordinary talent. You can make friends with anybody you want, anywhere in the world. You certainly don't need me. And once Sally dies, you'll likely be gone from here in the blink of an eye."

"Wait. You're inferring I have talent and you don't? You notice things. You see people, I mean, really see them. You rally people. I'm fairly certain, you're here in between. In between Los Angeles and New York, yes, but this is your stepping away. Your refining period. You got off a train in between who you were and who you will be. You're morphing from one thing to something else. The dross is burning off. And once it does, the world will go blind from looking at you."

If I hadn't been terrified of him before, I was now. "I have no idea what you're talking about. But... it's been a rough day. It's good to have you here."

"Rough day? How?"

"This morning I was reamed out by Alma Eddings, Brian's mom. And then," I took a deep breath. "My Mormor, my gran died."

"Today? She died today?"

"Yes."

"Why didn't you say anything? Why didn't you tell me?"

"I wanted a respite. A little time when it wasn't the focus."

"Avalon, I'm sorry. Come here. Can I hold you for a moment?"

I climbed out from under the covers and crawled across the bed. He opened his arms and I settled in against his chest, my head on his shoulder. He kissed the top of my head and stroked my hair.

"I'm sorry," he said.

We sat, melded. It was overwhelming.

"How is your wound?" I asked.

"Much better. Wanna see?"

Since I'd been there to save him from exactly that gunshot wound, I felt an odd ownership. "Um, sure?"

He carefully peeled back the tape and lifted the gauze. It looked much better. The puncture wound was still, if not angry, at least ticked off. The thin crust of blood around the sides was a dark crimson/purple. I assumed that was from our adventures at the Edison mansion. What did Davy Edison call it? Brimstone.

"I'm so glad you're on the mend," I said.

"I was so lucky. An inch either way."

"I'm grateful." And I kissed his wound. Or near it.

He nonchalantly re-covered it and pressed the dressing tape back down as I came up to sit against him, my head back on his shoulder.

Then he tilted my head up.

And he kissed me.

We'd only kissed once before, but his mouth was familiar.

I'd constructed space around me so carefully. It meant the whole world to me to keep my distance, to not ever be in a position to have my heart shredded.

Damn him. Damn him very much.

Every inch of my body wanted every inch of his body.

"This is why I'm terrified," I whispered.

"Me, too," he said.

"Can you do this? Will it hurt you?"

"Not if I'm careful. And go about it slowly. And inventively. And..."

The t-shirt was my last defense and it was soon gone.

"I adore you," he said. "I adore every inch of you."

Damn him. Damn him to hell, for taking me to heaven. When I first saw Philip with Rachel (may her name disappear from my mind), I could tell he'd be a thoughtful, joyful lover, just by the casual way he slung his arm around her shoulder, and smiled at her, and appreciated her with his eyes.

I was correct.

It was as if he couldn't believe his good fortune that I was there, that he was making love to me, that he was free to explore and delight in my body, that this was a powerful happening, larger than either of us, that he wanted me and I wanted him and he would take me and I would take him and we would both finally explode till the cows came home.

Afterwards I wept. I wept for Mormor, I wept for all I'd lost, especially Winsome and my father. I wept because someone *saw* me. Because someone made me fall in love, put my heart and my whole self in mortal danger.

Philip held me. Together, we situated ourselves into bed.

It was very late. Well, very early. He fell deeply asleep.

I was wide awake.

I got up, pulled my clothes back on, and headed out to sit by the lake and figure out my life.

COAT OF ARMS

World's Best Chocolate Martini

Ingredients

> 1 ½ oz vanilla vodka
> ½ oz creme de cacao
> ½ oz Godiva White Chocolate liqueur
> 1 ½ oz frozen hot chocolate mix (just the powder)
> half & half (optional)

Method

> Put into shaker. Mix thoroughly.
> Strain into glass.
> Descend into bliss.

$$23$$

LIGHTNING LAKE

I WALKED OUT through one of the kitchen doors, crossed the front terrace, then descended the rounded stone steps into shadows. Behind me, the mansion was dark except for three windows of Planton's large office. Out of sight on the lower terrace and under the cover of night, I felt safe from his gaze. I didn't want him wondering who I was and why I was outside his house in the middle of the night. I perched upon the wall nearest the lake.

I thought I wanted to think.

Turns out I didn't.

Unexpected sheets of lightning illuminated the far shore, back in town. Seven seconds later came thunder, low and rumbly. It was still clear on this side of the lake. I lay back on the wall and watched the show.

I began to drowse. But going back to bed meant going back to Philip. Perhaps it sounds odd, since we'd already made love (and we had "made love;" we hadn't just had wild animal intercourse, though I bet some of that was in our near future), but getting back into bed with him and waking up next to him felt like a larger step even than the one we'd taken.

If he didn't terrify me before, he certainly did now.

Not physical intimacy.

Those crazy things he'd said. Those things that implied he saw me. He knew me. And what was there was worth knowing. Worth loving.

That's what gave him power over me. If I believed him, believed any of those things, if he then chose to leave, or to attack, it would be shattering.

A man like him was dangerous.

Bursts of light from the sky became infrequent. I found myself nodding off. I guessed it was time to face the music and head back in.

I climbed the terrace steps and stopped.

Planton's office lights were off.

On the plus side, I probably wouldn't run into him.

On the minus side, what Philip said about the house being locked like the Louvre was correct. As I stepped onto the main patio, outside spotlights clicked on, their beams surrounding me, undoubtedly triggered by a motion detector. I shrank back and headed around to the side door I'd come out. On the wall inside was a flashing red light. I tried two more doors, only to find the same situation.

I was locked and alarmed out.

And my cellphone was upstairs.

Alrighty then.

As I pondered my situation, a stiff breeze swept across the lake. I'd need to find somewhere at least partially protected to sleep.

I thought of the playhouse near the cove. The cushions on the couches inside looked comfy enough. Chilly and exhausted, I headed over.

Even the damn playhouse was locked. It had one of those number-punch-locks. It was the same model Tomás, Analise, and Philip had installed on the upper balcony of the Edison's mansion. I studied it to make sure no one had put the combination on a tag on the back, but no such luck.

Out of ideas, I walked over to the cove and sat looking at the darkened hulk of the Edison home—the murder mansion. I began to zone out. Another lightning blast illuminated the sky, and I turned to see how close it was across the lake.

Not close.

As I turned back, my eye was caught by motion—a moving light inside the mansion across the cove. It wasn't an electric light or a flashlight or even a phone face, but a tiny, fairy light. Maybe a ghost light.

It was most likely the reflection of lightning bouncing off a window. I urged myself to remain rational, but my adrenaline had already surged. I watched the shadowed mansion. And watched. No repeat. Maybe I hadn't seen it. Maybe it was an early firefly.

Maybe it was the ghost Marta talked to. Maybe it was Jane.

Granted, Marta had a "gift" and saw spirits. But Philip and I had heard spirits weeping, hadn't we?

There's a character flaw often present in horror films and murder mysteries that Hollywood types diagnose as TSTL: Too Stupid to Live. The scantily-clad co-ed who runs into the dark basement. The horny young couple who go to have sex in the deserted cabin. The exhausted bartender who doesn't believe in ghosts but hunts them anyway...

I was awake, filled with a spike of short-term energy and tired of not understanding what was going on.

If an actual person was over there, I had the advantage. I knew he might be there and he didn't suspect I was coming.

Was I?

When again would I be awake at four in the morning, across the inlet from answers?

I got the canoe, dragged it to the water, and started to paddle. As I did, a large flash exploded through the sky, with thunder hard on its heels. Good lord. All I needed now was ominous music, and the scene was set. I paddled as fast as I could.

I left the canoe where Philip and I had ditched it before. Marta said she'd gotten in through the front sliding door that we'd not locked. I slid along the side of the house, wondering if I should turn around and huddle hidden under the porte cochere by the kitchen till morning.

A layered sword of lightening split the sky and hit the lake just beyond the mansion's closed pool. To this day, I've never seen anything like it. The electricity turned the lake into a series of huge fountains, and waves, and sprays.

The overwhelming din of thunder was on top of me—and deafening.

Then the rain fell in a torrent, so hard and fast I could no longer see the lake at all.

There was no other choice. I rolled the sliding door open two feet, let myself stumble through, and closed it.

I slid to the floor, the deluge behind me. I sat in silence, facing the room. If anyone—or anything—was here, I could be outside boiling in that lightening lake before their machete could be raised.

I sat in silence as my breathing calmed. The house was utterly still.

Then, in a middle-of-the-night waking stupor, I said, "Misty, if you're here, it's me, Avalon."

Nothing.

"Jane, if it's you, I'm a friend of Marta's."

Still silence.

"Person hiding out, I'm unarmed so I'm no danger to you. Machete-wielding madman, don't bother killing me, I'm a lot of trouble and it will gain you nothing."

Okay, so what was I going to do?

Obviously, get no sleep crunched against a glass door in a typhoon.

I looked toward the skylight at the top of the atrium. The residual light from the storm was impressive. And then, to the side of the middle staircase, near the door leading to the family quarters, there was again a dart of light.

This time I knew I'd seen it.

"Tinkerbell?" I asked.

I stood and walked through the first-floor door to the family quarters.

The family living room was quiet. There was no light.

I followed the corridor into the kitchen, where Philip and I had shared our unexpected kiss and he'd nearly reopened his wound.

I turned and spoke into the room. "If you're a presence here, and you'd like to communicate with me, let me know," I said. "If you're also waiting out the storm in here and don't particularly want to interact with me, just pick a wing. I'll let you be."

If I heard nothing, would I feel safe enough to sleep on a sofa?

Upstairs, a door banged shut. I jumped.

It was a for-sure door-banging. In this storm, of course, if a window was open, any number of doors could bang shut.

No windows were open.

Damn. I'd said if the presence wanted to communicate with me to let me know.

I hadn't really meant it.

The retort had come from up the back stairs between the kitchen and the children's floor.

Why didn't I have my phone? I couldn't even text my goodbyes.

The stairs were carpeted; my footfalls barely made a sound.

On the second floor, open doorways lined the shadowy hall.

One door was closed.

I slipped past the first open doorway to one guest suite, then another.

Misty's bedroom door was the one that was closed.

This was my chance to run and hide.

This was my chance to get some answers.

I opened the door.

LIGHTNING LAKE

Iced Mexican Hot Chocolate Martini

Ingredients

1 ½ oz white tequila of choice
½ oz white creme de cacao
½ oz milk chocolate liqueur
1 dash of fresh cinnamon
1 dash of cayenne pepper

Method

In cocktail shaker add all ingredients with ice.
Shake together creating a nice milky foam and pour into
martini glass.

24

AWAY

THE ROOM WAS pitch black. The storm was still stalking; torrents of rain assaulted the glass panels of the French doors to the balcony.

The brilliant illumination of sheet lightning threw the room into the relief of a black and white movie.

She was sitting on her bed, holding the pillow against herself, a shield, as used by many a sixteen-year-old.

"Hello, Misty," I said.

Isabella Richards, the reporter with whom I'd zip-lined K120, turned to look at me.

"How long have you known?" she asked.

"Only since yesterday. I saw your photo in the high school yearbook. Then I looked you up online."

The darkness was again impenetrable.

"Who have you told?"

"Nobody. I was texting you when I got a call telling me my grandmother died."

"Oh. I'm sorry."

"Yeah, me, too."

Behind her, outside the balcony doors, the mini-typhoon raged.

"May I sit?"

She patted a spot next to her on the thick comforter.

"Have you been staying here?"

"A few nights. But I'm partial to electricity and running water so I really do have a hotel room in Plattsburgh."

She was sitting against pillows stacked by the headboard. I followed suit and stretched out. Her golden blonde hair had obviously been cut and dyed the very striking and memorable shade of copper, making it the first thing you'd mention about her. It went well with her sapphire-blue eyes.

"Are your eyes really blue?" I asked. In this light it was impossible to tell.

"Contacts," she said. "They're green."

"From what I can tell, since you've been here, you've done a good job of avoiding people who might have known you back in the day."

"Staying on the fringes was the idea. If someone I knew showed up, I ghosted."

"So to speak."

"So to speak."

"When Marta came exploring, she found you here, and you talked?"

"Yes. I like her a lot."

"She works with me at the Battened Hatch."

"I put that together."

"It's funny because Marta is a sensitive. She can see ghosts. I asked her point blank if she'd talked to you and she said yes. I never bothered to ask if you were flesh and blood."

Misty laughed.

"You told her something about Jane Rodriguez. What was that about?"

She sighed. "I didn't go into the whole thing with Marta. It's a long and complicated story."

Oddly, at times like this, I don't remember that I am... obsessive... about collecting stories. I simply ask one question, and then the next, and the next, with no intention whatever of giving up before I get the full scoop. But this time, I was so curious, and so freaking close to the answers, I was very aware of the full-on buzzing in my brain.

I was scared she wouldn't talk to me. "Lightening hit the lake about twenty minutes ago," I said lightly. "I'm not going anywhere for a while."

"You promise you won't tell anyone, at least until I decide what to do?"

"I'm a bartender. We take an oath."

"Really?"

"No. But it's part of my personal code of ethics. Also, I owe you a great debt for climbing in the truck and changing the tenor of my conversation with Jeff. Anyway, I won't tell. So, what happened?"

"I don't know what you've heard about what happened here. I'm assuming the story goes that I lived a wonderful life with my wonderful family in an incredible home and had a life of promise ahead when I disappeared."

"Yes. That's pretty much it. At least, that's what I read in the story about your brother."

"Davy?"

"Yes. As a matter of fact, he's here for Brian's funeral. Two nights ago, he was at the Battened Hatch. He said he came to town to pay his respects because you and Brian were close."

"How did he look?" She had perked up.

"He looked good, for someone whose life was devastated as a kid."

"Oh, God." Misty brought a spare pillow in front of her again and wrapped her arms around it. "I never meant for things to turn out the way they did. But you have to know, my life... wasn't perfect."

"No?"

"It was pretty awful. I've had years of therapy and even become a counselor myself, but it's still hard to talk about. My father sexually abused me. My uncle did, too. My father knew about his brother, I'm sure. It started when I was four. By the time I was sixteen, I didn't have any will to keep living.

"I knew Brian because our last names were so close: Eddings and Edison. We were seated next to each other in nearly every class. He had a good sense of humor. He was friendly but distant from nearly everyone. I liked his smile. Then one day in English, under the cuff of his shirt I thought I saw... cigarette burns. Round red spots the size of the end of a cigarette. I went over to him at lunch as soon as he sat down so there was no one else around, and I asked him about it. Long story short, we slowly began to trust each other. He told me about his parents. I told him about my dad and uncle. We became friends. Eventually, more than friends."

"Wait. If this... your father and uncle... went on for so long... did you tell your mother?"

"Yep. When I was eight or so. She slapped me so hard it made my ears ring. She told me she never thought she'd have a liar for a daughter."

"I can't imagine. I am so sorry."

"By my junior year, I was in a deep depression. I would have been suicidal if I could have contemplated any actions at all. Brian was worried. He said we should run away together. It sounded like an out, and a plan someone else could make for me. I agreed.

"Brian's brother, Frank, was also abused, physically and mentally, by their parents. He and his girlfriend, Jane Rodriguez, said they'd run away with us. Frank and Jane were seniors. It was close enough to the end of the year that they'd probably graduate in absentia, though frankly, I don't think either of them cared. I knew who Jane was because we were in band together. She was tall and skinny and had longish brown hair. She didn't talk much. It sounded like her parents weren't exactly abusive, more absent. They didn't know or care what she was up to, one way or the other.

"So, Brian and Frank planned it. We chose a night my parents would be out, which meant they'd come home drunk and I could sneak off. I didn't pack much except cash I'd been secretly saving.

"As hoped, my parents came home, went upstairs to their bedroom, and passed out. The others came for me at two a.m. We were just about gone—I always climbed down the tree outside my balcony, it was perfect—but somehow Davy woke up and came into my room. Frank met him and made up some story. I didn't actually hear most of it, but somehow Davy didn't follow us or tell anybody.

"We made a clean getaway. It was me and Brian and Frank and Jane. We walked through the woods and walked and walked. Five miles, at least. Then we slept in a lean-to, and the next night we walked five more miles, this time to a hunter's cabin. It didn't have heat or running water. It did have a fireplace, but we were afraid to use it because someone might see the smoke and find us. Brian and Frank had loaded in some food, mostly junk that didn't need to be refrigerated. The first couple of days, they went 'hunting' during the day. They had Bowie knives and BB guns. Once they caught a squirrel, but they had no idea how to skin it and we couldn't make a fire. Once they caught a fish, but same thing. It dawned on me pretty quickly that Frank, the mastermind, didn't really have a plan beyond us living in the cabin.

"He and Brian started arguing. Then Frank and Jane began to fight. I knew my parents were probably frantic that I'd run away, and I was fine with that. In fact, the thought started to bring me back to myself. They thought I was their obedient child, their captive, but I took control and left. I made up my mind that if we were found, I would tell the authorities the whole story of what my dad was doing.

"As I came to my senses and slowly began thinking more clearly, I saw I needed to make a plan for myself, since these guys weren't exactly on top of things. I really did like Brian, we were close, perhaps the people closest to each other. But when he and Frank got into fights, I saw a whole other side of him. They both descended into fits of rage, and I thought they could easily hurt each other or one of us.

"Same thing when Frank fought with Jane. She often yelled at him that he'd promised to take her away, that he said he had a car, that they were going to go to South Carolina and live in a little house, and instead here we were stuck in the woods, eating Cheetos.

"She had a point. She definitely had a point. Even though it was June, she was always cold. I leant her my extra sweater and a scarf I had. I hadn't pumped Brian for details, but I, too, assumed we would be far away from here, somewhere that had a mall where I could buy clothes to replace the one t-shirt and pair of shorts I had on.

"On like the third day, Brian and Frank got into a fight about the plan Frank had claimed to have. Finally, Brian went stomping off. Jane and I had heard the whole showdown. It proved to us that the boys were incapable of getting us into a better situation. Jane went to find Frank to give him a piece of her mind. Given his state, that didn't seem very smart to me. I stayed in the cabin.

"After an hour, I heard Frank coming back. I went outside and hid so I didn't have to meet him. Maybe fifteen minutes later, Brian came back. Frank was actually crying. He said Jane fell off a cliff. He said, it wasn't a cliff, really, but it was a sheer, long drop off. That she wasn't moving. Brian started asking questions. He said they had to go get her and take her to the hospital. I wondered for a moment if I should help, but they both went charging off through the trees.

"I was terrified.

"I realized then that no good was going to come from this. I didn't want to be there when the ambulance came. This stupid, Cheeto-filled taste of freedom made me realize I didn't have the strength to go back and deal with the fallout of me making 'crazy claims' about my dad. I just wanted to be gone. On the other hand, if Brian and Frank called the paramedics then hightailed it to some other cabin, I didn't want to be the only girl hiding out alone with them.

"So *I* ran."

"Holy smokes." I was flabbergasted. "Where to?"

"I knew the ridge they were talking about, where Jane must have fallen. From there you could see for miles. I remembered you could see a road and the K120 ski jump. That at least gave me a sense of direction. Also, there had once been a road that led to the cabin where we were staying. By then it was overgrown, barely a path, really, but I figured it must lead to a larger road at some point.

"So I ran. Frank and Brian were consumed with Jane, so I got a good head start. By the next evening, I'd made it to down to the outskirts of Tranquility. My hairdresser, Renata, had recently quit her job at our salon to move down south to go to nursing school.

"I snuck into Tranquility and into Renata's house. She was shocked to see me, to put it mildly. She told me everyone thought I was kidnapped and was looking for me. I told her why I'd run away and couldn't go back home. She finally agreed to help me. I stayed at her place—not even stepping outside—for a week until she was ready to go. Oh, my gosh, when she cooked me spaghetti that first night, I must have looked like a starving cavewoman eating everything I could lay my hands on. I also remember standing in her shower, under hot water, crying. Just crying.

"We moved down to Charleston, South Carolina, where she was accepted at nursing school. Her cousin lived down there and had a business doing hair and makeup for weddings. Renata worked for her.

"Renata cut and dyed my hair—black at first, though I didn't like it. I got a job as a waitress. My full name, Melissa Isabella Edison, was on my social security account, so I went by Bella. No one ever connected me with the missing girl, "Misty," from upstate New York. I got my GED. I found a better waitressing job at an upscale restaurant and became friends with one of the sous chefs. I didn't want to become a chef, but I loved the restaurant. I ended up going to the Culinary Institute of Charleston to study Hospitality and Tourism Management. One thing led to another. Twenty years later, I have my own restaurant in Key West."

"Wow," I said. "That's quite a story."

"Yeah. I know. It wasn't easy. As I said, I've had a decade of therapy and now I volunteer with survivors of abuse."

"You didn't follow what was going on up here?"

"I couldn't stand to. None of it was good news. I was sorry my parents were hurting but they caused it, to my mind. I wished there was a way I could get in touch with Davy, but he was so little. I thought for sure Brian and Frank called 911 about Jane. Turns out they didn't. I didn't find out till I came back here last week. Her parents thought she'd run off. No one ever looked for her. That made me sad. That's why I asked Marta to look into Jane's disappearance."

"Did you know hikers found your scarf and saw a coyote with a hand—I guess it was Jane's, God bless her—which is what led everyone to think you were dead?"

"I didn't know that till this week, either. When I say I avoided the story altogether, I really did. I assumed Mom and Dad thought I'd run away but got over it. I wished I'd found and contacted Davy when he was old enough to understand and keep such a weighty secret. I didn't know my family would move and leave the house like... this."

"Pretty spooky."

"You think?"

Misty looked sad. She put the pillow she hugged down, then picked it up again.

"So what happens next?"

"I'm not sure," she said. "Maybe we catch a few hours' sleep?"

It was 4 a.m. I wasn't coherent enough to make another suggestion. It was with relief that we climbed under the comforter. Within five minutes we were both out cold.

AWAY

Strawberry Champagne Punch

Ingredients

> 1 bottle bubbly
> 1 bottle ginger ale (diet or regular)
> Large bag frozen strawberries.

Method

> Mix and share.
> (The frozen strawberries serve as ice cubes as well as, well,
> yummy champagne-soaked strawberries.)

25

UNFINISHED BUSINESS

INSTEAD OF WAKING up next to Philip, I woke up next to Misty Edison.

It was 7 a.m. The rain had stopped. Gray clouds still skittered away over the house. Across the lake, small rays of sun hinted at a blossoming June day.

Misty stirred and then sat up.

We took turns using her bathroom to pee, then stepped out onto her balcony.

"So, what's next?" I asked again.

"I don't know. I'd really like to talk to Davy if I can. I'm not sure how to get ahold of him. I can't go to the memorial service. Someone is bound to recognize me."

In the morning light, she looked wan and exhausted. "Boy, I never saw all this coming that day I ran. But I had to. I wouldn't be alive now if I hadn't."

"I'm going to the memorial," I said. "I can try to find Davy for you. Failing that, I know where he's staying. You want him to come meet you here?"

"No, that would be too weird. I don't know where else to suggest, though. Where it would be private and safe."

"You know where I live. It's very private. I can tell you where the key is and you could wait for him there."

Misty looked at me with a hint of hope. "Really? You wouldn't mind?"

"Not at all. There's even... if you want to read it... an interview with Davy giving his side of the story on my kitchen table. It's in a manila envelope. Up to you."

"If I go to your house, will anyone be there to ask who I am and what I'm doing?"

"My landlord gets home from her travels tomorrow. She might have some friends over then. But if you tell anyone you're my guest, there will be no problem." I glanced at my watch. "Meanwhile, I'm supposed to be staying next door at the Cavalleros's. I should get back."

We walked downstairs together and back out onto the terrace. "I bet you guys had some amazing parties here," I said.

"Here's the funny thing. The whole house, the atrium, the kitchens, it was all planned for entertaining. Yet we hardly did any."

"I'm getting the message things aren't always what they seem."

"That's one of the themes of my life. See you later, then. Thanks for the use of your place."

"Help yourself to a cup of tea and anything else you find."

She gave me a quick hug and headed back inside.

Early rising fisherfolk were out on the lake. It seemed there weren't lasting effects from the lightning strike. I paddled back, stored the canoe, and headed for the Cavalleros house.

There was a cook in the kitchen, and the door was open. "Hi, I'm Avalon, I'm a guest," I said perkily. I guess I didn't look too dangerous as no one stopped me.

Philip was still asleep. I closed the door to my suite's bathroom and was more than grateful to take a shower. Our hosts provided fluffy white bathrobes, of course, and the floor was heated.

By the time I was finished, Philip was not only up, he'd gone to his room to shower and change. He'd already returned and stood fully dressed by a long window in my living room. I came and stood in front of him; he casually wrapped his arms around my waist.

The smell and feel of him enveloped me with a perilous sense of home.

"It looks like it rained last night," he said.

I laughed. "Yep. It certainly did."

"Why do you say it that way?"

"There's a story. I'll tell you as soon as I can, I promise."

"A story? Having to do with the Cavalleros family?" He was confused.

"No, no. I got locked out. I took the boat and went to the Edison's. Lightning struck the lake."

"Holy smokes! You're okay?"

"Obviously." I smiled. He picked up the "holy smokes" from me.

"The memorial is at eleven, right? Let's go see about heading back over."

Tomás wasn't yet stirring. Philip, a frequent guest, knew to present ourselves at the private family breakfast room. It was a small, well-lit room with ten-foot windows; each boasted four rows of nine panes topped by a semicircle. Tall green plants gave spots of color, and the table with only six chairs was centered on a ten-foot circular rug. Philip and I made omelet and beverage choices and were served forthwith. It was fun to sit in the room in which every inch was meticulously designed and eat with him.

"Thanks for inviting me," I said.

"Thanks for coming," he said.

"Believe me, it was my pleasure," I answered, and we both giggled into our plates as the kitchen door swung open.

It was a gentleman who'd come to announce a boat was crossing in ten minutes, should we care to take advantage.

We took advantage.

We didn't talk much in the car as Philip drove me home. We'd said more than we'd expected to the night before.

Brian's memorial would be down at the Olympic Complex on Main Street. I expected I'd see Philip there.

He dropped me at the end of Cherry Lane. I strolled up, changed clothes, and straightened the cottage quickly in case Misty and Davy arrived before I returned.

Then I drove to MacTavish's and parked in the employee lot. I decided to do as much bar setup as I could, as we were close to the venue and would likely get slammed after the service.

I entered the Battened Hatch through the lobby door, using the big, old-fashioned key. It was always an interesting transition. For some reason, the light switch for the small entry hallway was all the way inside the pub, hence the first person arriving walked the hall in darkness, except for the exit light. I often pretended the short excursion took me back to olde Scotland, into the spirit of the beautiful dark-wood pub.

As it did today. Lazy sunlight filtered in through windows on the lakeside. I didn't turn on the lights, because I didn't want anyone to think we were open.

Hence, it took me maybe three minutes to realize there was a shape in the deep shadows of a corner table. I jumped.

"Hello, Avalon," said the shape.

It was a male voice, deep and raspy.

"I've come to talk to you."

"How did you get in here?" I asked.

No answer. He stood up. And started limping forward.

Ray. It was Ray.

Damn.

"I believe you and I have some unfinished business," he said.

And he pulled out a gun.

UNFINISHED BUSINESS

Pineapple Habanero Old Fashioned

Ingredients

2 oz of preferred rye/whiskey
Dash of bitters
Dash of sweet vermouth
½ oz of habanero simple syrup
Fresh cut pineapple (about 2 chunks)

HABANERO SIMPLE SYRUP

Method

Bring equal parts of sugar and water to a boil. Turn down heat on stove top and add fresh or dried habaneros. Simmer ingredients together for about 10-15 minutes so the oils from the peppers have time to release their heat into the syrup.
Let habanero simple syrup sit until cool and then poor into desired container. Leave peppers in sugar water as they will make it spicier. (Make sure to label and wear kitchen gloves as needed while making this. The oils from these peppers will get into your skin and leave a burning sensation.)

COCKTAIL

Method

In a rocks glass muddle fresh pineapple, add ice, habanero simple syrup, rye/whiskey, bitters, and sweet vermouth.

Stir ingredients together. (Do not shake these ingredients as you may bruise your rye/whiskey.)

26
HELL TO THE NO

HELL TO THE *no.*

Two former bartenders of the Battened Hatch were murdered. I wasn't about to become number three.

I darted for the hallway, throwing on the lights in the pub as I
passed. In the lobby, I ran for Nigel, the concierge. "Call security," I
said. "There's a trespasser with a gun in the pub."

His eyes widened.

As I said that, Ray came limping out. His gun was pocketed, his
arms held aloft.

"No danger," he said. "No danger."

"Call security," I said to Nigel. "Hold off on the cops."

First, no establishment wants a bevy of officers arriving, weapons
drawn. Second, local law enforcement was probably all at the
Olympic Center, and who knew who'd we get.

"I need to talk to you." Ray continued toward me.

"There are better ways than breaking-and-entering and pulling a
weapon," I said.

He took his revolver out of his pocket, holding it with only two
fingers, and put it onto the concierge desk.

Nigel shot me a look that clearly read, *This is not in my job
description.*

Yeah, well, not in mine, either.

"I didn't break-and-enter. The door to the Breezy was unlocked.
Went through the kitchen."

"Anything you need so say to me, go ahead. Say it right here," I
said.

He motioned to a circular Victorian conversation sofa in the middle of the room.

"Leave your gun."

"It's not loaded."

But it remained on the concierge station as Ray headed for the sofa and sat.

I followed, but looked back at Nigel, mouthing "security."

I stood in front of Ray, allowing us privacy of conversation, but giving me both the upper hand and the ability to bolt.

"What?"

"I don't like you."

"I'm aware."

"If you want to get me fired from the Cavalleros job, fine. But I support Alma."

"It never occurred to me to get anyone fired, until you showed up five minutes ago, waving a revolver."

"Then, leave her alone. She's had a hard enough time of it. She doesn't need anyone poking around or opening old wounds."

"What old wounds?"

He thought for a minute. "Any of 'em."

As he spoke, Milton, our head of security, came through with Dan, the parking valet. We only had one security guy, but Dan did add to the display.

Milton marched over. "Avalon, did this man point a gun at you and threaten you? If so, I have no choice but to call the police."

Damn. What to do? Because he certainly did. And I wasn't sure he wouldn't come for me again.

"Yes," I said. "The gun is over there. He says it's not loaded. He only wanted to get my attention."

"Still, they'll want to talk to him," Milton said, and without further ado, he kept staring at Ray but went to Nigel's station and called the police. He made it clear the situation wasn't ongoing and asked them to send an officer in without making a show.

I sat next to Ray. "I won't press charges," I said. "Nor will I tell the

Cavalleros family about this. But if you ever come at me again, there will be a different outcome." Unless, of course, he shot first and rendered the point moot. "So, if there's anything else you want to say to me, say it now. Because you're not coming near me again."

I studied Ray. He suddenly looked very old. His skin was creased and shrunken to his skull. His beard, usually well-trimmed, was stubble in shades of white and gray.

"I'm only looking out for Alma," he said.

"Got it." We sat. I realized this might be our last chance to chat. "Why are you looking out for her?"

"Are you kidding me? Does it look like she can take care of herself?"

"I mean, why you?"

"Who else?"

True enough. Her husband was dead, her son was dead, her other son lived many states away.

As we sat in silence, the adrenaline whooshed out of his body, and he kind of caved in. When he spoke, it was still gruff, but the volume was lowered. "Alma is my cousin. I told her not to marry that man. Then I told her to leave that man. I don't know how many times. He didn't treat her right. He couldn't hold a job. He didn't provide. Once he caught me dropping off some venison, 'cause we had a good hunt. I thought he was going to rip my head off. So even though we wanted to share what we had with Alma and them boys, we never could. She saw some lean years. So now that I can help, I do."

"Okay," I said. "You could have said that without a gun."

"It seemed like you were determined to make her talk about stuff best left alone. I only wanted you to let her be."

I said, "I will leave her alone."

"All right."

Joe Cooper, a town police officer, was the one who showed up. Joe still fit nicely into his uniform. He was middle-sized, not tall, not short. His hair was shaved; his skin was white and so far without a summer tan. He was a good choice to send when an officer had to listen before acting. He had kind blue eyes. I made a statement, giving him a blow-by-blow. He said I might be called in to answer questions. I asked if there was any way Ray could be permanently relieved of his weapon. I didn't relish the possibility of a repeat.

He said he wasn't sure.

Joe handcuffed Ray, which was mighty satisfying.

I took a deep breath and went back into the bar. Was that really all Ray wanted to say? The first thing he'd said was he didn't want anyone "opening old wounds." Which old wounds? And why was he so worried about Alma and wounds being opened, unless she was the wound-inflictor?

And how about Robyn? Was she too close to opening old wounds? If so, whose wounds?

Damn.

I did a few minor things to set up the bar, then looked at the time. I left, turning out the lights and locking the door. Milton from security had swept the Breezy and the kitchen that linked us. Things were now well-locked.

I headed outside and turned toward the Olympic Center. It was a clear day, fortunate for a memorial. The sun was bright but not hot.

As I walked the sidewalk around the hill that defined downtown, I pondered the fact that I held two huge secrets.

Misty Edison was not dead.

I was in love with Philip Young, and he with me.

Holy smokes, as Philip would say.

I was full up. On basically every single front.

At that moment, it didn't seem anything could happen to ruin my happiness, or the fact that at least some of today's questions had happy answers.

HELL TO THE NO

Honeydew Mojito

Ingredients

1 ½ oz of preferred white rum
1 teaspoon of simple syrup
2 oz fresh honeydew puree
Fresh lime wedge
Fresh sprigs of mint

Method

In a rocks glass muddle fresh lime and fresh mint. Add
ice, rum, simple syrup, and honeydew puree.
Shake ingredients together and finish with sparkling
water or soda water and fresh chunks of honeydew.
Garnish with a lime wedge.

27

MEET THE MONSTERS

I'D MISSED THE opportunity to arrive early at the Olympic Center. The parking lots were jammed, and seating inside was hard to come by. I decided to stand and went to the entry that gave me the closest, best view of the proceedings.

Chairs and a large table were set up on the floor cover of the rink, which was well below the banks of seats in the former Olympic skating and ice hockey venue. The table displayed Brian's medals, large sprays of spring flowers, and a large smiling photo of him.

I couldn't believe he had to die for me to find out so much about him.

Would anyone say the same about Robyn, or, now that her mother was failing, would she depart with much less fanfare?

Not to mention Jane, whose departure had hardly been noted, at all.

I thought of Mormor, who left this life in the midst of a large, boisterous family. Her passing left a hole in the hearts of her loved ones, as well as in the fabric of history. Although I guess everyone's passing does, whether we acknowledge it or not.

The memorial was to be televised. The participants filed in to their seats on the floor five minutes before the beginning of the service. I recognized Jeff and other Olympians as well as Arthur Bristow, the mayor of Tranquility, and Brian's brother Frank.

They spoke one by one. Jeff made nice remarks about rivalry turned friendship.

The hundreds of mourners paid attention and shifted in their seats as folks usually do during large-scale events. After Jeff finished and sat down, I saw a woman in an aisle seat halfway around the venue from me get up and head for the exit nearest her. The woman was Jeff's wife, Charlotte. She left her son sitting with the woman next to her.

The next speaker was Frank Eddings. I was curious about what he'd say, but I was also determined to take the opportunity to talk to Charlotte alone. This would likely be my only chance. I was certain she held important, missing pieces of the puzzle.

I ducked back out of the huge open arena doorway and headed toward the exit Charlotte had used. The long, wide hallways were empty.

I pushed open the nearest exit door but found only a cluster of state police overseeing the venue.

Back inside, I made one last try and went into the closest women's bathroom. And there Charlotte stood, over a sink, splashing water on her face. She wore a dark-green top with black slacks and a long black jacket on top. I guessed she'd had a middle-class upbringing, took care of herself, had some kind of job that entailed intermingling with Olympians, and voilà.

Besides the two of us, the cavernous room was empty.

She grabbed a paper towel, then saw me in the mirror.

"What? What are you doing here?"

"I wanted to talk to you."

"It's Brian's memorial, for God's sake."

"I know. I'm sorry. I know you were close to him at one point. It's also clear you have strong feelings about me. I'd like to understand where those are coming from."

"You have to ask?"

"Apparently."

"I want you to leave me... leave all of us... alone."

"I'm not looking to tell anyone anything about your family. It looks like you have a great son. I'm simply trying to understand what's going on. Why Robyn Forsyth was killed. Was it a coincidence she dated Brian? What happened in the Eddings house when the boys were growing up seems unhealthy, to put it mildly."

"Of course Robyn's death had something to do with Brian," Charlotte said, her voice nearly a hiss. "So far, I've been left out of it, so I don't appreciate you roping me in! I have a family and a young son. I'd like to watch him grow up!"

"Does it have something to do with Misty Edison?"

"What? How? Why would that be?"

I guessed not.

"Something that went on in the Eddings home when they were growing up, then?"

"What does it matter anymore?"

"It matters if people are being murdered. Does it have to do with something when you and Brian were together?"

"The honest truth is, I don't know. You're right, Brian had a messed-up childhood. Their parents were monsters."

"Both of them?"

"I'd say so. The father was the punisher. He'd decide one or the other boy deserved to be punished—tortured really. The mother would help and force the other boy to help hold his brother down."

"That sounds awful. I wish they'd felt they could tell someone."

Charlotte opened her purse and took out a cigarette and lighter. "I don't smoke," she said. "But I figured I might need one today." She lit the end and took a long drag.

"It seems Brian didn't have trouble getting girlfriends," I said, knowing I was pushing. This was my one chance. "But he had trouble keeping them."

"More the other way around. If you got too close to Brian, he'd send you packing."

"Is that what happened to you?"

"Look, Brian was a good guy. He was thoughtful and funny. He prided himself on funny. Had some rough edges, but nothing that couldn't be worked with. We were together for several months before I saw one of his rages. It was scary. It wasn't directed at me, thank God. He hardly knew I was there. He hardly knew anything rational, except he was mad. He threw things. He broke things. I'd warn anyone who dated him not to keep stuff they're really fond of sitting out in the open."

"Why do you think he did that?"

"Oh, come on. It doesn't take a genius to put together his parents' tempers with him flying off the handle."

"So that's why he'd break off relationships?"

"He felt he couldn't control that part of himself. But, personally, I think that was his excuse. He had... he had a very deep-seated guilt that continually made him punish himself. Some of the ways he did were productive—he never let up on his Olympic training, not when he was exhausted, not even when he was so exhausted, it was counterproductive.

"But he also made a categorical rule that he would never have a family. He said it was because he didn't trust himself. I'm pretty sure the real reason was he was punishing himself for what he considered his unforgiveable sins."

"Which were?"

"Brian and Frank ran away once, both boys together. But it didn't work out."

Charlotte stubbed her cigarette out in the sink, then took out her hairbrush and went after her highlighted brown hair furiously.

"Yeah?" I said, even though I thought I knew the time she referenced.

"When the boys came home, their parents were furious. Brian told me about it once when he was drunk—and, yeah, he used to drink. He quit not because it fueled his rages but because it unleashed his guilt. And he thought it made him talk too much.

"Anyhow, their dad was going to beat them. He was so mad, both boys were afraid he might not stop. He might actually kill one of them. He was going to start with Brian. So he went out to the garage to get his punishment implements. He made Frank come along, 'cause Frank would get the same punishment after Brian. As he went back toward the house, dragging Frank with him, Frank wrenched away and shoved him down the concrete stairs to the basement."

"Did it... kill him? If it did, I'd call that self-defense," I said.

"Yeah, me, too. But the fall didn't kill him. Broke one of his legs. Frank took a sledgehammer and went down and broke his other leg. Then hit him upside the head with it. Still, he didn't die immediately. He lay there for two days, slowly dying. No one called for help. They all went about their ordinary lives. They could hear him moaning, sometimes."

"Dear God."

"I know. Brian said he knows he killed his dad, just as much as Frank did. He didn't actually push him, or hit him with the sledgehammer, but the hate he had in his heart... he said he would have. And he could have saved him, could have called for help. But he didn't."

"How about the mom?"

"I don't know. All I know is, no one called."

"How does it play into Robyn's death?"

"Look, I've got nothing to go on but a feeling that bad things happen to people who know too much about the Eddings. There. I've told you everything I know."

She held her purse defensively in front of her body and stood ramrod straight. I might as well get right to it.

"Who do you think killed Brian?"

"I have no idea. And I'm not going to talk about this again. So don't cite me as any kind of source because I won't back you up. As soon as this service is over, me and my family are getting out of town. I just wanted to come so someday when my son is older and we tell him about his biological father, he'll know he was there to pay his respects."

"Got it," I said. "Thank you."

Charlotte tossed her hair back, took one final look in the mirror and flew out the door.

To err on the side of safety, I pushed open all the stall doors. They were truly empty.

I went out into the hall. Television monitors every few feet broadcast the service inside. The last speaker suggested they give Brian a final round of applause, and everyone was soon on his or her feet.

Then they piped in "The Star-Spangled Banner." The camera panned the crowd as they sang. I squinted to see, searching for Misty's brother, David. I'd promised to bring him back to my place. No luck. I walked back in through a side tunnel entrance, this time angling for the best view of the crowd rather than the speakers.

I thought I saw him as the song ended, but the crowd broke immediately and I lost him in the melee. I guessed I'd have to track him down at Brent and Susan's place.

I waited inside, pressed against the inner wall of the hallway as the crowds shuffled toward the door. I wondered if Misty was at my cottage. I wondered if Sally was back from India.

I wondered if Philip told Rachel he was moving on.

As the flow of people thinned, I joined the exodus and stepped again into the sunny day. It's tough when a town has only one large thoroughfare, and I was genuinely grateful not to be in one of the thousands of cars angling to get onto Main Street and either through or out of town. Lots of folks were walking, a good number possibly heading for the Battened Hatch. I joined their throng.

As I did, my phone vibrated with a text.

I pulled it from my pocket and stepped into the shade of the awning of a local craft store to read it.

The text was from Hannah: *I'm helping scatter some of Brian's ashes. Don't have my car. Could you pick me up in half an hour?*

Seriously? I had to get to work. Until days ago I had no car and couldn't be painted into corners like this. Normally, sure. But... the roads were glutted. Thousands of people trying to leave town.

Where?

K120. It's the big ski jump outside of town.

Oh, I knew what K120 was.

Marta had probably already opened the pub, and I had the full crew coming in: Davros, Mauela and sons, Sandy the former Breezy waitress. They could likely hold on for half an hour.

It wouldn't be bad to wait for Hannah in the parking lot, if I could get there. A big if.

I sighed loudly, glad Hannah couldn't hear. *Who are you there with?*

Frank Eddings.

Who else?

No one else.

Just you and Frank?

And Brian's ashes.

My stomach lurched.

I had a bad feeling about this.

A very, very bad feeling.

MEET THE MONSTERS

Pumpkin Martini

Ingredients

2 oz Death Wish Coffee Pumpkin vodka
1 oz Cold Brew Coffee
1 1/2 oz Pumpkin Cream Liqueur

Method

Fill cocktail shaker with ice. Add Coffee Pumpkin vodka, cold brew coffee and pumpkin cream liqueur. Shake all ingredients together and strain into a martini glass.
Add a pinch of fresh ground cinnamon for garnish.
Enjoy!

28

ASHES, ASHES...

B E CAREFUL. DON'T trust Frank.
    What?
I'm serious.
Okay.
I'm heading over.
Thanks.

I thought quickly about whether I should call the police. All I had was a thirdhand accusation of Frank killing his abusive father twenty years ago. And the mysterious demise of Jane.

So probably not.

Still, I didn't trust him. And I definitely didn't trust K120.

The employee parking lot for MacTavish's opens out onto two side streets. The wider one led to Main Street and was packed with cars. The smaller one led to an alley, which emptied onto neighborhood streets.

It's a good idea when you move somewhere new with a car to chart out the back roads and get to know shortcuts and options.

I'd had my car for two seconds, and it hadn't yet happened.

My car had a GPS but I had no idea how to use it, so I used the one on my phone. I turned onto the alley that led into a neighborhood. The route I took was apparently nonsensical to the woman in the phone, and she kept urging me to make a "legal U-turn."

I hoped I was making the correct turns.

At one point, I texted, *Hannah?* but got no reply.

Watching the map, I turned onto one small street, then another. Wrong guess. Dead end.

Turned around, went the other way, then the *other* other way. Finally got to a long road that eventually crossed Route 536, the road everyone was using to leave town.

Route 536 has no traffic light, only a stop sign on the smaller roads that intersect it. There were three cars in front of me wanting to cross.

We waited forever until a kind heart stopped and waved the first guy through. The second car gunned the motor and followed on his bumper.

Having witnessed a good Samaritan, a few cars back, another kind heart paused and let the car in front of me go. Following example, I crossed also.

Then I had a choice. I could either stay on this road and over-shoot the Olympic Jumping Complex or turn off onto surface roads and try to wind my way down. If I overshot, I'd have to turn left to make my way back, and would be at the mercy of the auto brigade again to let me cross. On surface roads, I'd still have to hope some-one would let me turn right and join traffic.

I muttered a short prayer and took to surface roads.

Muttered a prayer? What was happening to me? As long as I was praying, I added one for Hannah. Surely God would honor that one. She worked for the firm.

On a normal day, it's a ten-minute drive to the Olympic Jumping Complex. It took me twenty.

I hoped Frank and Hannah were also slowed by the mad rush.

On the way, I called Marta and told her I'd be late. She sounded plenty surprised but took my cues and asked no questions.

Several cars were in the parking lot even though the complex was opening late. I had no idea which was Frank's.

I texted, *I'm in the parking lot. Where are you?* not expecting a reply.

And there was none. For several minutes.

Then, *Up top.*

Are you kidding me? What to do?

Could be she was fine, there were lots of worker-folk up there; they'd scatter ashes and return down. I thought of texting, *Should I come up?* but that invited her to say yes.

Instead, *Do you need me up there?*

Although the day was sunny, once out of town the wind blew downright chilly.

Still having no answer, I climbed the wide stairs to the ticket lodge. The gondolas behind it weren't yet working.

Instead, I stood at the foot of the steep, narrow wooden worker's stairs I'd hoped never to see again in my lifetime. The ones that were for employees only. I looked around. No one was aware of me.

I took a breath and started to climb.

No one was there to meet me at the cabin where the stairs ended. A quick look around showed that attendants were over by the gondolas, apparently ready to get them started.

Hoping to stay unnoticed, I stalked to K120 and opened the ground floor door. I went through the nondescript entrance into the building. Once inside, I went over to the elevator. The car was up top. It seemed the least I could do was bring it down, in case I needed to ride to the rescue.

No. Please God.

I heard gears begin to grind as the elevator car began to descend.

All the while, I heard nothing from Hannah.

I knew we weren't alone. Employees both up here and down below were setting up for the day's business. In my mind, I tried to recall and count how many cars were in the parking lot. Then I tried assigning the workers I'd passed to those cars.

My conclusion: if anyone else was up top with Hannah and Frank, it was only one or two people at most.

A man in coveralls swung through and opened the door to a janitorial closet. He looked at me in surprise. "We're not opening until two o'clock today."

"Got it," I said. "Thanks."

The elevator car reached the bottom and the doors opened before me.

Should I get on?

Everything was likely fine. No reason to go up.

But what if Hannah needed me and the elevator left again? I'd have to wait forever for it to return.

I stepped into the large, glass-sided rectangle but didn't press the button for either floor. The doors slid shut. I sat on the floor, hoping it wouldn't move.

It didn't.

I sat.

And sat.

I heard the man in coveralls open the outer door and leave.

Maybe ten seconds passed when that same door swung open all the way with a squeal reserved for Olympians in a hurry. The haste was odd as the attraction didn't open for an hour. It was probably an employee, late for work, held up by traffic. I didn't stand up to check it out.

My phone vibrated with a call. The ID said it was Hannah.

Exhaling, I hit accept and started to say hello.

But there was a conversation already in progress. I quickly figured out that Hannah had called me so I could hear it. It was muffled, as though the phone was inside her pocket.

"Okay, we're finished," she said. "Thanks for letting me be a part of this. I hope it was meaningful."

"Oh, it was meaningful, all right."

"I'm glad. I have a ride waiting below. Safe travels as you leave."

"Not so fast."

"What?"

"I mean, there is something else I need from you, Mother Hannah."

"Reverend Bricksford is fine."

"Sorry. Catholic. Used to having Fathers and Mothers."

"What do you need? And please, if you don't mind, don't hold my arm."

"I'd like you to hear my confession."

"That's more up Father Collum's alley. I'm sure he'd be happy to speak to you."

"Ah, but I don't want to speak to Father Collum. I want to speak to you. Like Robyn Forsyth did."

"What?"

"Robyn. That poor girl. Didn't she speak to you shortly before she died?"

"Yes. I helped her get a lawyer."

"That's it? She didn't mention my brother?"

"Brian? Of course she mentioned him. He'd just died."

"So you Episcopalians don't confess things? I might need to sign up."

"We do. But not in a confessional."

As she said that, the door to the elevator slid open and the person who had banged the outside door open ran in and pushed the button to the zip-line landing. Then he pushed the "close door" button six times in rapid succession. Something was on this guy's mind. He didn't even seem to notice a woman sitting on the floor behind him.

The elevator briefly scoffed at his hurry, then closed in a calibrated, almost lackadaisical way.

Then we lurched into rising mode.

Oh, hallelujah.

Meanwhile, up top, Frank's tone had changed.

"I'm sorry, Mother... Reverend." He spoke more slowly and softly, cajoling. "I would feel so much better if you would let me repent. Is that the right word?"

"Yes. But only if you truly mean to turn away from whatever it is you've done." I heard her relent and put on her clerical persona.

"What was that? Oh, there's people on the level above us," Frank said. "Come back over here, just for a minute. I don't want anyone but you hearing."

I looked more carefully at the man who'd joined me in the elevator. He wore a well-tailored gray suit and black leather shoes. It was Davy Edison.

Well, that made my life easier. I wouldn't have to go looking for him.

But right now, I was concentrating on hearing Hannah.

"No one can hear us here, certainly. What is it you wish to be absolved of?"

"Did I say absolved? Does that mean forgiven? I don't want that. I know I can't have it."

"Why?"

"It's not a sin for which I can repent. It's a habit. That I was born with. It's just something I do."

The elevator climbed. Out the side of the glass wall, I could see the line of cars snaking all the way back into Tranquility. My heart rate accelerated from terror, to terror plus twelve stories.

"What do you do? And please, let go of my arm."

I held out my phone, squinting at it. My adrenaline was rising. "How?" I murmured.

"How what?" Davy asked.

"How can I record this?"

He deftly perused my phone and punched a button.

Then he looked up, willing us to go faster.

Frank's voice stated, "I push people."

"I'm sorry. I don't understand."

"Down things. Off of things."

"You've injured people?"

"Naw."

"You've killed people?"

"Naw. What I said. I push people. It's the gravity that pulls them. It's the ground that kills them."

I caught my breath.

"Who?" asked Hannah. To her credit, it didn't sound panicked. "Who have you pushed?"

"I pushed… I pushed this girl I knew named Jane. She was acting up. She accused me of stuff, stupid stuff, which she shouldn't have done, 'cause she was my girlfriend. She didn't listen to me when I told her to shut up. So I pushed her."

"Did she get hurt?"

"She was standing by a drop. A long drop. I didn't hurt her. It was the gravity. It was the ground."

"Where? Where was this?"

"Doesn't matter now."

"Was Jane the only one?"

"Hell, no. That's the thing. I also pushed my father. Down cement steps. He was fine when he left my hands. Not so fine when he hit the ground. Although there, there… I did help out some more. But it wasn't me that hurt him. It was the sledge hammer."

"And he died?"

"He was a son-of-a-bitch. The world is better without him. Let God sort 'em out, as they say."

"Anyone else?"

To Hannah's credit, she didn't sound shocked, she sounded interested, counseling.

I looked at Davy, to see if he was hearing this.

He stared straight ahead. No reaction.

"Well, yeah, now that you mention it. That bitch Robyn. I pushed her into a ditch."

"With… a car?" Now there was a slight tremor in Hannah's voice.

"Yeah. She was Brian's girlfriend. He likely told her stuff. That she likely told you."

His tone had changed.

"At Brian's wake. That bartender was talking and said Robyn confided in you."

"What are you implying?" asked Hannah.

I snapped my fingers in front of David's face. "Call 911," I hissed. "Now!"

He saw my fingers and looked at me. I didn't want to stop the recording of what was happening long enough to use my phone.

"What?"

"Call the cops!" I was quiet so as not to be heard by Frank.

David looked at me, confused, then he handed me his phone.

I held it, wondering what on earth was going on in his head that kept him somewhere else with murder confessions happening in his hearing.

"Whatever," he said.

How could I call and still hear what was going on?

I put my phone on the floor and dialed David's.

"911, what is your emergency?" It was a woman's voice.

I hissed, "Send help now to the Olympic Jumping Complex. Hannah Bricksford is on top of K120 and her life is being threatened by Frank Eddings. Now! He just confessed to previous murders, including Robyn Forsyth! I can't talk. He's going to kill her!"

And I hung up. I handed the phone back toward David, who just looked at it. I turned off the ringer and shoved it into his pants pocket. Then I picked up my phone from the floor.

"Let go," Hannah said to Frank. "Let me go!"

ASHES, ASHES...

Ingredients

1 oz of citrus vodka
1 oz orange liqueur
1 oz grapefruit juice
2 fresh basil leaves cut in half
1 1/2 oz of white cranberry juice
1/2 capsule of activated charcoal (Available in any specialty food store. Squid ink can be substituted.)

Method

In cocktail shaker, add ice and all ingredients.
Shake until charcoal capsule is dissolved and cocktail looks dark gray to black
Strain cocktail into martini glass and garnish with fresh grapefruit slice and fresh spring of basil
Enjoy.

29

ALL FALL DOWN

WE WERE NEARLY to the top.

How was I going to do this? How was I going to make myself step out of this elevator?

From the speaker on my phone, Frank said, "You know, the crazy thing is, I do feel better getting that off my chest. Thank you, Mother. And thank you for helping scatter some of Brian's ashes. Such a pity you slipped and lost your balance trying to get those last ashes out."

"No, you son-of-a-bitch!"

"Yeowww!" yelled Frank. "Damn you! If I didn't think you deserved it at first, now—"

That was the last thing I heard.

The elevator door opened.

Before I could plan my move, David Edison pitched past me at full speed, like a cyclone.

Without allowing myself to think, I charged out, following David, who rounded the corner to the entrance to the zip line.

At the far end, Frank and Hannah struggled together in a dance of death, right where you stepped off in the zip-line harness.

David barreled toward them.

He did not pause.

He said nothing.

He did not give them a moment to see he was coming.

To issue a threat or a warning.

He reached them. He broke Hannah's arms free from Frank. He threw Hannah backwards to the wooden floor.

And he shoved Frank Eddings backwards toward the edge of the platform.

Then he shoved Frank off.

The tableau froze. The three of us were suspended in time and space.

To this day, I do not know if Frank Eddings screamed.

The twelve-story drop was much too far for us to hear the impact as his body turned into an empty shell.

Hannah regained her composure first. She stood up and went to David.

He was going toward the edge. To look down or for other purposes, I do not know.

Hannah put her arm around him and walked him back away from the loading platform.

"Thank you," she said.

David looked at her, surprise evidenced in his eyes.

"You saved my life," she said.

"It was him," David said. "When he said the first two words at the memorial service, I knew. I will never forget that voice, the voice of the guy who took Misty, and threatened to kill me and my parents. The things he said to me were awful. His voice... had gravel.

"I hear that voice every night when I go to bed. It's in my mind. It's in my dreams." He slid to the ground along the wall of the enclosure. "Son-of-a-bitch has tormented me every day of my life since I was freaking seven years old!"

Hannah sat down beside him.

I went and crouched next to her. "Are you all right?"

She held out her arm. It was trembling.

I held out my hand to David. "Give me your phone."

"What?"

"The one I used to call 911."

"You called 911?"

But he fished his phone from his pocket and handed it to me.

I redialed.

I told them the perpetrator had fallen and was on the ground. That Hannah was safe. That the incident was over. Everyone was safe except Frank. The operator asked my name and said the police were en route and would arrive in three minutes.

I considered whether it was my duty, as a witness, to stay put at the scene of the crime.

Hell, no.

I was shaking worse than Hannah was. I was not going to spend my day talking to the police on top of K120.

"Come on," I said. I somehow got both Hannah and David back to the elevator. We got inside. As I pushed the "down" button, we saw multiple police vehicles careen into the parking lot below.

David's phone rang. I answered.

It was the officer in charge. He asked who was in the elevator.

I told him it was just us, all unarmed. I told him Frank Eddings had brought Hannah Bricksford to the top of K120 for the purpose of pushing her and letting gravity take her and the ground kill her. I told him that David Eddings had saved Hannah.

I told him where to find Frank's body.

When we reached the ground and the elevator door opened, we were greeted by three officers, weapons drawn. Just to be certain I was telling the truth.

Fortunately, my phone held a recording that proved that I was.

I decided not to tell David Edison or the police that Misty wasn't dead. Not yet. Let them clear up one incident at a time. Let them think David was following his sister's killer. It was what David thought. What he'd thought all these years.

David and Hannah were taken back up to show the officers where everything had happened.

I called Marta and said I likely wouldn't be in. She said she would handle it.

God bless her.

Later, we went to State Police Headquarters to give recorded statements. Hannah and David were given a lift in an official vehicle.

I was allowed to follow in my own car, although another police car followed behind.

I wasn't curious to see Frank in his current state. Not at all.

All I could think was, *David didn't kill him. Gravity pulled him. The ground killed him.*

ALL FALL DOWN

Fatal Fruit Shot

Ingredients

> Orange flavored vodka
> Peach Schnapps
> Lemon Juice

Method

> In a shaker with ice, add equal parts vodka and schnapps
> and a squeeze of lemon juice. Mix.
> Distribute to shot glasses.
> Stand back.

30
UNEXPECTED GUEST

O NCE WE WERE dismissed by the state police, I offered Hannah and David a ride back into town. Both accepted.

Hannah sat in the front passenger's seat. "Hey, nice car. Is it yours?"

"Yes. And thanks."

She checked her watch. "Oh, good. I'll have time to change before my vestry meeting."

"You aren't going to cancel it? You were nearly murdered! Surely that warrants time off!"

Hannah smiled. "It does warrant time off. You might not believe me when I say this, but it will be much easier to get this meeting over with than to try to reschedule everyone and let some of the issues remain pending."

"I'll trust you," I said. "But, still."

"I know. I hear you. I promise to fall apart as soon as they leave."

I considered going in to work later and told Marta to call me if I was needed. But I had no interest, as yet, in telling the day's story again and again. I had no interest in telling it again, period. My multiple statements to the state police were quite enough.

In the past, I had found dead people, even murdered people. But I'd never before been with a person alive one second and then, simply not.

It had shaken me.

Even if it was Frank.

I pulled into Hannah's driveway and let her out in front of the house. "Good luck with the vestry."

"Thanks."

She held the car door open so David could move up to the front seat. I watched to make sure Hannah got inside the house, then drove down the back half of the U, where I paused and let the car idle several yards from the road.

"Would you mind driving me back out to the Olympic Jumping Complex to get my car?" David asked. "I know it's on the other side of town."

"Actually, finding you was on the top of my to-do list today," I said.

He looked understandably surprised.

"Would you mind stopping at my place for a while?"

"It's... been a rough day," he replied.

"I know," I said. "But you need to.'

He looked at me uncomfortably, and it occurred to me he might think I was making a pass at him on the day he killed his lifelong tormenter. "There's someone who wants to talk to you."

Now he looked even more reticent. I pulled out and headed around the lake to Cherry Lane. As I pulled off the Main Street extension onto my quiet road, I was surprised to find a short row of cars parked to one side. I pulled up behind the last one.

Who was here? Was someone looking for me? The press? The police? Or had someone found out about my guest and was stalking her?

Before I could work myself into a full-blown panic, another car pulled in behind. A woman I recognized from town got out with a wrapped gift that was obviously a bottle of wine.

She smiled at me and I put the window down. "Nice to have Sally back, isn't it?"

"Yes, indeed."

Ah, it was a welcome home for Sally.

I put my window back up. Then I turned to David.

Ever since Misty had asked me to tell David she was alive before they met, I'd been pondering how to do it. I didn't know this man, yet I would be involved in one of the most important moments of his life.

"If magical thinking was real, what would be the best news you could get?" I finally asked.

"What are you talking about?"

"If you could have one wish."

"That Frank Eddings had never been born."

"Why?"

"What the… ?"

"I think what you're really saying is you wish Misty was still alive."

His eyes narrowed and his irises darkened. They transmitted the thought, *Why is a stranger playing with me like this?*

This wasn't going as planned. I cut to the chase. "She is."

"Who is what?"

"Misty. She's alive."

He recoiled as if I'd physically slapped him.

"Why would you even say something like that?" There was anguish in his voice.

"What Frank said to you that night, the night Misty disappeared, was not true. How he treated you was unforgiveable. His threats were horrible. His lies were even worse. Because of them, all this time, you thought Misty was dead. But she's not."

"No, she is. She really is. Or else, she would have told me. She wouldn't have let my whole life be ruined."

"Things were going on you didn't know about. I'm not the one to tell you. And she had no idea what Frank had said or done to you. But I think… I really think I'm not the one to tell you."

He studied my face. His brown eyes focused on mine, as if trying to see through to my thoughts.

"Then, where is she?"

"In the house. My house. It's up ahead."

"Why would someone do this? Why would someone pretend to be Misty?"

"You need to see for yourself."

He pondered for a moment more, then sprang to life. "Why are we still sitting here?"

Davy abruptly opened his car door and got out. I did the same. We headed up the lane.

The trees parted to reveal an enchanting portrait. Sally had illuminated the acres with strands of fairy lights. Three long tables covered with gold-laced white cloths were laden with food, drinks, and desserts. Cushioned outdoor chairs and settees dotted the lawn, and a phonograph player piped music into small white speakers.

David dug his hands into his pockets and looked at the ground as we passed through.

Sally, tall and statuesque, was dressed in one of her flowing summer frocks covered by a flowered day jacket. "Ah, Avalon!" she said when she saw me. "Come, join us!"

"Thank you," I said, mustering a friendly wave. "Maybe later. I've got company."

"Very well. Later, my sweet!"

Only Sally could make "my sweet" sound like a feminist appellation. As I led David through the celebrants, I scanned the group to see who was there. Okay, to see if Philip was there. I certainly had interesting things to share about the events of the day. Perhaps once the brother and sister were talking, he could join me on my hidden terrace so I could fill him in.

As it turned out, Philip was there, and deep in conversation. He had not seen my arrival nor heard his grandmother's cheery greeting. He was standing, conversing with the lone man who was wearing a suit. Philip held a glass of Champagne in his left hand. His right arm was draped around Rachel.

My heart stopped.

The man in the suit said something, and the three of them laughed heartily.

As if feeling my stare, Philip's line of vision slid into mine.

He saw me.

He stood up straight.

But he didn't take his arm from around his girlfriend.

His girlfriend.

I turned my attention to Davy and kept walking.

David Edison and I walked across the bridge. I took him around back to the terrace so we could enter the cottage through the kitchen.

"Misty?" I asked. "I'm here with David."

Misty must have watched us arrive. It took thirty seconds for her to join us in the kitchen. She wore jeans and a white boatneck sweater. She stood, staring at the grown man beside me.

David, who had obviously been expecting a hoax, let his jaw drop.

"Banana cakes," he said.

"With icing," she replied.

Within moments, he was in her arms.

From the hug, Misty looked at me with moist eyes. "What took so long? I've been waiting for hours."

"You won't believe it when he tells you," I said. "I'll leave you. The living room is all yours. You've got a lot of catching up to do."

Misty took Davy's hand and together they walked into the other room.

UNEXPECTED GUEST

Spiked Cucumber Lime Seltzer

Ingredients

1 ½ oz of preferred vodka
2 oz of fresh cucumber puree
Sparkling water or soda water
Fresh cucumber lime puree

Method

English cucumbers work best for this puree as there are little-to-no seeds. If regular cucumbers are used, remove the seeds from the fruit.
Peel and dice cucumber into small pieces and put into food processor. Add juice of two fresh-squeezed limes. Puree ingredients together until you have a nice silky puree.

COCKTAIL

Method

Pour ingredients into a Collins glass over ice and stir. Finish with fresh cucumber slices and a fresh lime wedge. (Do not toss or shake this cocktail. Sparking water or soda water will create a fizzing effect.)

31

KNOCK AT THE DOOR

THE TWO OF them had been talking for an hour when there was a knock at my front door.

I stalked from the kitchen through the living room, saying, "Pardon me."

Misty, still undercover, stood and ducked around the corner. David stayed seated.

I opened the door to find Philip standing on my doorstep. He was tall and well-dressed and smelled like oranges.

"I'm sorry," he said.

I waited another ten seconds for the apology to be followed by, "I've broken up with her. Let's leave for Bali."

Crickets.

I slammed the door and threw the bolt.

"Sorry for the interruption," I said to Davy. "It was for me."

Misty reentered the room. "May we have a glass of wine?" she asked. She looked a bit sheepish. "I'd ask if you had any, but I had plenty of time to rummage through your alcohol."

"Sure," I said, and took their orders.

"Thanks. Then come join us."

Thus, we ended up in the living room, wine glasses in hand.

"Davy filled me in on Frank's confession," Misty said. "And what Frank did to Davy and how he threatened my family. I'm horrified."

"I wish I'd been old enough that you could have shared what was going on with you, with our father. And uncle," David looked sorrowful.

"I'm so sorry you thought I was dead, and that it was your fault," Melissa said.

"You were both kids," I said, "and the adults around you were acting in terrible ways. You each did what you had to do to save yourself."

"This is going to take years of therapy to unwind," David said, conversationally.

"Yup," I agreed.

"Do we think Frank also somehow killed Brian?" David asked.

"I got a text about a half an hour ago from Brent Davis," I said. "Toxicology reports aren't back yet, but results of the rest of the autopsy have been released. It turns out that Brian's body was banged up from years of training and competition. His system was filled with ibuprofen. Apparently, he downed a lot of it on a regular basis. There were about ten over-the-counter pills still in his stomach at the time of death. They now know that drugs like ibuprofen, the NSAIDs, double the threat of heart attack or stroke. They think he had an undetected heart problem. That's likely what happened."

Misty looked sad. She put down her wine glass and hugged a blue sofa pillow to herself. She put it down, then picked it up again. "That's another thing. I think I killed Brian."

"*What?*"

"I watched his career for decades. Gold medals! Who'd have thought? I was proud of him. For a while, I'd been wanting to come back to Tranquility, to put old ghosts to rest. I also wanted to see him to tell him I was fine, to forgive him for the cabin, to see if he held anything against me for leaving. I guessed he and Frank just went back home after the disastrous runaway attempt, though I couldn't imagine how their parents would have welcomed them." She shuddered. "Things apparently went worse than I even suspected they would."

She took a long breath.

"Last week, the night I got to town, I found out he was at your pub with the Olympic newbies. I hung around outside. Saw them all come out onto the porch and slide into the lake. It was like the best version of the old Brian. It made me happy. When he left, I followed him home.

"It took a little while for me to get up my nerve. When I tried his door, it wasn't locked. I didn't knock because I didn't want to call attention to myself with any neighbors. I went in quietly. He was sitting in his bed, with a cup of tea and a bowl of tortilla chips. I stood in the doorway, watching, happy to see him happy.

"When he finally looked up, it took him a minute to figure out who I was. When he did, he was shocked. I think he thought I was a ghost or something. He started to say my name, but then, all of a sudden, he was gone. He didn't clutch his chest or anything, he was just gone. Not breathing. Not... anything. I didn't want to get caught, not like that, not after all these years. I was completely freaked out. I started to run downstairs and outside to call 911. But when I got out to the end of hallway, another woman came up the stairs and went in. Now I know it was his former girlfriend, Robyn. I was relieved and decided to let her handle it. I ran."

"Holy smokes," I finally said.

"Yeah," answered David. "This whole day. Holy shit."

Misty accepted my offer to spend the night in my guest room, and David decided to crash on the living room sofa instead of going back to Brent's.

I left them talking and went outside to make a phone call.

"Hey," said Hannah, answering.

"Hey," I said. "Is the vestry meeting over?"

"Yeah. I was getting ready to fall apart."

"Good. When you said nearly being murdered warranted taking a few days off, did you mean it?"

"Yes. I've already told them I'm taking off this Sunday and most of next week."

"Well, I was thinking. I'm going to head for Brooklyn to go to my grandmother's funeral in about half an hour. But maybe afterwards, I'll go to Montauk for a couple of days. It's not quite the season, and there's a rental that's at a good price. Want to join me?"

"Girls' road trip?"

"Girls' road trip."

"I'm in."

"Meet me in Brooklyn, and we'll carpool."

"Deal."

"I'll text you the deets."

"See you soon."

"Yeah, see you soon."

I looked at my little cottage and headed for my bedroom to pack. But it truly felt like my cottage, and this was my town. While there are certainly annoying things about having relationships, one great thing about having a home—and a family—is that you can leave them, and they'll still be there, waiting for you to come back.

I'd be back.

KNOCK AT THE DOOR

Pomegranate Margarita

Ingredients

1 oz One with Life organic tequila (or any other white tequila)
1/2 oz Cointreau (or any other orange liqueur)
1/2 oz Pama liqueur (pomegranate liqueur)
2 oz homemade sour mix (or store bought)
Ice salt for rim
Fresh lime wedge (for garnish)
Fresh pomegranate seeds

Method

In a cocktail shaker, combine all ingredients.
Shake until you have a nice frothy consistency.
Rim rocks glass with salt.
Pour contents of shaker into rocks glass.
Add fresh lime for garnish.

ACKNOWLEDGEMENTS

FIRST THINGS FIRST. When visiting Lake Placid, you should surely visit the Olympic Jumping Complex. There is a zipline at K120, but it is beside the ski jump, not attached to it. Also, both floors on the top of K120 are enclosed (unless you're ski jumping). I have been advised that if you wish to hasten someone's demise, you would need to use K80, which is shorter and, perhaps fortunately, not open to the public.

Thanks to the good folks of Lake Placid, who have welcomed Avalon as one of their own, especially Sarah and Marc Galvin at the Bookstore Plus on Main Street, and Andy Flynn of the *Lake Placid News*.

Special thanks to Mimi Fader for her expertise in things not-quite-of-this-world.

Thank you to early readers, including Barb Sherer, Bob Scott, Mary Ann O'Roark, Sharrata Hunt, Cari Keith, and the women of Creators Haven: Crystal Paul Watson, Wendy Paul, Melissa Hinnen, Cassie Hinnen, Melissa Paul, Christine Farrell, Lisa Cullen, Claire Woodley, Valerie Paul Greenway, Theresa Ladd, Deborah Lee, Claire Woodley, Jean Stephenson, Laura Wise and Anne Harkness.

Thanks to the real Brent Davis, whose name was put into the book by alleged friend Pam Gatreaux. Brent, while not a newspaper man, is a fine writer and did, in fact, write the "clippings" attributed to him.

As always, thanks to Jonathan Scott with whom I attended bartending school and Linnéa Scott, whose advice makes books and life better.

Thanks to Ray, our favorite barkeep, who wanted to be an irascible character in one of my books. Hope this works for you. We miss you.

A huge thanks, as always, to Jamielynn Brydalski, mixologist and bartender extraordinaire, who has contributed most of the fantastic recipes. You can see her make many of them on Bartender'sGuideto-Murder.com. Thanks also to Kalen Griffen also used to bartend in Lake Placid. I must also mention my fellow Baptist, Sharrata, again, as we have worked hard to get those Baptists mortified and as delicious as possible.

Cheers!

START READING AVALON'S NEXT ADVENTURE

DEATH AMONG THE STARS

IN THE ADIRONDACKS

ONE MORE PIECE. Or seven.

The young man took a sip of Malbec and fitted the puzzle piece shaped like a fish into the larger work that created a sitting fox. A fox with a strange, knowing grin on his face. It was a long time since he'd done a jigsaw puzzle. The rental cabin had a stack of them, all wooden, with shaped pieces. This one was close to complete.

Rise was grateful to his manager for renting this Adirondack cabin. He'd flown across country from Los Angeles three days early, to rest, re-center and dismiss any jet lag. In Los Angeles there was a pile of scripts on his desk—he'd only brought the three most promising along to read—constant calls and texts, a demanding personal trainer, and, oh yeah, four stalkers, two of whom required restraining orders.

Ah, the life of a star.

Except he wasn't a star, only a guy who'd grown up on television in three different series. Enough folks were so comfortable with him in their living rooms they figured they should be married. To him. And became violent when he didn't agree.

It had been a wonderful couple of days. His assistant, Con Allred, had laid in supplies, his favorite food, and he'd been able to cook for himself. Con had then gone ahead to join Rise's agent, manager and publicity crew to lay the groundwork for the premiere of his new feature film.

A car would be sent for Rise in the morning, his hiatus over.

The tall actor ran a hand through his golden blonde hair, snapped another piece into the puzzle and groaned. Two pieces were missing. Why would you rent a cabin and offer your guests puzzles with missing pieces?

He took another large sip of wine. The fire was burning down, a bed of orange embers lined the fireplace floor. Add another log, or let it go out?

If he wanted to be fresh and rested for the film festival, he should probably take some melatonin and read awhile, then get some sleep.

Rise drained the wine glass, washed it out and put it to dry by the sink. The cabin was made of wood with antlers everywhere. He stepped outside onto the small porch, then sat in a dark-green Adirondack chair. Rushing water of the nearby Ausable River spoke of recent rain; the piquant, calming scent of pine melded with the loam of the earth. He breathed deeply.

Back in Los Angeles, his house was a fortress, alarms everywhere. Even so, one enterprising woman, a teacher for god's sake, had left a note on his bed when he was away filming. His agent had gotten a letter from another of his stalkers, a psychologist, explaining they were uniquely psychologically suited for each other. Therefore, if she couldn't have Rise, she'd have to hurt him. A young man had stopped his mother in the grocery store and introduced himself as Rise's fiancé. Someone had followed and confronted his mom. His mom!

Rise hated being on guard all the time. Which was why he was sorry to leave the solitude of the cabin to rejoin the world in the morning. It was rented under his manager's brother's secretary's son's name. No one knew he was here.

The actor stood and stretched, then went back inside, and locked the door. He headed into the bedroom where he pulled on pajama pants and a t-shirt. He scrubbed his face in the master bath and popped two melatonin gummies.

The queen-sized bed had a quilt with an Adirondack design featuring bears dancing around a campfire. Rise picked up a script from the bedside table at random, put on his glasses, and began to read. Within ten minutes, he couldn't keep his eyes open.

It was all he could do to turn off the light before falling into a dreamless sleep.

His phone rang at seven the next morning.

"The car's on its way. It'll be outside in twenty," said Isobel, his agent. "See you at the hotel for breakfast."

"Roger. Wilco," said Rise.

He wiped sleep from his eyes and went to shower and dress. He was already packed. It wasn't long before the crunch of tires arrived outside the cabin. A glance out the bathroom window showed it to be a Range Rover driven by Castor, Isobel's favorite driver. Rise was grateful she hadn't sent the stretch.

Castor knocked on the door and Rise came through the room, pulling his suitcase. The shorter, stockier man gave Rise a friendly nod and took the bag. Rise walked around the living room, doing one last visual check. The puzzle. Should he rebox?

He stood in front of the table. And stared.

Castor was saying something, but Rise didn't hear him.

The puzzle was complete. All the pieces were locked in. None missing.

The paper towel next to the puzzle, which had a small rim of Malbec from Rise's glass the night before on it, now also had a tiny heart, drawn by pen. Filled in with lipstick.

Castor came and stood next to him, looking at the puzzle and the paper towel. A knowing smile crossed his face. "Fun night?" he asked. "Come on, we've got to go, or Isobel will have our heads."

Rise grabbed the paper towel and stuffed it into the pocket of his jeans.

It was only when he got into the car that he began to tremble.

1
EVENING'S END

TRANQUILITY, NEW YORK, held a new spark of energy. I felt it as I walked the nearly-empty sidewalks at 11:30 p.m. on that clear September Tuesday evening. A brisk chill seasoned the air around old-fashioned streetlights whose bulbs flickered merrily as if the lamplighter had recently come by. The shops of Main Street also spoke of an earlier day. They were brick or clapboard, one story or two, although the Adirondack Adventure Hotel had dared climb to four floors, the village's version of a skyscraper.

The Tranquility Film Festival was opening that weekend and I was looking forward to it. First, because I had friends whose documentary was certain to create a stir. Second, with the first festival screening on Thursday, actors, directors, publicists, and journalists were beginning to descend in their limos and fancy rental cars. Their imminent arrival excited the locals, even those who claimed disinterest, and the crowd at the pub I manage and bartend was buzzing with anticipation. Food, drinks, and high spirits flowed freely all evening.

MacTavish's, the Scottish-style inn that housed that pub—formally named That Ship Has Sailed, but universally called the Battened Hatch—was on the south end of Main, while my cottage was nestled in a hidden glade called Mill Pond off the northern end. I'd decided to walk to work that afternoon, in the late-summer heat with the teasing hint of autumn leaves. Tonight, the mountains that rimmed town loomed as a backdrop, purple and protective. We'd closed the bar at 11. My barback, Marta, and I took some extra time swapping out the next day's drink specials in the holders on each table. Marta then hurried off on her bike, and I headed home, savoring the pre-festival calm by strolling the walkways of my adopted home.

Most businesses, including restaurants, were closed, their nighttime illumination offering a soft glow over wares displayed in shop windows. There was one notable exception: the Orpheum Theater, where the festival was soon to begin. Outdoor lights shone and the marquee was aglow.

I paused to study the listing of films with the dates and times of their screenings. *Salty Sally and Pepper: Truth Be Told*, the documentary featuring as yet unknown stories about two screen idols of Hollywood's Golden Age who'd lived in Tranquility, would show on Saturday afternoon, a prime slot.

Glancing inside the hall that led to the lobby, I saw posters for the festival's other films lining the walls. It was kind of odd that the lobby doors were still open. Surely the night's final screenings of regular movies were done by now? As I entered to study a poster for an independent feature, Kyle, the lanky teenager who ran concessions during the week and usually closed up, walked into the lobby. He saw me and waved. I waved back.

"Just perusing," I said, signaling my willingness to leave.

He joined me in the outer hall. "You work around here, right?"

"Yes, I'm Avalon. Nash. I bartend at the Battened Hatch. In MacTavish's."

"Could you help me for a minute?" He looked nervous.

"What is it?"

"The last movie's over. I need to close up. But some girl fell asleep in the theater."

"You can't wake her up?"

"I tried saying, 'wake up,' but it didn't work."

"If she slept through an action movie, I'm not surprised. Did you try shaking her shoulder?"

Kyle looked uncomfortable. "I don't want to touch her or anything. We've had harassment training."

"Okay." How could I not help such a well-meaning kid?

The Orpheum was a grand movie palace back in the day. Now it was carved into three theaters, the largest of which was downstairs, in the footprint of the original. The once-commanding balcony was split in half to create two smaller screening spaces, but each remained large and raked with the original stairs going down each outside wall.

The sleeper was in theater three, upstairs. I trotted up the carpeted steps behind Kyle, who was obviously eager to get on with things.

All the theater lights were on, including the harsh work lights, which took away any golden veneer of the magic of storytelling. I headed down to where the young woman was seated, fifth row center, and walked across row four to be squarely in front of her.

The movie-goer was petite, perhaps in her mid-twenties, with the carefree good looks of youth, wearing a form-fitting white cashmere sweater that showed off her flawless tan skin, and jeggings. Her small popcorn was settled into the seat beside her. She hadn't enjoyed much of it before dozing off.

"Excuse me," I said. No reply.

"Miss?" I put my knee onto the folded seat bottom in front of me and leaned forward, reaching out and shaking the young woman's leg. I shook harder. Her naturally curly brown hair jostled, but she didn't move. "Hello?"

I glanced up at Kyle, who shrugged, *see what I mean*?

Willing myself not to think the worst, or even the second-worst, I walked back a row and across it. I put a hand firmly on the girl's shoulder and shook her. "The movie's over."

She fell forward.

Her popcorn spilled over her seat and onto the floor.

That's when I thought the worst.